choosing
charity

choosing charity

terri ferran

bonneville books
an imprint of cedar fort, inc
springville, utah

ISBN 13: 978-1-4621-1065-0

Published by Bonneville Books, an imprint of Cedar Fort, Inc.
2373 W. 700 S., Springville, UT 84663
Distributed by Cedar Fort, Inc., www.cedarfort.com

LIBRARY OF CONGRESS CATALOGING-IN-PUBLICATION DATA
Ferran, Terri, 1962-, author.
  Choosing Charity / Terri Ferran.
    pages cm
  Summary: Kit Matthews Bridger is newly married to her sweetheart Adam and adjusting to married life, but everything gets turned upside down when her birth mother, the one who left in her in a dumpster twenty years ago, contacts her to ask her to donate her liver to the daughter she didn't "throw away." It takes a lot of prayer and perspective for Kit to forgive her birth mother and open her heart to let new people into her life.
  Includes bibliographical references and index.
  ISBN 978-1-4621-1065-0 (alk. paper)
  1. Donation of organs, tissues, etc.--Fiction. 2. Parent and child--Fiction. 3. Foundlings--Fiction. 4. Mormons--Fiction. I. Title.

  PS3606.E734C48 2012
  813'.6--dc23

                          2012010871

Cover design by Angela D. Olsen
Cover design © 2012 by Lyle Mortimer
Edited and typeset by Melissa J. Caldwell

Printed in the United States of America

10 9 8 7 6 5 4 3 2 1

Printed on acid-free paper

To Chantelle, DJ, and Savannah
You complete our family. Mommo loves you.

preface

22 YEARS AGO

Baby Girl Found in Trash Bin at Bus Station
By Victoria Guerrera
Originally published in *Los Angeles Daily News*

WOODLAND HILLS—A newborn baby girl was found in a garbage can of the women's restroom at the Presidio Hills shopping center in Woodland Hills on Wednesday evening.

Police said a janitor cleaning the facility heard noises coming from the trash receptacle at 6:30 p.m. and investigated.

He found the baby girl partially covered by a pile of crumpled paper towels.

Police state the infant had been born earlier in the day. The baby, whose umbilical cord was not attached, was not wrapped or bound in anything.

The baby was taken to a nearby hospital and treated for dehydration. She is expected to be released into CPS custody.

Investigators are asking for any witnesses who have information to call (818) 449-2770.

This is the fourth newborn abandoned in Los Angeles County this year. Two of the four babies were deceased by the time they were discovered.

Advocates continue to push for a Safe Haven law to be passed allowing "safe" drop-off locations for unwanted newborns.

Although there are no national statistics compiled on infant abandonments, last year there were newspaper accounts of 17 reported cases of newborn abandonment in California and 118 cases reported nationwide.

chapter one

Being dumped in the garbage as a newborn set the bar fairly low when it came to improving the quality of my life. Over the past twenty-two years, it had definitely taken a turn for the better.

Since I was adopted as an infant, it wasn't until my teens that I questioned my self-worth and wondered how God could let a baby be thrown away. Counseling helped, but it wasn't until I moved to Logan, Utah, from Ventura, California, that I learned how to heal.

The move four years ago, which seemed tragic at the time, turned out to be a life-changing blessing. I met the Bridger family: Janet Bridger, who befriended me and introduced me to the idea that everyone was worth something; Adam, who captured my heart and kindled my faith; and Justin, who stood up to my stubbornness and baptized me.

Adam Bridger and I had been married for eight months, and other than not having much time with him, I loved married life. Since then I'd graduated from college and gotten a good—albeit a little bit boring—job at a CPA firm in Logan.

My best friend, Tara, was getting married in a month, and although I didn't care for the nonstop wedding talk—Adam and I had "eloped" to the temple—I was excited for her. Maybe the fact that my parents were going through a divorce while I was engaged left me with a negative association concerning wedding plans.

3

"Kit Bridger! Are you even listening to me?" Tara demanded as we walked out of the movie theater.

"Of course." I tried to recall what she was talking about. No luck. "I just missed the last part. What was it again?"

"Carrot cake." She ran her fingers through her tousled blonde curls while barely missing a stroke of the text she was sending.

I still drew a blank. "What about carrot cake?"

"Honestly, I listened to everything you said about Adam." She was right—although I doubted I rambled on about Adam like she did about Eric. Well, maybe I rambled a bit while Tara and I were in Romania together and I thought Adam had found someone else. And perhaps I carried on just a little when I found out my parents were separated, and again when I got an unexpected marriage proposal. Come to think of it, Tara *deserved* my full attention.

"I'm sorry, Tara. Will you tell me again?"

"Eric's mother makes great carrot cake. She wants to make it for our wedding cake. Ick. I don't want it, but Eric loves the idea. What do you think?"

"I think any cake made with vegetables as an ingredient is a crime against nature."

"Exactly! It should be a fluffy cake. Chocolate or white—I don't care—as long as it's fluffy. Carrot cake is heavy and feels dark and foreboding—I think it could jinx our marriage."

"Just tell him what you think. The cake should reflect the bride—light and full of air. Maybe Eric's mom could add nuts to the carrot cake—nuts would be a proper reflection."

"I think you just insulted me." Tara's thumbs flew across her phone keypad as she texted Eric. "There, I've put my foot down. No carrot cake."

"Another wedding crisis averted."

She ignored my sarcasm and kept talking about the wedding until she dropped me off at my apartment.

I walked in and encountered a familiar sight—Adam lying on the couch reading a textbook.

I kissed him and offered to make dinner. "Peanut butter sandwich or ramen noodles?" It was a good thing Adam didn't marry me for my cooking skills.

4

"I already had a sandwich. I'll take ice cream though, if you'll dish it. How was the movie?"

"It was good, but I worried we'd get kicked out because Tara couldn't stop texting."

As I scooped the ice cream, he asked, "How was the rest of your day?"

"Oh, the usual. I never see my husband. Work was dull. I never see my husband. My mother called. I never see my husband."

"Your mother called? Why?"

"Why did you ignore the part about 'I never see my husband'?" He reached for his bowl. I slapped his hand. "Wait for the hot fudge. Don't you *care* that I never see my husband?"

"Not really. I see him too much. His wife is overly dramatic, I hear."

"His wife pines for him—*pines*. Doesn't that tug at your heart strings?"

"I miss you too. But school won't last forever. You know that."

I drizzled the hot fudge over our ice cream and pushed a bowl toward him.

"I forgive you. I just want to know that you pine for me too."

"Oh, I pine. Men just don't verbalize it over and over like women do."

"You just said I talk too much!"

"Shut up and eat your ice cream, woman!"

We snuggled on the couch as we ate our ice cream and I focused on the moment. I wanted more of them.

He ruined the perfection by bringing up my mother. "Did your mom have a reason for calling, or did she just want to talk?"

Adam knew things were still strained between my mom and me. My parents' divorce was final, but I still hadn't fully forgiven them. I didn't blame *her* for the split—it was my dad's fault. I was angry with my mom for moving back to Ventura before the divorce was even final. She was so caught up in her own life that I felt abandoned during an important time in mine.

"She wants me to visit." I hadn't been to her new home, despite her frequent invitations. She called at least once a week. The conversations were consistent and always ended with an invitation from her, urging me to fly down and visit.

"I think you should consider it," Adam said, interrupting my musings.

"Seriously? We'd argue the entire time. She's not happy I'm married, and I'm not happy she's divorced."

"Maybe the situation isn't ideal from your viewpoint, but I think she's trying to re-establish her relationship with you. You should give her a chance."

"Adam, she's changed. She isn't the mother I thought I knew."

"Everyone changes. Maybe they're good ones. I'm all for it if you want to go for a week or two." Adam always thought the best of everyone—it was quite sickening sometimes.

"I don't want to be apart that long. I'll go if you will. I already told her I won't go without you. Today she offered to buy your ticket too." I knew he couldn't go right then because of finals coming up, but I didn't mind waiting a little longer.

"I can't go right now, I have school and work."

"I have work too. I can't just waltz in and say I want to go to California for a week. I've only been there a few months." The work excuse could work for both of us.

"Weren't you just complaining about how slow the workload is right now? They'd give you the time off, if you ask. I think you're just afraid." Adam cut right to the heart of the matter.

It was true—I was afraid. Afraid that the relationship with my mother could never be repaired. I didn't think a trip to California would help. My dad still lived right there in Logan, and I was having a hard time with him too.

Adam sensed my wavering. "When does your mom want you to come?"

"She'd send my ticket tomorrow if I asked. You're serious, aren't you?"

"I think your mom needs you out there. Besides, it would be a fun break for you. The sun, the ocean—just make sure you come home again!"

The thought of the beach convinced me. "I guess a week wouldn't hurt. On Monday I'll ask for the time off. But I'm coming home sooner if she drives me crazy."

chapter two

Adam was born and raised in Logan, and his parents still lived in the same house he grew up in. We went there on Saturday so Adam and his brothers, Justin and Mark, could help their dad, Hal, install a new fence around the Bridgers' backyard. My job was a little easier—sitting around the house watching his mom, Barbara, bottle peaches.

At least, I had planned on just watching. But when I got there, Justin's wife, Michelle, had pitched right in, helping. I liked my sister-in-law a whole lot more now than I did three years earlier when she dated Adam while she waited for Justin on his mission. I was past my jealousy of her—and her practically perfect natural beauty—really I was. I simply felt peer pressure watching her help Barbara slice peaches. I rolled up my sleeves and offered my assistance.

"Kit, that would be wonderful." Barbara motioned to the pantry. "The aprons are on the hook in there." She had to instruct me in every step because I'd never canned fruit before.

I glanced at Michelle, who smiled at me. Her makeup looked expertly applied and she wore lipstick. I didn't know canning peaches was a dress-up affair.

The kitchen was stifling. I noticed that Michelle was glowing—she didn't sweat. "Hey, Michelle, have you canned peaches a lot?" I never pictured her as a Molly Mormon sort, but sometimes she surprised me.

"Never by myself. Barbara taught me what little I know."

"I'm happy to teach," Barbara said. "I'm so glad you're both here. Lily is usually my right-hand man, but she's at youth conference today. Beth, Travis, and Sarah are out picking more peaches."

I glanced around the kitchen. The sink was full of peaches, and two loaded boxes were on the table. I kept my complaints to myself. "So you got Lily to go, then? I thought she was trying to get out of it."

"She wasn't happy. You'd think we were making her go for a root canal the way she pouted and carried on." Barbara shook her head. "I don't understand her lately. She used to love Young Women activities. Now she hates them and everything is a battle."

Michelle said, "I remember going through a phase where I didn't like going. I was a Laurel and thought the whole thing was boring. Now I'm glad I stuck with it."

"She's only fifteen and giving us fits. I don't know what she'll be like when she's a Laurel. She's not anything like Janet was. Janet always loved the activities and the classes on Sunday. Even Beth doesn't complain half as much as Lily, and she hates anything that requires her to dress up."

I had nothing to add. I'd never been to a Young Women activity in my life. I could think of a few activities I'd been to as a newly baptized adult in the Church that I wish I would have opted for the dentist instead.

"At least she didn't have to stay home and peel peaches," I said.

Barbara smiled. "She wanted to stay home and help with the peaches, which she always tries to get out of. She'll be the first to make a pie, but canning is torture for her. She's negative about everything lately." She placed lids on each full jar. "Let's talk about something else. Michelle, how was your doctor appointment yesterday?"

My ears perked up. Michelle and Justin wanted to have a baby, but she had infertility problems. Michelle talked openly about the different tests and procedures she had undergone. I hadn't realized how many she'd been going through until she detailed the latest disappointments.

"If nothing happens within the next three months, our next

8

step will be in vitro fertilization. That's going to be expensive. Justin thinks we should wait until he's finished with school, but that's another year. I don't want to wait that long." Her tone said she would win that argument.

Beth and Travis came inside, each lugging a box of peaches. "Mom, Sarah's just running around and playing," Beth complained.

Travis agreed, plunking the box down. "She should have to pick the next box. She doesn't even check the ones she puts in the box. If you see some with worms, it's her fault."

Beth dropped her box and whined, "Can we be done? We picked all the ones we can reach. I'm sick of peaches."

Barbara didn't give her much sympathy. "Sure. You can be finished outside, if you stay in and help me here in the kitchen."

"No way! That's even worse," Beth argued.

"I'll tell you what," Barbara said. "You and Travis each take one more empty box and pick up the good ones off the ground. Double-check the tree branches you can reach. As soon as you have your box filled, you can play."

"Mom, we've done all the work. Can't you make Sarah help more?" Beth complained one more time as Travis picked up an empty box and headed out the door.

"Don't worry about Sarah. She'll have to do her share of work. You'd better hurry because Travis is already gone and he'll beat you to the easy ones." Barbara said the magic words; Beth was so competitive she couldn't stand Travis beating her at anything. She grabbed the box and sprinted out the door.

Barbara laughed as we heard Beth yell at Travis to wait for her. "Thanks again, girls, for your help. I pay in peaches."

"Can I get the peaches in the form of a pie?" I asked.

Barbara nodded. "Of course. Michelle, what about you?"

"I love your peach pie, but what I'd really like is peach cobbler. I haven't had it in years." As she mentioned it, a shadow crossed Barbara's face and she stopped filling jars.

"That was Janet's specialty. Her peach cobbler was better than any I ever made." She paused. "You'd think it would get easier, but it doesn't. I don't think you ever get over the loss of a child."

Two years had passed since Adam's sister had died in a car

accident, but it still felt like she should walk in the door any minute. At moments like this, I felt the loss of my best friend keenly. I couldn't begin to imagine how Barbara felt.

Barbara must have recognized the heavy silence that had fallen over us. She brushed a tear from the corner of her eye.

"Don't worry," she said. "You don't have to walk on eggshells around me. I hope you know that by now. It just hits me hard every now and then." She sniffed and her face brightened. "Do you know who I heard from last week?"

"Who?" Michelle and I asked in unison, glad for the change in subject.

"Ben."

The subject wasn't much of a change—Ben and Janet were engaged when she died.

"What's he doing now?" I wondered how he went on after she died. I couldn't survive without Adam.

"He's got one more year left in premed and then he'll go on to medical school. It was a short email, but I was so glad to hear from him." Barbara was busy filling bottles again, the difficult moment having passed.

"Justin hears from him every now and then," Michelle added. "He asked him if he's dating anyone, but he always says he's too busy. I wonder if he'll ever find anyone else."

Michelle was tactless for bringing up Ben dating in front of Barbara, but I was also curious to know if he was seeing anyone.

Barbara didn't seem to mind. "I hope he finds someone. He's too young to spend his life alone. Janet would have been the first to tell him that." Barbara was right. Janet was the most selfless person I'd ever known.

"Yeah, she's probably on the other side trying to nudge Ben to start dating," I said.

Barbara laughed. "You're right! That's exactly what she'd do."

"Guess what?" I asked, wanting to change the subject. "I'm going to visit my mom in Ventura." They both knew I hadn't seen my mom in awhile, but neither of them knew about my issues with her.

"That's wonderful," Barbara said. "When are you going?"

"I haven't booked the ticket yet, but I probably will within the next couple of weeks."

"Is Adam going with you?" Michelle asked. "You can go between semesters."

"One of us has to work, and he volunteered to stay."

"I'm sure your mother will be thrilled to see you." Barbara was more enthusiastic about the visit than I was. I felt unsettled again and regretted bringing it up. I wished I could just forget about my mom and stay there in that sunny kitchen, canning peaches.

If only my mother was like Barbara Bridger, life would be so much easier. I loved Lily like a sister, but she didn't appreciate what an amazing mother she had.

chapter three

I dropped Adam off at work and stopped by the store to buy groceries. While I was standing in aisle eight, weighing the merits of Lucky Charms versus Magic Stars, someone called out my name.

"Kit! I can't believe it! It's so awesome to see you again!" I knew the voice instantly: Claire Anderson—my friend who had shocked everyone by unexpectedly taking off to California with her boyfriend, leaving behind only a short note.

It had been more than two years since I'd seen her. Although her voice was the same, her looks had changed dramatically. Claire had always been a sturdy girl—bordering on chunky—but now she looked thin and unhealthy. Her bleached blonde hair hung in limp, greasy strands past her shoulders, ending in black tips that looked like they'd been dipped in a can of paint.

The biggest changes, though, were in her face and on her hip. The Claire before me looked ten years older, and had I passed her without her speaking to me, I wouldn't have recognized her. On her left hip perched a baby who looked to be six or eight months old. I realized I was staring without saying a word.

"Wow, Claire, it's been a long time," I said. She hugged me, and I tried not to pull back. It smelled like more than just her hair needed washing. "Where have you been?"

"Mainly in California. I got back a couple of days ago. You

look great. I still love your hair." She reached out to touch it, and I stepped back without thinking.

Embarrassed, I tucked a strand of dark blonde hair behind my ear and mumbled, "Thanks." If I was vain about anything, it was my hair, which was naturally sun-streaked and reached halfway down my back. "Is this your baby?"

"This is Braxton." She talked to him in a sweet voice. "It's just Mommy and Braxton, huh, baby?"

Braxton smiled at his mother's voice. The toothless grin reminded me of the photo Claire had once shown me of Tommy, the baby boy she'd given up for adoption three years ago.

"So what happened to Alex?" It was so weird to have Claire show up like this. I hadn't heard from her since she left with her boyfriend, Alex—or Axel, as he liked to call himself.

Claire's face hardened as she talked about her ex-boyfriend. "I finally left the jerk. I'm such an idiot for ever going with him. The only good thing he ever gave me was Braxton."

"And Tommy," I said without thinking.

"Yeah, and Tommy. I lost track of his family after I left. Axel wanted me to have an abortion both times." She swore, calling him a name that made my eyes widen. She saw my reaction and apologized. Claire had never talked like that before—at least around me.

"Are you living back here in Logan?" I asked.

"Yeah. My mom bought me a bus ticket and said I could stay with them until I get on my feet."

Her answer surprised me since it was her mother who had kicked her out when Claire got pregnant the first time.

"So, you and your mom are okay? You've worked things out?" I didn't understand how a mother could be so hot and cold.

"She's glad I'm back. She really loves Braxton. She's not happy about the things I've done, but she's trying to help—and I need her help. I need to find a job so I can take care of myself."

"Well, I'm glad things are working out with your mom. So much has changed in the past couple of years."

"I know. I can't believe Janet's gone. My mom told me about the car accident you two were in. It's so sad that it happened a month before she got married. You and Janet are the two people

I've missed the most. I'm glad *you're* okay." Whatever else had changed, she was still blunt and honest.

"I miss her too. Did you know that Adam and I got married?" I held up my left hand to show her my ring.

"No! That's awesome! When did you get married?" She admired my ring as she jostled Braxton on her hip. He was starting to fuss.

"Last December. I graduated in May and I'm working for a CPA firm now—I get all the grunt work. Adam's going to school and working." A wave of gratitude enveloped me as I updated Claire on my life.

Braxton wasn't settling down, and Claire said, "He's tired and hungry. I've got to pick up formula and diapers. Will you write down your address and phone number for me?"

"Of course." I dug in my purse for something to write on. I had used the last scrap of paper for my grocery list so I tore a piece off that. "You need to come over and visit. Call me and we'll figure out a time. Adam is usually at school or work, so I have a lot of free evenings."

Claire shoved the paper into the pocket of her jeans. She smiled and said loudly, over Braxton's crying, "I'm so glad I saw you, Kit. I just know life is going to get better again."

She gave me another quick hug and this time I hugged her back tightly. "I'm glad too. I've missed you."

She walked off down the aisle with a crying baby in her arms and a big smile on her face. I'd forgotten about Claire's eternal optimism.

Seeing Claire put me in a good mood. When I got home, I put my groceries away and pulled out the ingredients to make chocolate chip cookies—my one and only baking specialty.

I mixed the cookie dough and thought about Claire. I had so many questions for her. Seeing her brought back a lot of memories, and I was aching to talk to somebody.

I sent Adam a text, but I knew he wouldn't read it until his break. Tara didn't know Claire and was probably with Eric anyway.

I put a sheet of cookies in the oven and decided to call my mom. I couldn't remember the last time I had initiated the call, and I felt a tinge of shame.

"Kit! Is everything all right?" Her voice sounded anxious, and I felt even worse.

"Everything's fine, Mom. Adam's at work and I was making cookies and thought I'd give you a call. Are you busy?"

"Not at all. What kind of cookies?"

"Chocolate chip, of course. Guess who I saw at the store tonight?" I ate a spoonful of cookie dough as I talked.

"I don't know. Who?"

"Claire."

"Who?"

"Claire Anderson, my friend who worked at the mall with Janet. Remember, the one who had the baby and gave him up for adoption?" Come to think of it, Claire never hung out at my house. I guess my mom wouldn't remember. Disappointed, I changed the subject.

"I'm going to check with work to see if I can take a week off to come visit you."

Her voice brightened. "That's wonderful! When do you think you'll come?"

"I'm not sure. It's really slow right now. I'm thinking two weeks from now when the next semester of school starts. Adam won't be coming. He'll have school." *That wasn't so bad*, I thought.

"I'm excited! Let me know as soon as you have the dates, and I'll book your ticket for you. I'll clear my schedule as much as I can."

"Great. I'll let you know. I should go so I don't burn the cookies."

"Okay, dear. Thanks for calling. I love you."

"I love you too, Mom." I hung up, feeling my good mood deflate. *What's wrong with me?* Claire seemed to have forgiven her mother so easily, even after being kicked out when she was pregnant and alone. I still harbored resentment against my own mother for moving back to Ventura and leaving Dave and me so abruptly.

Clearly, I needed to work on my feelings; I just wasn't sure how to do it. It occurred to me that maybe I needed lessons in charity from Claire.

chapter four

The delicious smell of Sunday dinner wafted through the Bridgers' house. My mouth watered even though Adam and I had eaten a bunch of cookies before we came.

I offered to help Barbara with dinner, but she had it all under control. Sarah had just finished setting the table. I saw everyone else lounging around, except for Lily.

"Where's Lily?" I asked Barbara.

"She's down in her room. Would you mind letting her know we're about ten minutes away from dinner?"

"Sure, I'll go tell her."

I went downstairs and knocked on her closed door. Lily had moved into Janet's old room about a year ago and was thrilled to get away from her younger sisters.

There was no answer. I knocked louder. I heard her ask, "Who is it?"

"It's Kit. Can I come in?"

"Sure." I let myself in and saw her lying on the bed, listening to her iPod. She shut it off, and I sat down.

"Ten minutes till dinner," I told her. "Did you make me a peach pie?"

"No." She looked sullen. I wanted to cheer her up, which usually wasn't hard since even when Lily was mad at the world, she was nice to me.

"Why not? Yours are the best. I peeled about a thousand peaches yesterday while you were off having fun. The least you could do is make me a pie." I tried to tease her out of her mood.

She snorted. "I wasn't 'having fun.' It was torture. Whatever happened to free agency?"

"I take it you didn't like youth conference."

"Great detective work, Sherlock." Lily was dramatic, but usually not so negative.

"Did something happen?"

"Nothing that doesn't always happen." She rolled her eyes as she said it.

"So, what is it?" Something was bothering her, big time.

"All those perfect, little righteous young women are two-faced witches. I'm sick of their hypocrisy. I hate being around them." Her tone was acid.

"What did they do?"

"It's not just one thing. They act all perfect especially when the leaders are around. But they walk down the hall and whisper about you as they go right past you. We're not supposed to gossip, but it's all they do!"

I sat there silently as she continued her rant.

"Then they text each other all the time. I've seen a couple of their texts. They're so mean. And that's just at church when they're trying to behave all perfect. It's even worse at school. There they'll say things right out loud, and if they don't know any good gossip, they'll make it up! I hate them!"

I wasn't sure what to say. "I'm sorry. Have you talked to your mom?"

"Right. My mom thinks the best of everybody. Anybody can fool my mom. She'll just say, 'Take the high road, Lily' or 'You choose how you act and react' or something stupid like that."

I wanted to help but didn't know how. Lily kept on. "If I really got to choose how I *act and react*, I wouldn't be forced to go to the stupid activities or church every week. I'd have a cell phone, and I would be able to date!"

Lily had been clamoring for a cell phone for two years. I didn't realize she'd been pressing to date. I thought she'd accepted that she could date when she was sixteen.

"You're almost sixteen. You can date then," I offered.

"That's two months from now! By the time I can date, the guy I like will like someone else. I just want some freedom."

She sounded so dramatic; I tried hard not to smile.

"I know it seems like forever, but two months will pass pretty quickly. Hang in there. If the guy won't wait two months to date you, he's not worth it."

"You don't even know him," Lily said as she leaned in toward me and dropped her voice low. "You swear you won't tell my parents?" Her intensity caught me off guard.

"Not without your permission," I said, hoping I wasn't agreeing to something I would regret.

"His name is Cody. He's so amazing. He's eighteen and he likes me. A lot. And I like him."

Alarm bells went off in my head. "Lily, eighteen is a little old for a fifteen-year-old. Does he know you're fifteen?"

She looked guilty. "I told him I was sixteen. You said yourself that two months isn't that long. I'll *be* sixteen then. He's just so hot."

"Where did you meet him?" I didn't think Lily had many opportunities to meet guys, except at school and church. She'd been out of school for the summer, and my gut told me she didn't meet Cody at church.

"He works at Hastings. I met him while he was working."

That didn't sound so bad. Hastings was a perfectly respectable bookstore. I'd worked at a bookstore before I got the job at the CPA firm. I felt relieved.

"You shouldn't have told him you were older than you are. No wonder he wants you to go out with him. You should tell him the truth. If he likes you, he'll understand."

She groaned. "You sound like Mom. I thought you would be on my side. He'll think I'm a baby. Besides, in a couple more months, it won't be a lie. I'll be sixteen." She muttered under her breath, "If he doesn't dump me before then."

"How could he dump you if you aren't even dating?" I was

suspicious again. She wasn't telling me everything.

"Oh, you know how it is. We don't date, but we like each other, so we're kind of, you know, together." Her voice was casual, but I could tell it was forced.

"How can that be? When do you see him enough to be 'together'?" I wished I hadn't promised not to tell her parents. At least I didn't promise I wouldn't tell Adam.

"I go to Hastings when I know he's working, and he takes his break when I'm there. And we've had lunch together. We've talked a lot. It's like we're soul mates."

Holy cow! What was I supposed to say to that? It was beyond alarm bells in my head—it was full-on sirens. "Is this guy, um, Cody, one of the things the girls at church have been gossiping about?"

"Yeah. Like it's any of their business. We were having lunch together, and Savannah and Brielle saw me. They started all sorts of rumors. Bad ones."

"So does your mom know about these rumors?" I asked.

"Savannah's mom told her I went to lunch with Cody. I got grounded and a big lecture. So, yeah, Mom knows." Lily's pout returned.

"Did she tell you not to see him anymore? Does she know how old he is?" I didn't want to say or do anything against Barbara's wishes even though I'd given Lily my word.

"They don't know exactly how old he is, and you promised not to tell them."

"I know what I promised. What about seeing him? Did they forbid it?"

"They won't even give him a chance, Kit. They won't even get to know him. How fair is that? My whole life they preach to me about not judging others, and they won't even give him a chance?"

"I don't know about that, but I'll tell you this much, Lily. Your parents love you more than anyone else does, and they want what's best for you. The best thing you can do right now is to listen to them and be honest with Cody. I mean it. I know you're not a liar, Lily, but you've crossed a line and you need to fix it." I tried not to sound preachy, but I was worried. I understood why Barbara was concerned, and she didn't even know the whole story.

"I thought you would understand. I don't like you calling me a liar." She glared at me.

"Then don't be one." I stood up and reached for her hand. "I love you, Lily. I'm glad you talked to me. Let's go to dinner."

Her expression softened, and she took my hand and followed me out the door but whispered once more, "Remember, you promised not to tell."

chapter five

On the way home from the Bridgers', I told Adam about my conversation with Lily. He thought he should tell his mom, but I convinced him to wait. We decided I'd go to Hastings and check Cody out to get a better idea of what he was like.

We were barely home when there was a knock on the door. I knew that knock—it was my brother, Dave.

He rarely stopped by our apartment, and our communication usually took place in the form of texts with an occasional phone call. I sometimes wondered if our relationship would have been closer if we had been brother and sister by birth. My parents never treated me differently because I was adopted, but sometimes I wondered if they loved him more.

I opened the door and greeted him with, "Is everything all right?" *Yuck, I sound just like Mom.*

He laughed and said, "What? Can't I just stop by to visit?" I motioned for him to come inside.

"It's such a rare event, I wondered if there was an emergency."

"Nah, I'm just bored and wanted to see someone whose life is even more boring than mine." He said hello to Adam and flopped down on the couch. "Got anything to drink?"

"Water, milk, or diet cola," I offered.

"No beer? I was hoping for a beer." He always tried to push my buttons. I ignored the comment and got him a glass of water.

"So what's up?" I asked, sitting down next to him. Adam sat on the floor by my legs. I automatically played with his hair.

"Not much. I've been working and enjoying the summer. I went boating last week with a bunch of my friends and we had a blast."

"Where did you go?" I was jealous. Adam and I loved boating. We'd been out once this summer with his parents on their old boat.

"Lake Powell. We camped for a week and it was hot, but we were in the water most of the time so we didn't care. Gas was expensive. Even with six of us pitching in, I'm broke."

I'd never been to Lake Powell, but Adam had been several times. He and Dave spent the next few minutes talking about it. By the time they were finished, I wanted to go even more badly than before.

"I'm supposed to invite you guys to dinner tomorrow night," Dave said. He still lived with my dad and often acted as the intermediary between my dad and me.

"What's the occasion?" There was always a reason. Neither my brother nor my father would volunteer to cook.

"Dad wants you to meet Amberlie," Dave said casually.

"Who?"

"Amberlie. His girlfriend."

"Are you kidding? What kind of name is *Amberlie*? She sounds like she's eighteen years old!" I had tried to ignore that my dad was dating again. In fact, I'd avoided him as much as possible since the divorce. Up until this point, I'd been fairly successful.

"Nah, don't worry. She's old." My irritation flared at his flippant attitude.

"How old? Are they serious?" I was alarmed. My dad had never tried to introduce me to anyone he was dating.

"I haven't asked her age. You can if you want. She's just old— like a parent." It was just like Dave to be obtuse.

"But are they serious?" I pressed. "I want details." Guys were not good at giving details—it was like pulling teeth.

He shrugged. "I guess. They're always hanging out together. She's cooking dinner tomorrow, and she's a pretty good cook. A lot better than Dad."

"That's horrible."

"Not if you have to eat as much of Dad's cooking as I do."

"You know what I mean. He can't be serious about her. The divorce has only been final for a few months. Why haven't I heard about this before?" I didn't bother hiding my anger.

"Don't get mad at me," Dave protested. "You're the one who hardly talks to Dad. It's not like he's been hiding it or anything."

He had a point—I kept communications with my dad short. Quite simply, I was still angry with him for cheating on my mom and breaking up our family. I blamed him and wasn't ready to get over it. I knew it was unrealistic to expect them to get back together, but I felt like he didn't even care about the havoc he had wreaked in my life.

I tried to speak calmly. "Do you like her?"

"She's okay. Dad likes her and that's what matters. I'm moving out of the house soon anyways, so I don't much care." Dave always accepted matters as they happened—another thing that bothered me about him.

"Is she divorced, widowed, pretty, ugly? What?"

"I dunno, I think she's divorced—or maybe a widow. She has two or three kids. I don't think she's ugly, but I don't check out old women, so that's all I can tell you about her looks. Ask Dad for the dirt."

I hoped Dave was never a witness to a crime, because his idea of details was not helpful. I told him so.

"What do you expect?" he asked. "It's not like you can't come see her yourself tomorrow night. Dinner's at seven."

"*If* I come," I huffed.

"You'll come. You can't stand the curiosity," he said smugly and then added, "Oh yeah, be prepared for a family home evening lesson—but you'll probably like that."

"What do you mean? You're not funny, Dave." He mocked me a lot about "getting religion," and this sounded like another jab.

"Dad's getting all religious on us too. Amberlie has the missionaries coming over, and he's listening to all their stuff. So, see, she can't be all that bad. She's a Mormon like you. I'll bet Dad becomes one pretty soon."

"No way. You're messing with me."

"I'm serious. He's even gone to church with her."

My anger boiled up again. Adam could tell. He grabbed my hand and gave it a squeeze, then responded before I could gather my thoughts. "Dave, thanks for stopping by. Tell your dad we'll be there."

I'm sure Dave saw the storm about to erupt, and he looked thankful for the reprieve. He was out the door in about five seconds.

He was gone maybe ten seconds when I let loose with my rant.

"How dare he? How can he stoop so low as to try to get to me with the church thing? He knows how much I wanted him and Mom to listen to the discussions. He never even considered it! Now some woman named *Amberlie* gets him to listen, and he's all ready to get baptized!"

Adam wisely let me vent for another five minutes or so. He just listened quietly.

When I finished spewing forth, I took a breath and asked him what he thought about it.

He hesitated. "I know you're really upset by this, and I can see why. I think you should consider this from a different viewpoint. Maybe your dad isn't listening to the discussions just because Amberlie is in his life. Maybe he really is ready to change."

I started to interrupt, and Adam placed his fingers over my lips. "Let me finish. More than anything, you've wanted your family to accept the gospel. With the divorce, you know it won't happen with them together, so why not be happy that he's at least willing to listen?"

"But what if he's just doing it for *her*? And why do it for her and not my mom or me? It's like he's left us all behind. That's not how it's supposed to be." I fought back the tears. "I just want a normal family."

"You want a perfect family, Kit. That doesn't exist," Adam said gently. "Maybe it's time for you to move on and forgive your dad."

He should take my side. The fact that he didn't made me mad. "That's easy for you to say because your family *is* perfect. It's all great for you to talk about forgiveness when you've never had to deal with anything like this!"

He flinched as though I'd struck him. "Maybe I haven't dealt with the exact thing you're going through, but everyone has their share of burdens."

"Like being a Bridger is such a burden," I said sarcastically, through my tears. "You were born to LDS parents who got married in the temple. Everything comes easy for you."

"You know that doesn't guarantee an easy life. My *sister* died in a car accident a month before she was supposed to get married. You know my mom has struggled with depression since then. Look at their struggles with Lily. Nobody's life is easy—or perfect." I knew the truthfulness of his words even before he said them. I just wanted to lash out at someone.

"See. You're even perfect in your reasoning." I wiped my tears, my venting done, finally exhausting itself.

"No, I'm not. That's why we're so good together, though. We balance each other out." He pulled me close and hugged me tightly.

"Yeah, I'm the unbalanced one." I returned his embrace. "I'm getting snot on your shirt."

"That's okay. You're the one who does the laundry."

"You work tomorrow night. You can't go with me," I reminded him.

"I'll trade shifts with someone. I'll be right there with you," he assured me.

"You just don't want to eat my cooking. You're probably excited to eat Amberlie's dinner."

"With a name like that, she's bound to be a great cook," he teased. So maybe he wasn't all that perfect. The thought was comforting.

"You know what would make me feel better?" I asked. "If you do the laundry this week." It was worth a shot.

"Nice try." He pulled away from me. "Now go blow your nose and wash your face so I can kiss you."

I obeyed—after wiping my face on his shirt one more time.

chapter six

During the staff meeting on Monday, our office
manager, Nadine, announced we were looking for a
new receptionist. I immediately thought of Claire and told them
I knew of someone. They were willing to interview her, and I
couldn't wait to call her.

After the meeting, I asked for time off to visit my mom in
California. My manager said yes so fast that I questioned my value
to the firm.

I scheduled my trip for the last week in August. Adam would
be back in school by then and work would still be busy for him. I
texted my mom and Adam with the dates, and my mom had the
ticket booked in less than fifteen minutes. I think she was afraid
I'd change my mind.

I called Claire to tell her about the job interview.

"Kit! What's up?"

"You said you were looking for a job. I found out our firm has
an opening for a receptionist. Are you interested?"

"Yeah, but I've never done that before. Will they even consider
me?" She sounded uncertain.

"You worked at the Hallmark store and answered phones and
talked to customers there. I know you can do it." I encouraged her.
"I already told them you were interested and could start immediately. They'll give you an interview at least."

"That would be awesome! What do I need to do?"

"Do you have a résumé?" I asked.

"No, I've never done one." I heard Braxton fussing in the background.

"I'll help you. Can you come over tonight around 5:30? I have an hour before I'm going to my dad's for dinner. We can do it then." I was excited to have something to think about besides dinner with my dad and Amberlie.

I saw Adam at lunch and told him about the opening at work and my plans to help Claire.

"I think it's a good idea," Adam said. "Remember though, just because she gets an interview doesn't mean she'll get the job."

"I know, but she might get it. She needs a break."

"I have a suggestion," Adam offered as he swallowed the last bite of his sandwich. "Don't take it the wrong way, but your description of how she looks now doesn't sound very professional. Maybe you could coach her on that. The first impression will stay with them."

"You're right." I pulled out some cookies and offered them to Adam and bit into one myself. "I need to think of a way to bring it up. I'm sure she doesn't have any clothes that would work for an office. There's not a lot of time."

"Did you already set up the interview?" Adam asked.

"Yeah, it's set for Wednesday afternoon."

"Work on the résumé tonight and then maybe tomorrow night you can go to DI and find some clothes for her that won't cost very much."

I liked Adam's suggestions. I hadn't even considered Claire's appearance, but he was right—it wouldn't really fit in the CPA firm atmosphere. "Good idea. I don't know if she'll even have any money to spend, though. If she doesn't, are you okay if I spend a little money to get her some clothes?"

"You're the number cruncher around here. If you can squeeze the money out of the budget, I don't mind at all. I want to help her as well."

The afternoon at work passed slowly. I kept thinking about Claire and what I could do for her. I tried not to think about the dinner afterward, but the hard feelings crept up throughout the day.

Claire showed up promptly at 5:30, out of breath. "I rode my bike over, and I'm way out of shape. Can I get a drink of water?"

"Of course. You're probably dying of heat stroke. It's hot today." She followed me into the kitchen, and I got her a drink.

She gulped it down and said, "Thanks. I thought I might croak." She looked around our living area. "This is a cute apartment." She walked over and peered at the portrait of Adam and me in front of the Salt Lake Temple, taken on our wedding day. "I forgot how cute Adam is. You two are perfect for each other."

I refilled her cup with water. "Thanks. I feel pretty lucky to be married to him." Adam was everything I'd hoped for in a husband, and I sometimes felt like he'd married down when he chose me.

"He's the lucky one," Claire said. She smiled at me. "Thanks so much for helping me."

I booted up my laptop and opened a new document. "Do you want to type it up, or do you want me to?" I asked.

"You do it. I'm not that good with computers." She chewed her fingernails. "I don't know if I can do this job, but I really want to work in an office, like you."

"You'll have to use computers, so you can't be afraid of them," I told her. "But it's not all computer stuff. You'll answer the phones, file, make copies, and stuff like that. Have you worked with Word or Excel before?"

"I did in high school. I don't know how much I'll remember, but I'll do my best."

Claire didn't have a lot of experience. She'd worked at the mall before she went to California and had several random jobs, mainly at fast food places, while she was gone. Her résumé was short.

I printed off half a dozen copies for her and slipped them into a folder.

"My first résumé," she said, smiling. "It feels so professional."

"Speaking of that," I said. "I think we should do something to help you look more professional for your interview." I didn't want to hurt her feelings by saying so, but she needed to know.

"Yeah. I was going to ask you what I should wear." She didn't seem the least bit offended.

"You can wear a skirt or dress pants with a nice top. You want to look your best for the interview. Do you have clothes that will work?"

"Not really."

Claire was shorter than me—most women were. She used to be chunkier, but now she looked thinner than me. Although my pants would be too long, maybe a couple of my skirts and some tops might work for her. I suggested it.

"Really? Are you sure?" Claire was excited by the prospect, and we went back to my bedroom and I dug out the skirts I was thinking of. I added two more and found half a dozen tops that would go with them. I was embarrassed at how many clothes I actually had when Claire had so little.

I looked at the time. I needed to pick Adam up on campus at 6:45, and we were going to go straight to my dad's from there. We had a few minutes left.

"Why don't you try these on, and if they fit you can have them," I offered.

"Awesome!" She scooped up the clothes. "Can I use the bathroom?"

"Sure. Or you can try them on in here. I'll go out to the living room."

She came out ten minutes later carrying the stack of clothes and wearing a big grin. "They're great! Are you sure I can have them?"

"Definitely. Sorry they're all skirts, but my pants would be too long. What shoe size do you wear?"

"Seven."

"Oh. All of mine are eights. Do you have shoes?" I asked.

"I'll bet my mom has a pair I can borrow that will go with skirts. Thanks so much, Kit. You have no idea how much this helps."

"You're welcome. Let me get you a couple of bags." As I pulled out some plastic grocery bags for her clothes, I figured I might as well mention the hair. "Claire, I think you should get your hair cut before the interview on Wednesday. How attached are you to the dark ends?"

"You don't like it?" she asked.

"It doesn't matter if I like or not. It's just the receptionist is the first person a client sees when they come into our office. They are pretty conservative there." I felt bad, like I was judging her, but I knew the environment.

"If you think I should do it, I will." Her face turned red and it wasn't from the heat. "I don't have any money right now. Would you mind cutting it for me?"

I knew my talents didn't include cutting hair, so I was reluctant. "I would, but I'd be afraid I'd mess it up."

"I'll have my mom cut it then." Claire separated the pile of clothes into two neat stacks and transferred them into the bags.

"What if I take you to get a haircut tomorrow night after I get off work?" I asked, not wanting her to feel like I was pushing her but wanting her to get a professional cut. "My treat."

"You've already done too much," she protested.

"I'd really like to. And not to be rude, but you need more than just a trim." Subtlety has never been my strong point.

"Okay," Claire said. "What time should I be here?"

"I'll pick you up after I get off." She gave me her mom's address. I wrote it down, and she gathered up her bags to leave.

"Thanks for helping me, Kit. You're awesome!" She opened the door and gave me a quick hug.

Her comment embarrassed me, yet made me feel wonderful. "I'm glad you're home, Claire," I called out as she left.

"Me too! See you tomorrow!"

My good mood lasted until we pulled up to my old house, where my dad and Dave still lived. The "For Sale" sign was a stark reminder of all the things I'd tried to ignore. My parents had put it up for sale in May, right after Dave graduated.

The unfamiliar green car in the driveway must be Amberlie's—I hated green cars.

As we walked up the driveway, Adam smiled and said, "You can do it, Kit. Give him a chance."

I tried to smile back, but my dark thoughts got in the way.

We walked in to the smell of something Italian cooking. It smelled good, but I wouldn't admit it to anyone else—not even Adam.

No one was in the living room, so I called out, "Dad, we're here."

My dad came out of the kitchen, followed by a woman who was obviously Amberlie. They wore matching aprons. *I want to throw up*, I thought.

As my dad made introductions, I forced a smile and shook hands. Adam kept his arm around me and didn't have to force his charm.

I looked at her critically. She didn't look like a monster or a bimbo. She looked normal—like somebody's mom.

"Kit, I'm so glad to meet you. I hope you like lasagna." Amberlie had wavy blonde hair. If it had any gray in it, the blonde masked it well. Her smile looked genuine and there were lots of crinkles around her eyes when she smiled—if I'd met her some other way, I probably would have liked her immediately.

My dad knew I loved lasagna. He probably put her up to it. "I like it," I said, shooting a glare at my dad, but he didn't seem to notice.

Adam said, "It smells delicious."

"Amberlie makes the best lasagna I've ever tasted," my dad said. He turned to her. "What do you need me to do?"

I seethed inside. He didn't wear perky little aprons when he was married to my mom, and he didn't offer to help in the kitchen, either. He made me sick.

Once again, Adam came to the rescue, "What can we do to help?"

Amberlie waved Adam away. "It's ready. I just need to set it on the table. I hope you two aren't roasting. I told Paul it was too hot for lasagna, but he insisted."

I *knew* it was his doing. My second glare was also wasted on him.

"It doesn't feel too hot to me," Adam said. "Kit and I both love lasagna. Don't we?" He squeezed my shoulder to prompt me. They were all looking at me.

"Yeah, we do. Where's Dave?" I asked.

Amberlie answered. "He's downstairs, playing video games." I wasn't asking *her*, and it irritated me that she was the one who replied.

"I'll go tell him it's time for dinner," I offered, wanting to escape for a minute or two.

The food was delicious, and I managed to be civil through most of dinner—probably because I kept my mouth full. I honestly couldn't pick out anything wrong with Amberlie herself—it was her association with my dad that was the problem. I wondered if she was the one who broke up my parents' marriage.

"How long have you two known each other?" I asked between bites.

"One month yesterday," my dad answered. *So not that long ago.*

"Where did you meet?" I asked. "Do you work together?"

Amberlie laughed. "No, it was a singles' dance, of all things. The first one I ever went to—and the last."

My dad at an LDS singles' dance? I found it hard to believe. I turned to him, "What were you doing there, Dad? Picking up women?" It sounded a lot harsher when I voiced it. My dad didn't seem to notice, but Adam kicked me under the table and Dave snickered.

"No. I went with a friend from work. Charles Eckley? I doubt you had any classes with him." My dad grinned and looked silly doing it. "He kept asking me to give it a try and meet new people. I'm glad I did."

Amberlie blushed, and I felt a little nauseated. *Old people love—gross*, I thought. Aloud, I asked Amberlie, "You said 'first and last' dance, why?"

"First of all, I'm not a dancer. I'm clumsy, but so is your father." Another fond look at my dad. *Yuck.* "I'd been to a few other single activities since my divorce, but I always avoided dances. My friend, Evelyn, convinced me to go that night. I saw your father, and he looked even more uncomfortable than I was, so I took pity on him and talked to him."

"She even asked me to dance," my dad said.

"I did not. You asked me," she argued playfully.

"But you said yes."

"My sore feet can attest to that. Not only did he look more uncomfortable than me, he was also a worse dancer than me. *That* made him stand out."

It was strange to hear their bantering. It reminded me a little of Adam and me. I didn't like that.

My dad helped himself to more lasagna and said, "I thought it was my personality that made me stand out."

She laughed again. "No. Your personality is what convinced me to go out with you. It definitely wasn't your dancing."

There was a pause in the conversation, and my dad seemed to realize he'd been flirting in front of his children. His face flushed.

Amberlie covered up the awkwardness by standing and saying, "I've got homemade brownies in the kitchen. Who would like one?"

Dave and Adam said yes at the same time. *This woman knows all the tricks.* I couldn't resist chocolate either. "Do you want to save them for after the lesson?'

"What lesson?" my dad asked.

"Family home evening. Don't you have a lesson prepared?" I was confused. Dave had forewarned me, after all.

Dad and Amberlie exchanged glances. My dad spoke up. "We weren't planning on it, but if you want to, we can."

I looked at Dave, who was trying not to laugh—and failing miserably.

"You jerk!" I shrieked at him. "You set me up."

He didn't bother to deny it, which made me even angrier. I looked at Adam for support, but he was trying to suppress a smile too.

Red-faced, I turned away from them both. I spoke to Amberlie. "I would like a brownie. I think I deserve Dave's share too."

She maintained a straight face and said, "Come and help me. You can cut them."

Dave got the smallest brownie, but he didn't say a word. I'm sure he figured he'd slither in later and grab more. I laughed all the way home as I imagined his face when he went into the kitchen to snag another one. I looked at the plate on my lap that contained the rest of the brownies. I would take the small victories.

chapter seven

When Claire came in for her interview on Wednesday, she looked like a totally different person from the one I'd met in the grocery store a few days earlier. The blunt, shoulder-length haircut suited her.

I gave her a little wave as she walked past my cubby. She waved back and flashed her bright smile. I noticed the little jewel in the side of her nose was gone, and I silently cheered her. She looked like she would fit in just fine.

Nadine, the office manager, walked Claire back to the front when the interview was over, so I didn't get a chance to ask Claire how it went. I twitched with curiosity all afternoon.

Just before five I gathered up the courage to ask Nadine how the interview went. She had been with the firm for longer than anyone except the partners, and we all joked that she must have come with the building. I knew if Nadine liked her, Claire would get the job.

When I stepped into her office, Nadine was talking to one of the dozens of plants that adorned her office. "That's right, princess, I've got special food for you. We want your royal purple to fill out those leaves, now, yes we do." I knew Nadine was aware of me standing in the doorway, but she ignored me until she finished the conversation with her plant. She smiled at it and patted a fat, purple-veined leaf. "There now, get your beauty rest."

34

Nadine turned her attention to me. "Kit, what can I do for you? Would you like a plant start?" She was always offering me plant starts since I had unwittingly said yes the first time she'd offered. I didn't have the heart to tell her that every plant I owned had died, including the half dozen she'd already given me.

"I wondered how the interview with Claire went." I tried to avoid answering the plant question. I didn't know if she'd tell me anything. Nadine could go on and on about some things and keep completely mum about others.

"Oh, that young girl needs a chance, I think." Nadine nodded to herself and started looking around her desk for her glasses. She did that a lot. I pointed to her wiry gray hair, which I think she permed herself. She patted the tight frizz and found her glasses. "Yes, that's what I think."

Nadine often sounded like she wasn't quite right, and it was easy to be fooled into thinking she was absentminded. I quickly learned that she rarely missed anything that went on around her.

"So, does that mean she'll get the job?" I ventured to ask.

"I have to get the okay from the Partners," she said. She referred to the two partners like that—as if it were a revered title. Of course everyone knew that if Nadine thought something should happen, the Partners would concur.

"When do you think you—I mean, the Partners—will decide for sure?"

"Her qualifications aren't the best," Nadine pointed out.

"I know, but she'll be reliable." At least I hoped she would.

"I don't think you need to worry about your friend, dear." She smiled at me. "Go on home to that young man of yours. Scoot!" I turned to go then she said, "Wait!"

I stopped, turning toward her, hoping for more information.

She thrust a little pot out to me. "Here's another plant start for you. It's Fluffy Ruffles."

"Okay." I took it from her automatically.

"It's a variety of Boston fern. Bright light, but no direct sun." She waved me away. "Try not to kill this one, Kit," she added as I walked away. I swear, that woman knew *everything*.

Adam was already home and laughed when he saw the plant.

"Do you want to bypass the neglect and throw it away now?"

"You should be in charge of the plants." I argued.

"I think I'd be worse. Why do you keep bringing them home?"

"Nadine gave it to me. It's a Boston fern. A fluffy something or other." I set it on the counter and pushed it away from me. "What's worse—she *knows* I kill plants but still gives them to me. She thinks everyone can be a plant whisperer like her."

"Maybe she hopes you'll get better at it. Have you tried talking to them like Nadine does?" He pulled it toward him and started talking to it in a high-pitched voice. "Hello, little plant. Do you know you're about to meet your maker? You've been given to the plant killer. I'd try to save you, but she's just too good at what she does."

"You and Nadine are accessories to the crime. You both know I can't keep a plant alive, yet she keeps giving them to me, and you keep letting them die at my hand. I'm just not a nurturer."

"Not a plant nurturer maybe." Adam left the plant and came up behind me, pulling me close. "How was your day other than picking up another victim?"

"It was good. Claire came in for her interview, and she looked great. I didn't get a chance to talk to her. I was trying to find out if they were going to offer her the job when Nadine forced that innocent baby fern on me."

"Do you think she'll get the job?" Adam asked.

"I think so, but Nadine wouldn't tell me for sure. If they hire her and she's not reliable, I wonder if they'll blame me."

"You just have to worry about something, don't you? You knew Claire before. She was reliable when she worked with Janet." I stepped out of his embrace and turned to face him.

"Until she took off with 'Axel' for two years without telling anybody."

"She could take off again, but that's her issue, not yours. They wouldn't hire her strictly on your word anyway. What's for dinner?"

"Tacos. I'll start it right after I change. Will you go check the mail?"

Adam came back in as I headed for the kitchen. He was thumbing through the mail and stopped at one envelope. He frowned as he looked at it.

"What is it?" I leaned over to see what he was staring at.

"There's a letter addressed to 'Katherine Matthews Bridger' from an attorney in California." He handed me the letter. "What do you think it is?"

"I don't know." I looked it over. *Bernacchi Graves & Chandler* from Oxnard, California. I felt kind of sick. *What can it be?* My mother was in Ventura, California, but she'd said nothing about me receiving any legal paperwork. It didn't feel good. I stood frozen, my thoughts in turmoil. Adam's voice broke my trance.

"Open it, Kit."

"You do it." I shoved it at him. "It's something bad, I just know it."

Adam didn't take it but pushed it gently back toward me. "It's your letter, you open it. Let's sit down. You don't know if it's bad news or not, and even if it is, I'm right here with you and we'll deal with it together." He led me over to the couch.

It's just a letter. It won't bite. I opened it and unfolded the expensive linen-bond paper.

> *Dear Katherine,*
>
> *I am corresponding with you at the request of my client who, at this juncture, must remain anonymous. There is no delicate way of saying this, so I will put it as simply and forthrightly as possible: My client believes she is your birth mother and desires to make contact with you.*
>
> *Normally, California law requires the mutual assent of both parties prior to adoption records being unsealed. In this case, the unsealing of those records would not reveal your birth parents as they were unknown to the court at that time.*
>
> *My client has submitted to a DNA test and would like you to agree to the same. All costs for this test will be borne by my client. If the results prove that my client's assertion is correct, my client would like to arrange a meeting with you as soon as possible.*
>
> *As time is of the essence, we are requesting that you contact our office as soon as possible for directions in setting up the DNA test collection and other pertinent information.*

Please give careful consideration to this request, as my client is most anxious to get this issue resolved.
Very truly yours,
Arthur Bernacchi, Esquire

Of all the things I worried about, a message from my birth mother had never even crossed my mind. She'd abandoned me at birth. Literally thrown me in the garbage. I reconciled myself years ago to the fact that my birth mother had likely lived and died on the street. I never expected to know who she really was, and I rarely thought about her.

Stunned, I looked at Adam. He finished reading and met my gaze. I whispered, "Do you think this is a joke?"

"Why would anyone joke about this?" he reasoned.

I agreed. Blindsided at first, I started to consider the possibilities. "Adam, I could find out why she did it. Why she threw me away. My birth mother is still alive."

"So, you want to call him? Set up a time for testing?" Adam spoke cautiously, trying not to let his own opinion influence me.

"I want to know what you think."

"Kit, you need to do what feels right to you. If you want answers, I think you deserve to have them."

"So you think I should call them?" I prodded.

"Yeah, if you feel good about it. But remember this—Paul and Nora Matthews are your parents. They've loved you and cared for you your whole life. I know you're mad at them for getting a divorce, but I wouldn't want you to hurt them." Adam's words brought me back to reality.

This had nothing to do with my parents. It was about getting the answer to a deeply personal question I'd carried around my entire life. I doubted they would see it that way and had no desire to cause them pain.

"You're right. I don't want to tell them about this right now. I want to take the DNA test though. I have to know. Let's keep it between us for now." This was all so new and raw, I wasn't ready to discuss it with anyone else.

"It's your news to tell, if you choose to tell it. It's 5:45, that means it's 4:45 in California. Do you want to call right now?"

I suddenly felt nervous. "No. I need to wait a little bit. I have to think about it more."

We sat there a few more minutes as I reread the letter and again voiced my thoughts to Adam. He listened patiently as I argued back and forth with myself.

He sometimes joked that he wasn't really necessary to our conversations because I carried on both sides just fine by myself. I decided to call the attorney back tomorrow.

Adam's stomach growled loudly enough to remind me that I needed to cook dinner. I browned the ground beef and shredded the cheese while Adam chopped tomatoes and lettuce. Cooking wasn't such a chore when we did it together. I savored the moment, eating together at our little table on our cheap dishes.

Just before seven my cell phone rang.

"Kit! Guess what? I got the job!" Claire sounded so excited, I could barely understand her.

"Really? Nadine called you tonight? I tried to get it out of her, but she wouldn't tell me." I bet she didn't even check with the partners. She was a sly one.

"She called a couple of hours ago, but I had to feed and bathe Braxton and get him ready for bed so I couldn't call 'til now. I'm so excited!"

"When do you start?"

"On Monday. Things are looking so much better. Kit, when I came back to Logan with Braxton, I was so depressed. I felt so worthless, like I totally messed up my life and wanted to give up. My mom let me come home, and I figured I'd have to work at minimum wage. Then you helped me get this job, and it just gave me hope again. Thank you so much." Claire's words brought tears to my eyes.

"You're welcome. You got the job on your own, you know. I'm so glad for you."

"Thanks. You never know what life will bring. Last week, I was homeless and jobless. Now I have both *and* a good friend. I was afraid I'd lost your friendship forever when I took off like that. You're a good person, Kit. I'm glad you forgave me."

"There's nothing for me to forgive, Claire. You're back, safe and sound, and you're making a new beginning. I'll always be your friend."

I truly harbored no hard feelings toward her. I simply hoped she would make better decisions in the future.

After we said good-bye, Claire's words came back to me. *I thought I'd lost your friendship forever when I took off like that.* Maybe that's what my birth mom was thinking. Maybe she regretted it all these years but wasn't able to make it right. She must've known the baby she left in the trash had been found and adopted.

Like Claire, it was probably hard for her to reach out again, after making such a huge mistake. If I was really the kind of person Claire thought I was, I could forgive my birth mother too.

chapter eight

I waited until 10:00 a.m. to make sure the law office would be open. I stepped out to my car to make the call in private. I convinced myself Arthur Bernacchi would be in a meeting or something, and I would have to leave a message, so when he picked up the line I was speechless for a moment.

I stammered a bit then my words came out in a jumble. "This is Kit—uh—Katherine Bridger, calling from Logan, Utah. I got a letter from you yesterday."

"Yes, Katherine." Mr. Bernacchi either recognized my name or was a good faker. "Thank you for responding so promptly."

"Um, I have some questions." I didn't know where to start.

"I would be surprised if you didn't. I'll do my best to answer them." He sounded professional and distant—but not unkind. I tried to relax a little bit.

"Can you tell me more about my—this client—who says she is my birth mom?" There, straight out with it.

"I'm afraid she has requested anonymity until the results of the DNA tests are back and the relationship confirmed." He hesitated then continued. "Naturally, she is eager to find out the results."

"Why did she wait so long? Why now, after twenty-two years?" I hated knowing so little.

"Katherine, I'm not at liberty to answer these questions for my client. I can say that there is a matter of urgency, however. There is a health issue that has recently come to light."

"What kind of issue?" I pressed.

"I'm unable to discuss it further at this point." He was very good at not giving answers. My silence must have concerned him because he said, "Katherine, are you still there?"

"I'm here. I want to do the test—the DNA test. So I guess I need to know what to do."

"Excellent. I will put my assistant, Jodi, on the line, and she will give you the necessary instructions. Please leave your telephone number with her. I will contact you as soon as the results are back."

I'd barely said, "Thanks," before I was transferred to Jodi. She was efficient and seemed to anticipate my questions even before I did. Before I knew it, I had the name and address of a lab in Logan, which would perform the test. Jodi probably had the lab on the phone before I went back inside.

I texted Adam to tell him I'd made the call and to let him know I was going in that afternoon for the test. I was sure he would call me back during his lunch break. I needed to talk to someone now. I called Tara to see if she could go to lunch with me.

We met at a fast food place, and Tara ordered a salad and a diet soft drink. "I only have three weeks to go, and I'm afraid my wedding dress won't fit," she announced. "You're so lucky you're thin, you probably never worry about what you eat."

"It's not that I'm thin, I'm tall. I hide it better," I said as I ordered a cheeseburger and large fries.

"Oh, so you're calling me short *and* fat!" Tara pretended to pout as she grabbed a few of my French fries before the server even pulled his hands away from the tray.

She shifted the subject back to her impending wedding. "We got the last of the invitations addressed and sent out." She flexed her right hand. "I still have cramps in my hand."

"I heard that carrot cake is good for hand cramps." I was dying to tell her about the letter and the call, but I didn't know how to interrupt her wedding talk with my news.

"We're not having carrot cake. You need a new joke. We're having chocolate cake—with caramel filling. Doesn't that sound yummy?" She kept talking about the wedding, and there was no graceful way to change the subject.

I took the last bite of my cheeseburger and washed it down with soda. "Seriously though, there is something that I want to talk about."

Her expression told me she sensed my mood change. "What's going on?"

"I got a letter yesterday from an attorney in California." Tara listened while I told her about the letter, my phone call this morning, and the DNA test I was scheduled to take that afternoon.

Tara's silence was a good indication of her shock. It took a lot to shut her up, but my story did it. I finally had to ask her. "So what do you think?"

"I can't believe it. What are the chances that she'd contact you after all this time? I mean, how did she find you? Do you think she's been keeping track of you all these years?"

"I doubt she's kept track or she'd know for sure who I am. I think something has happened. The attorney said there is some sort of medical issue." I had a hard time keeping my voice steady, which surprised me. I thought I had detached myself.

"Wait—I bet she's found out she only has six months to live and she's going through deathbed repentance. Or maybe she's rich and you'll inherit everything when she dies." Tara was in her element now—speculation. "I know. She's being blackmailed and has to come forward before her sordid past is revealed. Or *she's* the blackmailer."

I laughed at that one. "You watch too much TV."

"Maybe so, but it's *reality* TV. Maybe you could be on a reality TV show. It's like that Locator show." She clapped her hands. "I'll know somebody famous!"

Tara's theatrics actually had a calming effect on me. Her viewing it as an adventure shifted my own attitude a little. Maybe this would turn out to be something amazing.

After we said good-bye, I stopped by the lab to see if the paperwork was there yet. I wanted to get it behind me.

After checking in with the receptionist, I sat on the edge of a hard plastic waiting room chair. I was the only one there. I thumbed through the stack of magazines on the table next to me. A thin magazine caught my eye—*Adoption Today*. I stared at it for a moment and realized I was chewing my lower lip, anxious again.

The receptionist was gone for what seemed like thirty minutes—but was probably only a minute or two. She called me up and handed me a clipboard with a form to fill out and asked to see a picture ID. As she copied down my driver's license information, I jokingly asked her if they needed my fingerprints too. At least, I thought I was kidding.

She pulled out a fingerprint card and ink pad. I asked, "Are you serious?"

She didn't smile as she replied, "We take identification issues very seriously."

As I cleaned my fingers with the wet wipe she gave me, she instructed me to have a seat while I waited. I tried to relax, but I felt like the suspect of a crime. The process only lacked a mug shot and a pat down.

The medical assistant called me back and had me stand against a blank wall while she took my picture with a digital camera. At that point, a strip search would not have surprised me.

I thought after all that documentation and verification, it would be more involved than a simple cheek swab. "Are you sure that's it?" I asked the lab tech. She assured me it was and told me I was free to go.

I left the lab musing how my destiny could very well be changed by one soggy Q-tip.

chapter nine

My thoughts were consumed with getting the results of the test. Arthur Bernacchi said he would be in touch when he got the results, but I hadn't thought to ask the lab assistant how long it would take. I didn't want to call the lab from work.

I looked around to make sure Nadine wasn't lurking, and I searched DNA tests on the Internet to get an idea of how long it would take to get the results back. My best estimate was three business days.

Adam called and I tried to talk to him without letting the entire office staff hear what I was talking about.

"I went to lunch with Tara and stopped on my way back for the test."

"So what was it like?" he asked.

"Fingerprints, mug shot, and cheek swab." I marked off items on the bank reconciliation I was working on as I talked.

"Wait—did you go to the police station or a lab?"

"A lab, but they were very methodical and they know how to handle a Q-tip. It was very strange. I don't know how I'll be able to wait for the results."

"Did they tell you when that would be?" I could hear Adam eating his sandwich as he talked.

"No, and I forgot to ask. I googled it though, and I think I'll hear back around the middle of next week."

"I've got a few minutes before my lunch break is over. Can you talk for a couple more minutes? I want to hear about your conversation with the attorney."

"Yeah, I can talk while I work. I'm just checking off stuff for a bank rec."

I recapped my conversation with Mr. Bernacchi. I was a little cryptic and tried to keep my voice low. Adam figured out I couldn't talk freely in the office.

"I'd better get back to work," he said. "We can talk about it more tonight."

"I should focus on work too. I love you. See you tonight."

The rest of the afternoon stretched out before me as I tried to concentrate on my assigned tasks. I didn't mind the interruption when Nadine stopped by my cubicle.

"Kit, you haven't logged your time for yesterday," she reminded me. I had barely opened the email from her right before she walked in. Nadine liked to follow up her emails in person to make sure her message was delivered. I figured that was one of the ways she kept tabs on everyone and everything. "I can't finish my report until I have everybody's time."

"I just read your email. I'll get it done right now." I logged into the timekeeping software. "Sorry about that."

"It's just not like you to forget. Are you feeling well?"

Just what I need—yet another mother, I thought. Aloud I said, "I'm fine. Why?" I hoped she hadn't overheard my conversation with Adam.

"Forgetting your time, taking a long lunch, and I thought I heard you say you had some tests done."

I thought I'd been so careful. It would be even more unnerving if I didn't know she knew details like that about every single employee in the office.

"Oh, I'm not sick. My friend Tara and I got carried away talking at lunch. Her wedding is coming up next month and there's so much to do." I ignored her remark about the test.

She gave her vague smile that distracted you from her all-seeing eyes. "Just take care of yourself, dear." She turned to leave then paused. "Oh, your friend Claire starts working here on Monday. I thought you'd like to know."

"That's super! Thanks for telling me." I didn't let on that I already knew. Nadine liked being the bearer of news—good or bad.

Somehow I made it through the rest of the week. Adam patiently listened to me wonder aloud for the fiftieth time about what the results of the DNA test would be and what would happen next. I always prefaced my wonderings with, "If the test comes back positive . . ." because I was perfectly aware that there was a chance I wasn't who this woman was looking for.

Deep in my soul, though, I knew this would link me to my birth mother.

Adam worked on Saturday, which I don't think bothered him, since all I could talk about was "what ifs." I considered cleaning our bathroom or going over to the Bridgers' house. Barbara might be canning again and I didn't want to do that any more than I wanted to scrub a toilet.

I called Tara, but she already had plans with Eric. I hung up the phone feeling doomed to household chores. A call from Lily saved me from the drudgery.

"Hey, Kit, what're you doing?" She sounded more upbeat than I'd heard in a while.

"Bored out of my skull. I want to do something fun on my day off, but Adam's working, and Tara's with Eric."

"I'm bored too. I thought we could go shopping or something." Lily hadn't offered to go shopping with me for a couple of months. I pushed away the seed of suspicion that she was using me.

"Where did you want to go? I can't spend a lot of money." Knowing I'd be going without a paycheck for a week at the end of the month was incentive for me to be frugal.

"I have twenty bucks. Not much, but it's more an excuse to get out of the house than anything." Again I felt the vibe that Lily didn't really want to see me so much as she wanted to go some-where. I was probably one of the few people Barbara would let Lily hang out with that Lily would tolerate.

"Sure, I'll come get you in a little while."

To assuage my guilty conscience, I gave the bathroom sink a

quick wipe down and cleaned the toilet. I pulled the shower curtain shut to hide the soap scum.

When I picked up Lily, I ran in to say hello to Barbara. She was doing peaches again, and I felt bad when I saw she was alone. I offered to help. She must have seen the stoic look on my face because she laughed.

"Don't worry about it. I'm finishing up the last of them now." She indicated the row of filled bottles lining the counter. "Lily and Beth have been helping me all morning. I think that's why Lily's so desperate to escape."

"Good," I said with a big sigh of relief. Barbara just laughed again.

"Where are you guys going?" she asked.

"I don't know. Maybe to the mall, maybe a matinee. We haven't decided." I eyed the sliced peaches in the bowl. Barbara seemed to know what I was thinking.

"There's peach cobbler in the fridge if you want some before you go."

"Really? Did Lily make it?" I was surprised, given Lily's sullen attitude lately.

Barbara nodded. "Last night. It's almost as good as Janet used to make. I think she was buttering me up so I would lift her grounding."

I helped myself to the cobbler. "Do you have any ice cream? Why was she grounded?"

Barbara nodded toward the freezer as she spoke. "Her attitude."

"Oh. So is it okay if she goes with me?" I spooned a big portion of cobbler into my bowl and put it in the microwave to heat up.

"I am thrilled for her to go with you. We can use a break from each other. It seems all we do is argue." Barbara sighed. "I'm just tired of it."

The microwave beeped, and as I scooped the ice cream, I hesitated. I felt a wave of concern for her. "Barbara, are you sure I can't help you here in the kitchen. You look exhausted."

She managed to smile, but it didn't quite reach her eyes. "Kit, the best way for you to help right now is by being a friend to Lily. At least she's willing to spend time with someone in the family."

Before I could respond, Lily walked into the kitchen. She eyed my heaping bowl and said, "I thought we were going to leave sometime this century." Her sarcasm was intact, at least.

"We are, but I couldn't resist your cobbler. This makes up for the peach pie you refused to make for me." I took a bite. "Yum. I think this rivals your chocolate cake."

Lily smiled at the compliment. "Well, hurry up before Mom changes her mind and violates more child labor laws." Her tone had lightened up a bit, and I glanced at Barbara.

"Thank you," she mouthed silently, behind Lily's back. I honestly didn't know what Lily's problem was. She had a great mom. That thought brought back the whole letter thing and the DNA testing.

Lily dished her own bowl of cobbler and said, "I have to wait for you anyway and if I don't have some now, Travis will pig down the rest of it."

With Lily eating too, I didn't feel as rushed and the battle to keep my secret to myself was lost.

"So the weirdest thing happened," I said.

"You realized Adam was a mutant?" Lily asked innocently.

I ignored her comment and told them about the letter.

I had their full attention as I told them what Mr. Bernacchi said in the letter. Barbara stood still, hands frozen on the jar lid she was tightening.

"Did you call him?" she asked.

"I did." I took another bite of peaches and ice cream, enjoying the suspense.

"Well, what did he say?" Lily asked impatiently.

"He said," I paused dramatically, "That his client wanted me to take a DNA test to prove she's my birth mother."

"You're kidding. After all these years?" Barbara said.

"I know. It freaked me out."

"So are you going to do it?" Lily asked. Her ice cream dripped, melting, from her spoon.

"I already did," I said.

"What did you find out?" Barbara asked.

"Nothing, yet. I'm waiting for the results. It's driving me crazy!"

Barbara resumed putting the lids on the peaches. "What do your parents think?"

"I haven't told them. I've only told Adam and Tara. Now you." My own ice cream was melting into the cobbler. "Please don't say anything to anyone. At least until I get the results and find out if there is anything to tell."

"I won't say a word," Lily promised.

Barbara looked worried. "It seems like there's a pretty good chance that she's your birth mother, if she went through the trouble of having the attorney contact you and ask you for the test. Have you considered the ramifications if she is your birth mother?"

"I've hardly thought of anything else. I can't imagine what she wants from me at this point. The only thing the attorney would say was there was a health issue and 'time was of the essence' or something like that." I was worried about inheriting some dreadful disease but kept those thoughts to myself.

"Maybe that's an excuse so you'll willingly take the test. She's got to realize that you wouldn't be too happy to hear from her after she abandoned you. There may be legal issues." Barbara echoed some of my own concerns.

"I'm not sure what to think. I just feel like I have to know." I turned my attention back to my cobbler.

"Just imagine," Lily said, "what if she's rich or famous and that's why she's been anonymous all these years. Maybe you were her secret love child."

"Lily!" Barbara scolded her. "That's inappropriate."

"Throwing a baby in the garbage is inappropriate, Mom." Lily had a point.

"It could be anything," I said. "I just hate waiting to find out."

When Lily and I left her house, I asked her if she wanted to go to the mall and wander around.

"No! I'm not a mall kind of girl." Her protest surprised me.

"What kind of girl is that?" I asked.

"You know, the kind that's all about 'oh look at me.' Hanging out with all her petty little gossipy friends. That's not me." Lily's pout was back.

"I'm sorry. I used to hang out at the mall a lot. I didn't realize that's how I was."

She looked a little contrite. "I didn't mean you, Kit. You know that."

"Do you mean the girls in your ward?"

"Yeah, and it would be awful at the mall. School starts a week from Monday and they'll all be shopping today. I *don't* want to go there."

"That's fine. It was just an idea. Do you want to see what movies are playing?"

"Okay." At least her short reply was better than the vehement response to my last suggestion.

We drove by the theaters, but we'd missed the showings by about half an hour. "Any other ideas?" I asked her.

"Do you want to stop by Hastings?"

"You mean to see Cody?" My look was enough to make her squirm a little.

"You'll be there with me. What's wrong with that?"

I asked her straight out if this was her plan from the start.

She denied it. "I was willing to go to the movie with you. You're the one who just had to have peach cobbler and made us miss the matinee."

"Don't get snippy, Lily. I don't want to be used."

"I'm not using you. You asked for my suggestion and I gave it. If you didn't want it, you shouldn't have asked." Her voice softened. "I'd kind of like you to meet him. Then maybe you'll see he's not that bad."

"I'm not getting involved in you sneaking around behind your parents' back."

"I'm not asking you to sneak, Kit. I'm asking you to go to a bookstore with me and meet my friend who works there."

"Your *friend*?"

"My *friend*."

I thought about Barbara's trust, which I did not want to violate. I also realized that Lily would find a way to see him if she really wanted to. At least I would be with her if we went today.

"We can go." Maybe I could get a feel for their relationship. I would have gone to the bookstore at the mall anyway if Lily hadn't thrown a fit about going there. And Adam and I had agreed I'd stop by sometime and check Cody out.

"Thanks!" Lily tried to hide her smile, but she was obviously pleased with the results.

I tried to be polite as Lily introduced me to Cody. All I could think was, *Are you kidding, Lily?* After acknowledging him, I moved over to the nearest sale table and pretended to look at books while I kept an eye on them.

It wasn't so much that his ears were gauged and his pants were cinched below his butt cheeks—although I was surprised that Lily considered him "hot"—I was repelled by the way he checked out other girls—including me—while standing there talking to Lily. She didn't seem to notice his wandering eye.

I tried to see something good about him. Clearly Lily liked him. I failed to see the attraction he held for her. *At least he has a job*, was the most charitable thing I could think of.

When we left she enthusiastically asked me, "So what did you think of Cody?"

Like a chicken, I tried to hedge around the answer. "I didn't really talk to him that much."

"Nice try, Kit. Come on, I want your honest opinion."

"Are you sure?" I knew she wanted me to give her a glowing report of his charms, but I couldn't.

"Yes, I want to know what you think," she insisted.

"I don't think he's your type." That was the nicest way I could say it.

"What do you mean by that? Are you judging him by the way he looks?"

"Of course I am. That's usually the basis you judge someone on when you first meet them." We were both getting defensive.

"Kit, I would think you of all people would have more of an open mind. So what if he doesn't look like a Mormon-boy clone? Maybe Cody is *exactly* my type—did you ever think of that? Like maybe you don't know me as well as you think you do?"

"Don't get mad at me when you ask my opinion," I argued back.

"I don't like everyone telling me who I am and how I should be," she said. "I'm so sick of being compared to a perfect ideal. *I'm not Janet.*" She said the last bit with such force that it shocked me.

"I never said you were." I was confused by the direction this conversation had taken.

"Do you have any idea how hard it is to be compared to your perfect sister?" Her voice rose in frustration. "People do it all the time whether they mean to or not. 'Janet made the best cobbler' or 'Janet never hated young women activities.' I'll never be as good as she was."

It never occurred to me that Lily might see her older sister as the benchmark by which she was measured. Her recent behavior suddenly made more sense. "You don't have to be Janet—just be you."

"Then why is everybody trying to change me and control me? Why can't anyone trust my judgment? Like with Cody. Why can't you give him a chance?"

"What do you two have in common? What do you talk about?" I wanted to give her something to think about. "Maybe your crush on him is more about making a statement that Lily Bridger is different and you're using him to do it."

"I'm not using him! I care about him, and he cares about me. How can you judge him when you don't even know him? You're a hypocrite like my parents, Kit."

Her words stung, so I lashed out. "If he cares so much for you, why did he check out every girl that passed by when you two were talking?"

"He did not! You're so rude! I thought you were my friend." Lily was trying hard not to cry. I felt horrible, but I stood my ground.

"Lily, I'm your friend. Real friends tell you the truth, even when it hurts."

"Take me home, please," she said.

Silently, I drove her back home. She got out of the car, slammed the door, neither of us saying good-bye.

chapter ten

I was upset that things ended so badly with Lily. Adam assured me it would blow over, but at Sunday dinner, Lily wouldn't even talk to me.

Barbara asked me what was wrong, so I told her we'd had a fight. I thought about apologizing to Lily, but she was acting like a baby, and I didn't want to give in to her.

The week didn't start out much better. Claire was fifteen minutes late for her first day on the job, and I overheard Nadine giving her a lecture. Shortly after that, my dad called to invite me out to lunch. I hadn't spoken to him since the dinner where I'd met Amberlie.

"Will it be just the two of us?" I asked him suspiciously.

"Yes. Dave's at work and I'm assuming Adam will be working as well." He didn't mention Amberlie and neither did I.

I arrived at the restaurant first and waited for my dad. He walked in the door talking on his cell phone. He'd never been a cell-phone type of guy. I wondered if he was talking to Amberlie.

I refrained from asking him about it as the hostess led us to our table. We ordered lunch and made small talk about school, the weather, and my work. I told him I was going to Ventura to visit Mom.

"When are you going?" he asked, clearly surprised.

"I'm leaving on Sunday and staying a week."

"I'm sure your mother is excited," he said. "She's missed you."

"Well, she's the one who chose to move back to California—not me." I heard the bitterness in my own voice and toned it down a little. "Besides, I did see her in May when she came out for Dave's graduation."

"I know, but it's important for her to have you visit her out there, in her new place." My dad always stood up for her. I wondered again how they ever came to the point of divorce—they were both so mild-mannered.

"It will be strange. The whole thing still is," I muttered.

"I know. You've been pretty forthcoming about how you feel." He smiled but didn't seem to be baiting me, just stating facts.

"Are you glad you and mom got divorced?" I asked bluntly.

"I wouldn't say I'm glad, but it was the best thing," he said.

"I still don't get it. You two seemed happy," I pushed, trying to understand how it had happened.

"We weren't unhappy, but we weren't happy either. Rather than face the issue head on, I made some poor choices that ended up hurting the entire family. I'm very sorry for that, but I believe the resolution was the best for your mother and me." He looked uncomfortable talking about it, but he did look me in the eye as he spoke.

"Doesn't what Dave and I want matter to you?" I still felt cheated.

"Of course it does. But it was the marriage that dissolved, not the family. I'm still your father and Nora is still your mother. That will never change." He reached over and took my hand. "Kit, you're an adult. I'm sure you know that your mother and I are not going to reconcile. We need to move on."

I pulled my hand away. "Why is it so easy for you and Mom to move on? She moved back to Ventura, and you're already dating Amberlie—how can you both just forget all the years we were a family?"

"I haven't forgotten, but it's different now. Different can still be good, Kit. I'd like you to give the future a chance."

"Do you mean a future with you and Amberlie together?" I asked.

"Quite possibly. You've probably figured out that we're serious."

"Is this some sort of announcement? Don't you think it's a little sudden?" I wanted to run away.

"I'm not announcing anything. I just want you to be open-minded. Get to know Amberlie."

"If you want me to be open-minded, then don't push her on me. Don't rush into things—especially if you're doing it just for her."

"What makes you think I'm doing anything just for Amberlie?" Dad asked.

"Well, Dave said you're taking the missionary discussions. Is that true?" I demanded.

"It's true I've listened to the discussions. What makes you think it's because of Amberlie?"

"I'm not stupid, Dad. You wouldn't listen to the missionaries when I asked you to do it. Now you're dating Amberlie, and she's LDS. It's not hard to figure out you'd do it to please her."

"Oh, I see. Kind of like how you listened to the discussions and joined the Church for Adam." The comparison caught me off guard.

"No. That's not how it was, and you know it. I wanted to know for myself." I felt a little guilty even as I protested. "Well, maybe I listened at first because of Adam, but I was baptized because I believed it was right. Not to impress Adam!"

"So your motives are pure, but mine are suspect? Is that really fair, Kit?"

"You're twisting my words, Dad!"

"It sounds to me like you use one set of standards for yourself and a different set for me. You haven't asked me anything about what I've learned or what I believe. So how could you possibly know my motives?" He said all of this calmly, which agitated me more.

"It's the timing that makes me wonder, Dad. Why wouldn't you listen when I asked you to, but you did when Amberlie asked you?"

"First of all, when you asked your mother and me to listen to the discussions, we were going through a very rough time with our marriage. You didn't know it at the time, because we kept it from you and Dave. We were concentrating on making tough decisions."

"That's when you *should* have paid attention the most!"

"Right or wrong—we didn't. We couldn't at that point."

"But Amberlie changed your mind?" I asked bitterly.

"Yes. But not for the reason you think. When I met and got to know her, I realized that she had a sense of happiness—an inner peace—that I was missing from my own life. I started asking her questions. I asked *her* to set up the missionary discussions."

None of this was what I expected to hear. I wanted to blame Amberlie. "Why didn't you ask me instead of her? I would have set them up for you."

"Kit, why do you find it easier to talk to Adam or Tara instead of me? They're your peers. You can identify with their viewpoint much easier than you can mine. That's how it was with me and Amberlie. She's my friend."

I had no response. I knew he was right, but I still wanted nothing to do with Amberlie. And I was still bothered that he chose her as the one to introduce him to the gospel.

He tried to reason with me a little more. "Kit, we haven't gotten along very well for the past few months—you and I. I know I'm to blame for a lot, but I *am* sorry. I'm trying to be a better person. I want to make our relationship right—like it used to be."

I knew he wanted my forgiveness, but I wasn't ready to give it. "Dad, you said yourself—it'll never be like it used to be. It will always be different."

"I know that. But are you willing to work on making it a good kind of different?" He looked so sincere and I wanted things to be good between us again, but that core of betrayal twisted inside of me.

"I'll try." That's the best I could offer.

"That's all I ask, sweetheart." He pulled out the dessert menu and smiled. "Now how about a hot fudge brownie to top off our lunch?"

I felt better by the time I left, and it wasn't all due to the chocolate.

The week went a little smoother after that. Claire was on time for work and everyone seemed to like her. I worried about the typos in her emails though; it didn't look very professional. I had lunch with her in the break room on Wednesday.

"So how do you like your new job?" I asked as I ate my ramen noodles.

"I like it a lot, but it's really confusing. There's so much to remember. I hope it gets easier."

"I'll help you where I can," I offered.

"Thanks, Kit. But you'll be gone next week, won't you? I updated next week's schedule and it shows you're out. Are you going someplace fun?" Claire's comment reminded me that I was going to Ventura next week. I groaned.

"What's wrong?" Claire asked.

"I just remembered I have to spend the whole next week with my mother in California. I don't know if I'm ready."

"Well, the California part is good." Claire tried to cheer me up and talking to her helped me think more positively about my trip.

We finished eating, and I remembered the email errors. "Stop by my desk for a couple of minutes, Claire." I showed her how to use spell check before she sent an email. It wouldn't cure everything, but it would help.

She thanked me profusely, and I was glad she wasn't easily offended, because it seemed like I was always pointing out her faults.

On Wednesday afternoon my cell phone rang, displaying an unfamiliar number. I answered and instantly recognized the voice, although I'd only heard it once before. *Arthur Bernacchi, Attorney.*

Trying to ignore the pounding in my chest, I walked back to the vacant lunchroom for some privacy.

"Did you get the results of the DNA test?" I blurted out.

"Yes. The test confirms that you are the child of my client."

I stood there in shock, trying to process what I'd just heard.

"Katherine?" Mr. Bernacchi's voice brought me back to reality.

"I'm here," I answered. "What's next?"

"My client would like to set up a meeting with you—in person. I would like to make the arrangements now."

"Um, sure." I fumbled for words. "When?"

"She would like it to take place as soon as possible, at my office in Oxnard. She will pay for your expenses, of course." He discussed this like it was just another legal matter—which it probably was to him, but all I could think was, *My birth mother wants to see me!*

"Katherine?" His voice cut into my thoughts again. "How soon can you make the trip? My assistant can book your airfare and reserve a hotel room for you. One day should be sufficient."

What a strange thing to say. *How can we catch up on a whole lifetime in one day?* "I'll be in Ventura next week. Can we set it up for then?"

"You were already planning a trip to Ventura?" Mr. Bernacchi sounded surprised.

"My mother—Nora Matthews—lives there. I'm going to visit. I'll be there on Sunday and I'm staying for a week." I don't know why I felt obliged to tell him that.

"Let's make the appointment for Monday morning. If you need a rental car, please take care of it, and we will see that you are reimbursed for the expense."

"I think I can use my mom's car. What time on Monday?'

"How does 10:00 a.m. sound?"

"I can do that. Can you give me your address?" I quickly went back to my desk and grabbed some paper. I wrote down the address and the call ended. I was worthless at work the rest of the day.

chapter eleven

Adam drove me to the airport after church on Sunday.

When we landed, I texted Adam to let him know I made it safely and then called my mom. She was already waiting for me at baggage claim, which was no surprise. She always liked to be on time.

What did surprise me was her appearance. I did a double take, because I didn't recognize her at first.

She had never been one to spend a lot of time on her appearance and a new hair cut was a big deal for her. She not only sported a new cut, but it was colored from her usual brown to a warm cinnamon. She'd always worn it shoulder-length and straight, but now it was tousled in layers that framed her face.

When I recovered from the change in her hair, I noticed her face. She was wearing makeup! My mother *never* wore makeup. I remember having to beg for permission to wear it myself; she'd considered it a waste of time and money.

I stood there staring at my mother, not saying a word. Normally she would have hugged me and asked me a hundred questions, but this time she just stood there smiling.

She broke the silence first. "Well, Kit, what do you think?" She held out her arms and turned in a circle, giving me the full effect. "Do you like the changes?"

If I was speechless before, I nearly tripped over my jaw when she twirled. "Mom? You've, uh, grown . . . " That was the least embarrassing way I could describe my mom's new figure.

She laughed at my discomfort. "I like to refer to it as being 'surgically enhanced.' Are you shocked?"

"Do you mean *implants*?" I couldn't believe it—not my mother.

"I was hoping the hair and makeup would distract you." She stepped forward to give me the overdue hug.

"Seriously—what possessed you to do this? It's like *Extreme Makeover*—Mother Edition." I didn't mean to sound so judgmental. In my defense, I was in a state of shock. My words wiped the smile off her face.

"You don't like it, then."

"You look good—you just don't look like my mom." The hair and makeup took ten years off her, and she seemed to stand straighter with more confidence.

She smiled at my words. "I'm still the same person; I needed to do some things for myself. I hope you understand."

"I wasn't expecting it. What made you make the, uh . . . changes?" I tried not to glance down at her chest, but it was hard not to.

"Let's get your bag and we'll talk more on the way."

Once we were on the road, I brought up the subject again. "So, Mom, tell me why you did all this."

"It's no secret that going through a divorce is difficult. There are so many feelings of failure. It was hard enough to deal with my husband not wanting me, but then you announced you were getting married, and Dave was about ready to graduate. My identity felt stripped from me. I wanted to take control of who I was. I wanted a change." Although I could tell she was trying to sound lighthearted, there was an underlying bite to her words.

"Dave and I still needed you, Mom. *You* left us." I didn't bother to mask my own animosity.

She shook her head. "No. I didn't leave you. I wanted you both to come with me. You've built your life in Cache Valley. I needed to build mine here." She reached over and patted my arm. "Let's not dwell on it. You're here now. Let's have fun."

I kept my mouth shut, unable to switch off my emotions so easily. I wished I hadn't come.

My mom's condo was beautiful and contemporary. It looked great but felt superficial—it reminded me of my mother's new look. She showed me to the guest room, and while I unpacked, she got dinner ready—a delicious Asian chicken salad. My dad was a meat and potatoes guy, and we never ate like this when they were married.

"Would you like some wine, Kit?" she offered as she poured herself a glass.

"Mom! You know I don't drink!" I was offended she even offered.

"A little glass of wine never hurt anyone," she replied. "It would relax you and maybe you wouldn't be so uptight."

"No thanks," I said. The salad suddenly wasn't so good. I wondered if the entire trip would be a battle—me baiting her, then vice versa. "I'm really tired. I'm going to save my salad and get ready for bed."

"I'm sorry." She was instantly contrite. "I shouldn't have said that about the wine. I knew you wouldn't want any. I don't know why I did that."

The ringing of her cell phone saved me from answering. It sounded like a client, and it would take awhile. I finished my dinner without her. She was still on the phone when I cleared my plate, so I took the opportunity to call Adam.

He greeted me with "Hey, beautiful." The words warmed me.

"Hey, Bridger." I wandered into the bedroom so my mother wouldn't overhear.

"How was your flight? I miss you already."

"The flight was fine—it was bizarre seeing my mom though." I told him about the changes in her appearance and how we seemed to be bringing out the worst in each other. By the time I finished, I was about to cry. "I want to come home, Adam."

"It sounds rough. I'm not surprised it's awkward for you—this is really the first time you've been together, alone, since she moved to Ventura. I think you should hang in there for a couple more days at least. You have the meeting with the attorney tomorrow."

"I know. I need to stay at least until then."

"Are you going to tell your mom about the meeting?" Adam asked.

"I don't know. Right now I don't really feel like telling her anything. I'm tired and I have a headache. I probably should go to bed." I massaged my temple with my fingers. "I miss you."

"I miss you too. Hang in there; remember I'm rooting for you. I love you."

"I love you too. Good night." I hung up the phone feeling reassured. I could always count on Adam.

I left the room and saw my mom was still on the phone, but it sounded like she was wrapping up.

"Perfect. Shall we plan on Wednesday then?" She moved around the kitchen putting away the remnants of dinner as she talked.

"No, it will have to be lunch. My daughter is here visiting this week, I'm keeping my evenings free." She smiled as she caught my eye. "I'll meet you at 11:30 then."

I watched her. For a brief moment, I saw her as a person apart from being my mother. I rarely thought about her feelings and never considered that she had hopes and dreams of her own. That brief glimpse of a world—her world—that didn't revolve around me made me feel unsettled.

I found something to take for my headache as my mom finished her call. I decided to try harder to get along her.

"So, I take it that was a client." I figured work was a good neutral subject.

The next hour passed quickly as I listened to my mom talk about her job. She was an interior designer, and the firm she'd been with before we moved from Ventura had offered her a partnership to entice her back.

Although she had worked in the design field before we moved to Utah, I never remembered the passion in her eyes as she talked about work. She hadn't gone to work during the three years she'd lived in Logan, and I asked her why.

"It's difficult to re-establish yourself in a profession like this when you move to a new area. There isn't much demand for what

I do in Cache Valley, and I wanted to enjoy the last few years you and Dave were at home." She shrugged. "It was the right decision at the time."

"I don't remember you being into design like this when we lived here before."

"I've always enjoyed my work; I just never talked about it much at home." Her tone changed slightly, and I sensed she was trying to frame her words in a way that wouldn't offend me. "I needed something like this when your father and I separated. I needed to feel valuable again. In a way, I'm thankful for the divorce—it forced me to acknowledge things about myself and help me discover who I really am."

"I have to admit, you look better than ever. You sound happier too." It was hard for me to say that, but her animation when she talked about work was amazing.

"I'm trying." We were silent for a moment.

"I'm glad." I stood up and stretched. "I need to go to bed, Mom. My head is still hurting."

"I understand. Do you want me to wake you up tomorrow morning before I leave for work? If you drop me off, you'll have the car for the day."

"That would be great. I want to explore the old neighborhood, and I *have* to go to the beach while I'm here."

"I need to go to the office Monday through Wednesday, so you can just drop me off and use the car. I took Thursday and Friday off, so we can do whatever you want to on those days." She came over and hugged me. At least her scent was familiar—she hadn't changed everything. "I'm so glad you came, Kit. Make yourself at home while you're here."

"I will." I got ready for bed and booted up my laptop to write in my journal.

My mom has changed so much but seems happier now. Is she even the same person who took care of me my whole life? Does she still care about me? She's moving on with her new life. I had the same feeling when I had lunch with my dad. I'm so sad that my family has disintegrated. Sometimes I feel as alone and detached as the orphans I took care of in Romania.

chapter twelve

I checked the directions one more time. Having lived many years in Ventura, I wasn't a complete stranger to Oxnard, but I'd never been to this particular area. I'd also never been to an attorney's office before—there hadn't been a reason.

I was fifteen minutes early. I didn't want to go inside yet, so I sat in the car and tried to keep myself calm. I still hadn't told my mother where I was going or what I was doing, and I felt a little deceitful. *It's because I don't know how it will go, and I don't want to hurt her feelings.*

At five minutes to ten, I said a silent prayer and went inside. I introduced myself to the receptionist, who looked like she should still be in high school. She picked up the phone to notify Mr. Bernacchi I was there. She hung up the phone and said, "I'll show you to the conference room."

I followed her back through the massive wooden doors marking the entrance into a new phase of my life.

Three people were already seated in the conference room. Two men and a woman. One of the men stood to greet me, hand outstretched.

"Katherine?" I nodded, and he continued. "I'm Arthur Bernacchi. We've spoken on the phone." I mutely clasped his hand. He turned to the couple sitting next to each other on the far side of the conference table and continued the introductions.

"This is Alicia Haversham and her husband, Lawrence." They arose simultaneously, each offering a hand to me. I shook the man's hand first; his grip was warm and firm. Alicia's hand was small and cold, and her handshake was steely.

"I'm Kit—Katherine Bridger." The three sat down, and Mr. Bernacchi motioned for me to take the chair next to him, across from the Havershams. My thoughts raced. *So this is my biological mother. Is he my father?*

No mention had been made of my birth father, so I assumed my birth mother was single. I sat quietly, unwilling and unable to make the first move.

I couldn't take my eyes off Alicia Haversham. She met my stare with one of her own. I studied her intently, searching for similarities between us. Her white-blonde hair was pulled back into a twist at the nape of her long, slender neck. Green eyes were the focal point in a face expertly made up. She was stunning. She looked closer to thirty than forty. Biology suggested she must be closer to forty since I was twenty-one.

She sat erect, like a queen. One hand came up to smooth a non-existent stray strand of hair. A gigantic diamond flashed on her professionally-manicured hand. She didn't say a word either. I broke my gaze first and looked at the man.

Judging from the way he towered over Alicia, I guessed Lawrence was over six feet tall. He looked quite a bit older than Alicia, but was one of those men who aged well. *Maybe I got my height from him.*

I turned my attention back to Alicia. My brown eyes and dark blonde hair looked nothing like hers and I detected no resemblance between us until she turned her head toward Mr. Bernacchi and smiled slightly. From that angle, I saw her high cheekbones with a slight hollow near her hairline. *I have her cheekbones.*

"We should begin, Arthur," Alicia said. I detected no emotion in her smooth voice and I wondered what she was thinking. *Can she see a resemblance? Can she tell I am her daughter?*

"Of course." Mr. Bernacchi shuffled the files in front of him. He looked like he sounded over the phone—professional, yet kind.

"As we all know, it has been established through DNA testing that Katherine Matthews Bridger is the biological child of Alicia Everett Haversham. Mrs. Haversham has requested this meeting and, according to her direction, has asked me to explain why there is a certain amount of urgency involved."

I looked at Alicia. She sat rigidly still. Lawrence said nothing but reached his arm around the back of her chair and gave her shoulder a squeeze. I desperately wished Adam had come with me.

Mr. Bernacchi cleared his throat and continued. "I have a proposal here, Katherine, from Mrs. Haversham. We request that you keep the contents of this meeting confidential. As a matter of fact," he said, pulling some papers from his file folder and distributing one to each of us, "I would like to stop here and request that each of you sign copies of this non-disclosure agreement before we proceed further."

I took the paper and glanced through it. Alarm bells went off in my head. They had an unfair advantage over me. They already knew what this was about, and I knew nothing. I was naïve but not stupid. I spoke up.

"I tell my husband everything. He couldn't be here today, but I intend on discussing the meeting with him. We don't keep secrets from each other. I won't sign anything until I know what this is about. Then I'll consider it."

Mr. Bernacchi looked uncomfortable. "I'm afraid we cannot continue without your signature."

Disappointment swelled up like gall in my throat. I was so close to finding out the truth about my birth. *So close.* But I couldn't deny the strong feeling telling me I shouldn't sign the paper.

I stood up. "That's it then. Thank you for your time." I turned to Alicia and Lawrence. "It was nice meeting you, however briefly." Mr. Bernacchi reached for the unsigned confidentiality agreement.

Alicia's arm snaked out, stopping him from scooping up the paper. "Wait," she commanded. Mr. Bernacchi and I both obeyed.

"Arthur, I wish to continue. The agreement can be signed later." To me, she said, "Katherine, please stay." I sat down. Hope rose within me.

"I'll stay, but I can't promise I'll sign later, either."

Alicia's smile made me feel like she was trying to lull me. "Katherine, let me be frank. What happened years ago could be construed as a crime, and although the statute of limitations has expired and there is virtually no chance of my being prosecuted for it, I do not wish the details to become public knowledge. That is the reason for the agreement."

She wants to make sure I won't call the police because she threw me in the garbage. Of course she's covered the legal bases before contacting me. But she's worried about her reputation? Aloud, I said, "I can honestly assure you I have absolutely no intention of pursuing any legal recourse against you, nor in broadcasting it. *You* contacted *me.*"

She looked at Lawrence, who gave a slight nod. She turned back to Mr. Bernacchi. "I'm satisfied, Arthur."

"Would any of you like something to drink?" he asked. I wanted to scream at him to just get on with it, but I noticed he was tugging at his starched collar, and realized *he* probably needed a drink.

"I would like something," I said. He picked up the phone and an assistant responded in a moment with a tray containing a selection of soft drinks, bottled water, and glasses of ice. I took a Diet Coke, and the others chose water.

Mr. Bernacchi took a drink and seemed back in control. "This is an unusual situation. Katherine, my client has searched you out and confirmed your biological relationship for a purpose."

Somehow, now that I'd seen Alicia, I knew it wasn't because she had some latent rush of maternal feelings for the child she had thrown away. I couldn't imagine her reasoning, but I wanted Mr. Bernacchi to just spit it out.

"Alicia has a daughter who is suffering from a progressive liver disease. She is in dire need of a liver donor. Her condition has worsened and, as you likely know, the waiting list for transplant recipients is extremely long. A living donor presents the greatest chance for success—a close relative is likely to be the most suitable candidate. Mrs. Haversham requests that you be tested to see if you are an appropriate match and, if so, if you will consent to be a liver donor."

It took a few seconds for it all to register. Alicia had a daughter other than me—apparently one she acknowledged publicly—that needed an organ transplant. So *that* was the reason for breaking her silence after all these years.

"You want me to be an organ donor? For my half-sister—or is it sister?" I tried to keep my voice steady, to hide the hurt that pierced me at the realization that this woman only contacted me for my body parts.

Lawrence spoke first. "Katherine, I'm not your biological father."

Alicia barely let him finish. "Katherine, without meaning to sound harsh, I feel I must speak openly to you. I know you have parents who love you and raised you. I do not wish to interfere with that relationship at all. I see no benefit in dredging up past mistakes. I believe you're the match that will help my daughter. I'm in a position to make it worth your while."

Arthur Bernacchi interjected. "Mrs. Haversham is not saying she will compensate you for your liver donation—that would not be legal. She would, of course, cover all expenses of testing, the transplant itself if you are a match, and all other expenses for your travel and recuperation."

I was stunned at the businesslike manner in which they approached this whole thing. *Do they not even consider me as a person with feelings?* I wanted to make a scene—to *make* them acknowledge me.

Perhaps Alicia sensed my dismay. She said, "I know this is sudden, but my daughter is getting sicker and sicker. We need to move quickly."

"What's your daughter's name?" I asked.

Alicia looked surprised at my question. "Her name is Charity." I sensed her reluctance at revealing anything to me.

It was a beautiful name, but I had a feeling Alicia didn't know the meaning of the word. "How old is Charity?" I deliberately spoke her name, wanting Alicia to feel uncomfortable. She wanted to keep it on a business level, but I was determined to make it personal. It was extremely personal to me.

She looked displeased, but after another shoulder squeeze

from Lawrence, she answered. "She just turned sixteen."

"Does she know about me?"

"No!"

Her sharpness stabbed me. How could she put so much on the line for Charity, and not even acknowledge that I was her daughter too? It felt like a personal rejection. I wanted to strike back.

"Do you have any other children?" I asked, working to keep my voice even.

"No," Alicia said. "Charity is our only child."

Does this woman have any idea how cruel she sounds? I had just given her an opportunity to acknowledge me, and she made it clear she didn't consider me to be one of her children.

"You must be desperate for a donor," I said. "Desperate enough to dig up something you obviously want to keep hidden."

"Charity is very ill. I will do what is necessary for my daughter." Alicia managed to sound cool and detached, and I wondered how much was an act.

I could play her game. "You said it would be worth my while. Exactly what do you mean? Why would I put myself at risk for a complete stranger who doesn't even know I'm alive?"

Mr. Bernacchi spoke up. "As I mentioned before, the Havershams cannot pay for your organ—per se. However, based on the biological relationship that has been confirmed, Mrs. Haversham has requested I prepare documents that would provide you with a lump-sum settlement—an inheritance of sorts, that could be collected immediately."

"Immediately after the organ donation, you mean," I said.

"Of course, but it would be yours to spend, no strings attached," Mr. Bernacchi said smoothly.

"No strings attached to either party," Alicia added.

I knew what she meant by that remark. "So you're saying, after I donate part of my liver to Charity, I'll get an 'inheritance,' but I'm to go away after that and never contact you again. Am I understanding this correctly?"

"Yes." She didn't seem disturbed at all that I put it in those callous terms. "The paperwork will reflect the key points."

"So you're offering to buy my liver," I said.

"No," Mr. Bernacchi reiterated. "The two things are unrelated. They simply need to occur in a certain sequence."

I was outraged but tried to mask it. "How much?"

"Are you asking about the settlement?" Alicia asked.

"Yes. How much would my 'inheritance' be?"

"Fifty thousand dollars."

"So that's the price for a liver. Somehow I thought it would be higher." I doubted any of them caught the sarcasm in my voice. "Of course, livers grow back, don't they?"

"Are you saying you want more, Kit?" Alicia asked, totally misreading me—and using my nickname at the worst possible time. Enraged, I stood up and looked her in the eye.

"My name is Katherine. Only my *friends* call me Kit. I don't count you among them. As to wanting more, I can assure you that your money means absolutely nothing to me. Nothing!" I was almost yelling at the end, and I felt the tears welling up and threatening to spill over. I had to get out of there. I took a deep breath and spoke more calmly. "You'll have to find another source for your liver donor. Maybe you can track down another child you threw away. Good-bye."

I turned and walked out. If they called after me, I couldn't hear, because the sobs I'd held at bay overcame me. All I could focus on was finding the car—my *real* mother's car—and getting out of that place.

chapter thirteen

I drove back to Ventura and straight to Marina Park. Midmorning on a weekday in late August meant it was not very crowded, which was perfect since I was searching for solitude. I crossed the sand toward the *San Salvador*, a wooden and cement ship that had been there as far back as I could remember.

I sat down a little way from the ship, watching two children playing pirates on it. Their mother sat in a lounge chair not far away, a book in hand, her eye on her children.

My initial tears abated, but the anger and outrage remained. I replayed the meeting over and over in my mind. Alicia Haversham was nothing like I had imagined. Not that I dreamed of some fairy-tale reunion where I found out I was really a long-lost princess, but I had expected some sort of emotion from her. Especially considering she would obviously do anything for Charity, her other daughter.

I called Adam. I told him I'd call after the meeting ended—and it had definitely ended.

"Hey, Mrs. Bridger." The warmth in his voice was a balm for my raw emotional wounds.

"Hey, Mr. Bridger. So, the meeting's over."

"I figured it must be. Tell me about it."

"It ended early—I walked out of it." I was glad I'd cried it all out before I called Adam; I didn't want to worry him.

"Are you serious? What happened?" Concern was evident in his voice.

"My birth mother, Alicia Haversham, is unbelievable. She's beautiful on the outside, but she has the emotional depth of a paramecium. She doesn't care a bit about me at all as a person. She wanted to meet me for a 'business deal.'"

"What kind of deal?" He sounded confused.

I filled Adam in on the details of the meeting. I did most of the talking. Being Adam, he knew when to let me rant and when to offer comfort. When I finished telling him everything, he asked, "Are you okay?"

"Yeah. I'll survive. I really miss you, and I want to come home."

"What about your mom?" He hesitated then added, "Nora."

"Nora *is* my mom. You don't have to clarify—*ever*. I would never acknowledge Alicia Haversham as my mother after the way she treated me."

"I don't think you should punish your mom by cutting the visit short just because Alicia is such a jerk. She's waited a long time for you to visit her."

"You're right. The problem is, I don't want to deal with how imperfect my family is. I don't want to argue with her the whole time, and I don't even know what to talk about that won't end in an argument." My mom and I had never had a "best girlfriends" kind of relationship, and it was even more strained since the divorce.

"Why don't you tell her about Alicia?" Adam asked.

"I don't know, maybe I will. I feel so weird about the subject. I don't want her to think I went looking for Alicia. And how do I even bring it up? 'Hey Mom, today I met the woman who dumped me in the trash after birth.'"

"Don't you think she'd want to know? I know my mom would."

"My mom isn't like yours. And she seems so different now. She's more wrapped up in herself." When I said it aloud, I realized that was one of the struggles I was dealing with. My mother was putting her own interests first, which she'd never done before. I didn't know how to deal with it.

"She's done a lot of that out of necessity. She had to pick up the pieces of her life after she and your dad split up. I think she's pretty normal in that regard. It doesn't mean she doesn't love you, Kit."

"I know she loves me, but I think I'm just part of her old life and not her new. Why are you sticking up for her anyway? You're supposed to side with me."

"I'll always be on your side, but I know it helps me when you point out things I can't see for myself. I'm trying to do the same for you. Your parents are good people." For Adam, preaching came kind of naturally. I liked that trait when he wasn't using it against me.

"Okay, I get your point. I'll think about talking to her. Let's talk about something else."

"You said you were at the beach. Is the weather nice?"

I looked around for the first time that day really seeing the bright blue sky and feeling the sun on my face. "It's absolutely gorgeous. I wish I'd brought my swimsuit with me today."

"Go back and get it." Adam made things sound so simple.

"Maybe I will. Maybe I'll just go swimming in my clothes. Or I'll go to the mall and get a new one."

"I think you should do whichever you want. Take some pictures for me, since I'm stuck here in Utah while my wife lounges on the beach."

"Not just any beach—my favorite one. You know what? I'm going to go get a swimsuit and a book to read. I'm going to indulge myself in this little bit of paradise and ignore the rest of my life for a few hours."

"Have fun, but don't forget about me. I don't want you loving it so much you never want to come home." I could tell he missed me but didn't want to put pressure on me.

"I'll call you later, Adam. I love you."

"Ditto," he said.

One turquoise and black swimsuit, best-selling novel, and Jamba Juice later, I was back on the beach to enjoy the afternoon.

I picked up my mom at 5:30, and she was in a great mood. My attitude was considerably better after spending the day soaking up the sun and reading.

"So, sweetheart, how was your day? It looks like you've been to the beach."

"I've been at Marina Park. It was a perfect day for it. I've really missed living by the ocean."

"You and Adam need to move here when he graduates." My mom rarely grouped Adam and me together as a couple even though we were married. I was pleased.

"I don't know where we'll end up. He still has a couple of years to go, and I don't know if we want to live that far away from family." I loved Southern California, but it meant a lot to me to stay close to the Bridgers.

"Well, you have family here too. Don't rule out the possibility." It was just like her to push the issue.

"There's no point in discussing it yet. We have to just wait and see where Adam gets a job." I felt the tension start to fill the air.

She must have sensed it as well. She switched subjects. "Are you hungry? I'm starving. I skipped lunch to try to get everything done. I thought we'd go out for dinner."

"I'm ready to eat, but I came straight from the beach to pick you up, so I don't want to go anywhere where I have to go inside. Can we grab something and go home to eat it?"

"I want to go to Milanos while you're here, but it doesn't have to be tonight. What sounds good to you?" At least food was a safe subject.

"What about Cafe Rio? Is there one around here?" My mouth watered at the thought of it.

"There isn't one in Ventura, but there's one in Oxnard. It's about fifteen minutes away." She changed lanes, so she could get on the freeway.

"Oxnard? Never mind." The mention of the city brought back the memories of what I'd successfully suppressed all afternoon.

"Kit, it's fine. If we call ahead, it will be ready when we get there." She was being so nice about it, I either had to go with it or tell the whole story now.

"Okay. If you're sure you don't mind. Tell me what you want, and I'll call it in." I phoned in our order and tried to ignore the reminders of the morning's disastrous meeting.

Less than an hour later, we were back at my mom's condo eating our dinner. We managed to make small talk without picking at each other—a record for us, lately. I had to bite back one or two snide remarks—especially when she poured herself a glass of wine to go with her dinner. She wisely didn't offer me any this time.

"So did you spend the day with friends, or did you go it alone?" Mom asked.

"I just enjoyed my beach time alone. I forgot to take my suit, so I went shopping and got a new one. I picked up a novel and spent the afternoon reading." I purposefully left out the events leading up to the beach.

"You forgot your swimsuit? Why didn't you just wear it there under your clothes?" Leave it to my mom to pick up on the nit-picky details.

"I wasn't planning on going to the beach. I kind of ended up there, and once I saw how great it was, I wished I'd brought my suit. I could've come back for it, but I felt like treating myself to a new one." I hoped the explanation satisfied her.

She let it go. She talked about the project she was working on. Her design client was a developer who did a lot of commercial real estate buying and selling. It sounded like a big deal.

I tried to focus on what she was saying and ask the appropriate questions at the right times, but my mind was wandering. I kept thinking of Adam's advice to talk to my mom about Alicia and the meeting. I pushed the thought away, but it kept coming back.

My mom's voice interrupted my battle of thoughts. "Kit, are you even paying attention?"

"I'm sorry, Mom. What were you saying?"

"I wanted to know if you'll come by my work and have lunch with me tomorrow. I'd like you to meet everyone."

"Sure. What time?"

"Come at 11:00. That way no one will have left for lunch yet. I want to show you off."

I didn't expect that. Judging from her new look and outlook on life, I thought she wouldn't want to acknowledge she had a daughter as old as me. "Really? You want to show me off to every-one you work with?"

"Of course I do." She laughed. "You won't believe it, but I've bragged about how smart you are, and I have pictures of you and

Dave on my desk. People will want to meet you, even if it is just to shut me up."

"Thanks, Mom." I was touched. She had no idea how much it meant to hear her talk that way about me. I blinked back tears. I was entirely too emotional.

"Kit? What's wrong? You act like I'm not proud of you and Dave. Just because we live far apart doesn't mean I don't think about you and talk about you constantly."

I had to tell her. I just had to.

"Mom, I needed to hear that—in the worst way. You'll never believe what's happened."

She looked alarmed. "What? Is something wrong? Is it you and Adam?"

"No. Adam and I are fine."

"What is it then?" she asked.

"A couple of weeks ago I got a letter in the mail from an attorney in Oxnard."

"Why?"

"It was from Arthur Bernacchi, an attorney whose client claimed to be my birth mother. She wanted me to take a DNA test."

My mom's jaw dropped open. "How is that possible? If she's really your birth mother, why would she come forth now after all this time?"

"I asked the same question. I called the attorney and agreed to take the DNA test." I watched my mom's expression. She didn't say a word but took a long drink.

"Mom, are you okay?"

"Why didn't you tell me? Does your father know?" She looked hurt, but it was too late to spare her feelings.

"I told Adam—and Tara." There was no point in telling her about Barbara and Lily. "I didn't want to hurt you and Dad. I mean—it's not like I *hoped* she'd turn out to be my birth mother, but I needed to find out for myself first." I nervously picked at my food, wondering what her reaction would be.

"Do you have the results?" My mother had that look on her face that told me she was trying to control her emotions. I could hear it in her voice too.

"Yes. She's my birth mother. She wanted to meet me." I said it quietly, trying to soften the blow.

"When?"

"Today. I met with them this morning."

"Them?"

"Alicia and her husband. And the attorney." I wish she'd do more than ask me these short questions. I couldn't tell what she was really thinking.

"Both of your birth parents?"

"No, her husband's not my birth father." We sat in silence for a moment, and I couldn't stand it any longer. "Mom, what are you thinking?"

She sighed. "I'm shocked by the whole thing. I never considered it would happen. When you were abandoned, the police followed up on every lead they could find. Now to find out she's initiated contact—it's just hard to take."

"Are you angry that I did it behind your back?" I found old feelings surfacing, those of not wanting to disappoint her.

"No, I'm not angry . . . well, maybe a little bit. But I'm more concerned about what she wants from you. I don't want you to get hurt."

I snorted in disgust. "Don't feel threatened, Mom. I know what she wants—and she's not going to get it."

"What did she want?"

"She has another daughter—one she didn't abandon. Her name is Charity, and she needs a liver transplant. Alicia wanted to see if I qualify and am willing to be a donor." Amazingly, I managed to keep my voice steady.

"Are you serious?" My mother's eyes flashed with anger. "What nerve! How dare she ask that of you!"

"I know." The ferocity of her tone was validating. Behind the new façade, my old mother still existed. She loved me and would stand by me. I knew it. It felt palpable. "She offered me money. Like she could buy me off."

"That's illegal! You can't buy organs. What kind of an attorney would be party to something like this? That woman should be prosecuted for what she's done." Mom grabbed her cell phone and started scrolling through her contacts. "Our company has a good attorney. We can put a stop to this nonsense right now."

I reached over and covered her hand with mine. "Listen, Mom. I already ended it. They had it all packaged in a nice, neat legal way. They insisted the money was not tied to the transplant. Expenses of the transplant would be covered. The money was offered as an 'inheritance' for me, since I am Alicia Haversham's biological child. It just wouldn't be available until *after* I recovered from the surgery."

"Will she give you the 'inheritance' if you don't donate for her daughter?"

I shook my head. "I don't want it, anyway."

"Well, that sounds like semantics to me. They are essentially offering to pay you for your liver."

"I agree, Mom. I told them to find another donor, and I walked out." I laughed, but it sounded harsh and mirthless. "I would've liked to have seen their faces. I think Alicia Haversham is a woman who always gets her way. Well, she didn't this time."

"I'm glad you didn't fall for it. What kind of act did she put on—poor me?"

"No. She was cold and arrogant. She seemed so *unfeeling*. I think that's what hurts the most. How can she be so attached to one daughter and so detached from the other? What did I ever do to her?" I felt hot tears spill down my cheeks, and I wiped them away furiously. I would *not* let her affect me.

My mom came around the table and hugged me close. "We should contact the police. We need to report that we know who she is. It's a crime to abandon a baby. She needs to pay."

I pulled away. "There's no point in calling the police. Alicia and her husband are smart. She never would have revealed herself if there were any chance of her being prosecuted. She said the statute of limitations has run out on the crime. 'If there was a crime' as she would put it."

"If you don't mind, I'd like to make a few phone calls about it." My mom was rarely punitive, and it surprised me.

"No, Mom. I want to let it go. I told them I had no interest in pursuing legal action against Alicia. There is nothing I want from her, except to forget about her."

79

She mulled it over. "If you change your mind, let me know. If they bother you anymore, let me know. If they harass you, let—"

I cut her off. "I know. Let you know. I'm an adult, Mom. I can fight my own battles."

She pressed her lips together as if trying to keep the words from jumping out against her will. *So that's where I learned that trick.* Watching her try to keep control over her mouth almost made me smile. I realized I resembled my adoptive mom much more than I did my birth mother, and that was one of the most comforting thoughts I'd had all day.

chapter fourteen

Sleep eluded me even though I was physically and emotionally exhausted. I kept replaying the meeting with Alicia over in my mind.

My initial hurt and anger had faded away after venting so much to Adam and my mother, so that wasn't what was keeping me awake. Regret rolled around in my brain. I hadn't paid as much attention to Alicia, as a person, as I'd wanted to.

My feelings of rejection from her attitude and impersonal reaction kept me from seeing and finding out all that I could. Tossing and turning, I wished I'd learned more, since it was likely the only time I'd ever see her.

I should have written down my questions. Adam had suggested it before I left. He knew I'd get caught up in the moment and forget the things I wanted to know. I mistakenly assumed that her request to meet me was an invitation for some sort of openness.

There in the dark, I realized how few answers I really had. I now knew who my birth mother was—as far as name and physical appearance went. I still didn't have answers to the issues that burned within me for so long. *Why? Why did she do it? Who is my birth father?*

My thoughts turned to Charity. I couldn't believe I had a half-sister I'd never met. She was a little older than Lily. *What does she look like? Does she resemble Alicia or Lawrence? What if she looks like me?*

There were times growing up when I wanted a sister—someone to confide in and share secrets with. Lily had been like a sister to me for the past four years, until recently, when she started pulling away from everyone and obsessing over Cody.

Dave and I were never very close. Irritating each other was what we did best, and we weren't exactly friends. We never got together just to hang out; we ran out of small talk within ten minutes.

I envied the kind of closeness the Bridger family shared and wished I had it with my own family. Having to deal with my parents' divorce and each of them moving on was difficult for me. It was easier to distance myself from them.

Now this new dynamic had appeared—a birth mother and a half-sister. One didn't want me, and the other didn't even know I existed.

My thoughts kept spinning from Alicia to Charity, and back again. I wished I could go back in time to this morning. If I could have gone into the meeting better prepared, it might have ended differently.

Feeling unsettled, I crawled out of bed and opened my laptop. I logged on to the Internet and searched "liver donor." I couldn't remember the name of the disease Mr. Bernacchi said Charity had, but I thought I might recognize it if I saw it.

I searched for articles about living liver donors, liver disease, and I even checked websites about child abandonment and the law in the State of California.

After a couple of hours my eyes burned, and I shut down the computer. I closed my eyes and tried to process some of the things I'd read.

I'd assumed that the living liver donor had to be a blood relative, yet many sites stated that it wasn't necessary for the donor and recipient to be related. Blood type should be compatible, the donor should be healthy, and it was major surgery for both donor and recipient.

It was common for parents to be living liver donors for their children, and I wondered why neither Alicia nor Lawrence donated to save their daughter's life.

If she was driven to contact me, there must be a reason why they couldn't donate, but surely they had other relatives—ones they actually acknowledged—who would qualify. If not, they must have friends of the family. I considered what would happen if I needed a liver donation. I felt pretty certain that all of the Bridger family over eighteen, along with my parents—even Dave—would volunteer to be donors.

I could not fathom why Alicia would disclose my existence all these years later. It must be so embarrassing and humiliating to have to face a child you threw away. Reflecting on her businesslike attitude, she seemed cold and calculating. After meeting her, it was easy to imagine devious purposes.

I harbored no illusions that Alicia might soften her attitude toward me. She seemed like the type to insist on dictating the terms. She probably saw me as a tool to be used. I couldn't change what she did or how she felt about me, but the one thing I could control was making sure she didn't use me.

Is Charity just like her mother? I knew from personal experience that genetics did not necessarily make the person—I was living proof of that. I was *nothing* like Alicia. The thought invaded my mind, *What if Charity is nothing like Alicia? What if I can make a difference in her life?*

For the first time that day, my thoughts turned away from myself, and I concentrated on Charity. I imagined her like Lily—only blonde—and I knew without a doubt that if Lily needed help, I would be there in any way I could.

I knew and loved Lily, and she was not related to me by blood. Charity was. Did that obligate me? *Is it possible that Charity is just as much a victim as I am? Is it right to punish her because of what her mother has done? What would she do if the situation were reversed?* I would never know.

One thing I believed with all my heart—a person can't control the circumstances of their birth or even their childhood, but they can control the kind of person they are when they become adults.

I got down on my knees beside my bed. I poured my heart

out in prayer in a different way than earlier that night. This time the prayer wasn't about me—it was about Charity. I was about to make a life-altering decision and needed to know if I was making the right choice.

I received my answer and felt at peace.

I logged back on my computer and sent a long email to Adam, telling him what I'd decided. I knew he would understand and support me in my decision. When I crawled back in bed, I fell asleep immediately.

chapter fifteen

Adam called me the next morning to say he got my email and supported my decision. After I hung up, I made the phone call I needed to make. I knew what I wanted and it wasn't Alicia's money.

I told Mr. Bernacchi I wanted to meet with Alicia again—alone. I wasn't surprised when he called me back fifteen minutes later and set up the meeting for that afternoon.

When I met my mother for lunch, I could hear the pride in her voice as she introduced me to her coworkers. I vaguely remembered meeting a couple of them several years before, when we'd lived in Ventura. They commented on how beautiful and grown up I was. Although I suspected they were just being polite, the positive feedback strengthened me for what I was about to do.

I was careful not to mention the second meeting to my mother. After lunch, I drove back to the law offices.

I was better prepared for Alicia the second time we met. I refused to be intimidated and awed by who she was. I may have initially assumed because she had sought me out, she wanted me for me. I would not make that error a second time.

She was again seated in the conference room, looking regal as ever. I was glad I insisted we meet alone this time. Adam wasn't with me, and I didn't want Lawrence with her. I definitely didn't want an attorney sitting around in the meeting. I wanted it to be just me and her for a few minutes. Mr. Bernacchi and Lawrence lurked outside as I entered.

She stood as I entered but didn't offer me her hand again. I wouldn't have taken it, anyway. I sat down as she spoke.

"Kit— " I cut her off before she could continue.

"My name is Katherine." She had no right to call me Kit.

"Katherine," she corrected, unruffled. "I am so pleased you asked for this second meeting. I assume it is good news, otherwise a message would have sufficed."

It felt like she was talking down to me, again. I took a deep breath and began. "Alicia, I've considered what you asked of me . . . your 'proposal.' I was caught off guard and needed time to think. I'm willing to be a liver donor for Charity, if I'm a match. *Donate*— not sell. But I have a couple of conditions."

Eagerness flitted across Alicia's face before she could mask it. Maybe she was as nervous as I was, but she just hid it better. "I'm listening," she said.

"I don't want your money—except to pay for my expenses. What I want are answers—straight answers from you." She watched me, unblinking. I quickly added my final condition. "And I have to meet Charity."

Alicia plucked an imaginary piece of lint off her sleeve. "Of course your expenses will be paid for. And I'm willing to answer any questions you have. As for meeting Charity . . ." She shook her head. "I don't think *you* understand, Katherine. Charity is very ill. I don't want her upset by an ugly, thoughtless episode that happened when I was much younger and long before she was born."

I felt anger flare and struggled to keep my voice steady. "I don't think you understand, Alicia. I don't want you as a mother—I already have a mother. I don't have a sister—at least not until now. If my liver is good enough for Charity, then *I'm* good enough to meet her."

"It would be very disrupting for her." She gave me a look I could only describe as calculating. "Will you agree to meet her as a friend—a potential donor?"

"No." It came out sharp, but she needed to know I wouldn't bend on this. "Charity meets me as her sister. She gets to hear the truth."

"Half-sister," Alicia corrected.

"Whatever. I want to meet her, talk to her. I want her to know who I am. And I want answers to my questions—these are my conditions."

Alicia didn't respond for a minute or two. She studied her perfect, artificial fingernails as if searching for a flaw. A slight frown marred her professionally lined lips. It seemed like an hour as we sat there in silence. I was determined to wait her out. I wondered which would win—her pride or her love for Charity.

She finally looked directly at me and broke the silence. "What questions do you have for me?"

"Does that mean we have a deal?" I pressed her.

"Yes, it seems we do."

I pulled out a little notepad from my purse. This time I had written down the questions I wanted Alicia to answer. I didn't want to get sidetracked and forget to ask things that were important to me.

When Alicia saw the list, she asked, "Do you want me to fill out a questionnaire?" I recognized the sarcasm delivered in that cool voice.

"In triplicate, please." Her look told me she recognized sarcasm as well. "I made some notes so I wouldn't forget."

"Go ahead, I'm ready." She didn't look ready; she looked uptight and closed off.

"Alicia, please answer these questions truthfully. I need to know some answers."

"What will you do with the information?"

"I'm not going to *do* anything with it except satisfy questions I've had my entire life. Is that so hard to understand?"

"As long as *you* understand I'm not putting anything I say in writing. I'll answer your questions, Katherine, but you'll not use my words against me." She was the most mistrustful person I'd ever met. Again, the sense of loss—that she had no idea what kind of person I was—washed over me. I pushed it aside.

"Just please tell me the truth," I said quietly, looking her in the eye.

"Let's do this, then." She stared right back at me, unblinking.

"Who is my biological father, and does he know about me?"

"It would be hard for him to know about you when I don't know who he is." Alicia's voice was empty, devoid of emotion.

I thought, *How can you tell if a robot is telling the truth?*

"You don't know who he is? How can that be? You must have some idea." I wondered if she was holding out because he was someone prominent.

"You must be naïve, Katherine. It is possible to become pregnant without knowing who fathered the child. You are married, right? You do know how it works?" As sharp as her words were, I preferred the sarcasm to the hollow voice she started with.

"I know it's possible, Alicia. I want to know the circumstances. What happened to you?" I didn't want to voice the silent question in my head, but I forced it out. "Were you raped?"

She sighed and went on, "I wasn't raped, Katherine." The mechanical voice was back. "I was sixteen years old. My parents were wealthy and bought me everything. Same old story of trying to buy me off so they didn't have to spend time with me. I found ways to spend my time, which weren't appropriate or smart. I went to a lot of parties, with a lot of different people, and did things I'm not proud of. Things happened—teenagers aren't always discriminating, you know. That summer is a blur in my mind. The only thing I really remember is that I felt loved."

A trace of bitterness crept into her voice. "Sixteen-year-old girls don't know what love is, and they'll accept cheap substitutes. I did. It wasn't until Christmas time that I realized I was pregnant. There was no way I was telling my parents. They weren't around enough to hear my story anyway." Alicia leaned forward and something flashed in her green eyes. Although the conference table separated us, it felt like she was merely inches from my face.

"Do you know it's possible for parents to live with their teenage daughter and never know she's pregnant? I did it." A fierce pride filled her voice. "When I went into labor, I knew what it was. I took pain pills from my mother's personal stash and took enough to get through it."

I was horrified, yet mesmerized, by this insight into her mind. "Where did you give birth?" I asked.

"In my room at home. I had done research. I cut the cord, which was disgusting." She shuddered. "I stuffed the mess into a plastic bag, wrapped the baby in a pillowcase, and put it all in a backpack. I took a shower and then took a cab to the train station. I rode the train, caught a bus, and dropped off the plastic bag in a grocery store dumpster. I took another bus or two—I don't remember how many. I took the baby out of the backpack in a restroom and put it on top of the garbage and took the pillowcase with me. The pillowcase ended up in a different dumpster." She shrugged.

"The baby," I repeated. "You mean *me*."

"Isn't that what we're talking about?" she asked coldly, staring at me.

I looked away first. "I'm surprised I didn't suffocate. Then what did you do?"

Her tone implied the answer was obvious. "I went home. I never told anyone, until I told Lawrence and my attorney. Now you."

I felt horror at the story, and not only for myself. It was also for a sixteen-year-old who was so isolated, so detached, that she went through an entire pregnancy and birth alone. Someone who had so little respect for life, hers or her baby's, that she could be so unemotional about it.

"Did you ever wonder about me—about the baby?" I asked her.

"It was on the news briefly. I wasn't the first, and I won't be the last to do something like that. Now they have laws that let you drop a baby at the hospital without fear of prosecution, but they didn't then. My parents never knew."

"Why didn't you have an abortion? Wouldn't that have been easier for you?" I assumed that someone like Alicia would have taken that option.

"I considered it. By the time I admitted to myself I really was pregnant, I was too far along to be comfortable with it, and I would have had to tell my parents. It wasn't an option." She made it sound like a choice she made for lunch a long time ago—inconsequential.

"Did you ever think about what happened to me?" I could not

understand the way she viewed things. *How could a person give birth and then just throw away the baby?*

"You want honesty, and I'll give it to you. I blocked it from my mind. After a few years, it was as if it had never happened. I would have never told Lawrence if it hadn't been for Charity's need."

"What about your parents? Are you going to tell them now?" I wondered if she still thought she could keep it all a secret.

"They passed away five years ago in a car accident in London." She rattled it off like she was talking about strangers, and I guess in a way they were strangers to her. As an afterthought she added, "I was their only child."

We sat in silence for a moment—together but irrevocably apart. "Thank you for telling me, Alicia." I didn't feel horribly rejected. I thought I would, but I didn't. If anything, I felt sorry for Alicia. She still felt like a stranger to me, but at least I had some answers.

"Not exactly the kind of story you were hoping for, I suppose." She looked at her watch. "I'm not an unfeeling monster, you know. I was stupid, young, and thoughtless. I am a good mother to Charity. Anyone would tell you so."

How do I respond to a comment like that? I wanted to yell at her. *A good mother doesn't throw away her baby!* I kept quiet. My silence must have made her uncomfortable. She kept talking.

"It's not as if you don't have a good mother and father of your own, Katherine. You've told me so yourself."

"I do."

"Then stop looking at me like that. Nobody is perfect. Now, do you have any more questions?"

"Yes. Why aren't you and Lawrence donors for Charity?"

"We've been tested." Her tone told me I'd hit a nerve.

"And?" I pushed her—maybe I wanted her to suffer.

"We were declined. I won't go into the reasons, so save your breath." Her second answer confirmed my suspicion that it was a touchy subject.

"Don't you have friends?" I asked. Realizing how that must have sounded, I quickly added, "That could be donors, I mean."

"Believe me," she said, leaning forward, her green-eyed stare piercing me. "If there were any other options, I would have taken them."

I believed her. I looked down at my list of questions. Some of her answers had negated the need for me to ask some of the others on my list.

"That's all of the questions I have," I said. I again wondered if Charity was like her mother. I hoped not.

"I assume the first condition is met then." She was cool and collected again. "Let's get the others back in here now and work out the specifics of the agreement. Shall we?" She was already up, moving toward the door.

We spent the next hour working out the details and waiting for the changes to be made. I refused to sign a confidentiality agreement, and I insisted on meeting Charity before I would submit to any testing. Alicia insisted on moving everything at a rapid pace.

I arranged to meet Charity on Thursday and start the testing on Friday. I agreed to stay a few more days if necessary.

We parted ways with the understanding that I would visit Charity at their home in Santa Barbara. Alicia wanted time to tell Charity about me so she could get used to the idea before I showed up. Alicia offered to put me up in a hotel, but I took delight in telling her I would stay with my mother in Ventura. I accepted her offer to pay for a rental car though. I didn't want to leave my mom stranded without her car.

I drove to the beach again but stayed in my car as I called Adam. I told him what Alicia had revealed about the circumstances of my birth. While I was able to maintain an emotional distance while I was with Alicia, with Adam it all came bubbling to the surface.

I cried for being made to feel so inconsequential—like garbage. I mourned for the mother who didn't want me at birth and didn't seem to want me now. I now knew who she was and why she did it, but it only seemed to confirm my sense of nothingness.

Adam listened quietly. Eventually, I felt drained of tears and emotion.

"I wish I could be there with you," he said. "Do you want me to come?"

"I'm okay. She does not define who I am," I said resolutely.

"I'm proud of you, Kit," Adam said.

"For what? I'm a blubbering fool."

"No, you're incredibly brave. You asked the questions you had to ask, and you're still willing to help a stranger you've never met—even when you didn't like the answers you got. Even though Alicia has hurt you, you're still willing to help her."

"I'm willing to help Charity. Alicia benefits only by association." I was *not* doing it to help Alicia.

"I know that, but it would be easy to reject her and anyone associated with her. What she did to you was horrific. Even though it has to be devastating, you aren't letting it hedge your way and keep you from helping others."

I looked down at the wad of used tissues I was shredding as he continued.

"You know what?" he asked. "I'm glad she let you go, because I never would have met you if she didn't do what she did." His words lifted my heavy heart.

When I hung up the phone, I felt like a piece of my heart and strength went with him.

chapter sixteen

My mother wasn't quite as supportive as Adam when I told her what I was going to do. I updated her as we sat down to eat the pizza we'd picked up on our way home.

"Mom, I met with Alicia Haversham again today—it was my idea."

I saw the surprise on her face, but she didn't say anything.

"I wanted to know more information about my birth, and I want to meet my sister, Charity." I took a deep breath. "So I agreed to donate part of my liver if I'm a match."

She was quiet for a moment, and then she ripped into me.

"Are you insane?" Those were her exact words, and she added drama that was worthy of Lily. "What are you thinking?"

I knew she'd be upset, so I was prepared with answers. "First of all, know that I didn't decide this lightly. I spent last night doing some research and—" She cut me off.

"So now you're an expert because you spent a few hours researching this on the Internet. Donating an organ is serious business, Kit. It's not something you decide to do after a few hours of searching the web. Not to mention *who* you're doing it for." I sensed a full-on rant coming and tried to head it off.

"Mom, it wasn't just the research. I prayed about it and—" Again, she interrupted me.

"You prayed about it." She said it with almost a sneer. "Well, isn't that convenient? Who can question an answer to prayer? I'm sorry, Kit, I think prayer is an excuse people use when they don't have a logical reason for their decisions. I don't buy it."

Her mocking me for praying was like an unexpected slap across the face. I sat there, dumbfounded. "I can't believe you said that, Mom. You've always supported me, even when you didn't agree with me. When I decided to get baptized you were right there. When Adam and I got married, I knew you were upset, but I thought it was because you couldn't go to the temple with me. I didn't know it was because you don't believe in God. Is this part of your new look too?" Those last words were cruel, but I wanted to strike back at her.

"It has nothing to do with my 'new look,' as you call it. It has everything to do with stopping you from making a mistake that could ruin your life. I stood by and watched you get married without speaking up, but I won't be silent now." Her voice rose in anger as she cut me with her words.

I stood up, shaking with rage. "Are you saying that my marrying Adam was a mistake?"

"I know it was," she said stubbornly.

"Just because you couldn't make your marriage work, doesn't mean mine won't!" I yelled. "You may have made over your outside, but you need to work on the inside. Your bitterness is going to ruin more than your marriage!" I whirled and stomped off to my room.

I slammed the door and flung myself onto the bed. I had never been so angry with my mother before, and it was the first time she'd spoken to me that way. I wasn't a criminal doing horrible things, nor did I disrespect her way of life.

I didn't know what to do. I couldn't stay there, knowing how she felt about me, my religion, and my marriage. I couldn't go home yet. I was committed at least through Friday.

I remembered that Alicia had offered to pay for a hotel room for me. She could afford it, and I needed to get out of my mother's house. I searched for hotels on my computer and called a Holiday Inn. After I reserved a room, my next phone call was for a taxi.

I packed my things as I waited for the cab. When I went into the bathroom to gather my stuff, I saw my mom wasn't at the table anymore. I checked the countertop where she'd set her purse and noticed it was gone.

I hadn't heard her leave, but I checked the garage anyway. Relief washed over me when I saw her car was gone. I wouldn't have to talk to her. I went inside to finish packing and had my suitcase by the door before the taxi came.

She would be surprised to find me gone, but what did she expect? I thought about letting her worry, but I changed my mind and wrote her a short note.

> *Mom, I decided to stay at a hotel until I can make arrangements to go home. Kit.*

I heard the honk of the taxi, and I hurried out with my suitcase, backpack, and one last glance at my mother's beautiful condo. *So much for reconciliation*, I thought as I closed the door firmly behind me.

I called Adam as soon as I got to my room. For the second time that day, he patiently listened to me dump my pent-up frustration and hurt. I told him the hateful things my mother had said to me.

"I'm glad you left," he said, when I finally took a breath. "It sounds like you both need to cool off."

"What do you mean—cool off? You say it like we're going to make up and things will be fine. Didn't you hear what I told you? She thinks our marriage is a mistake. She mocked me for praying. I can't forgive her for that." I was adamant.

"Kit, listen to me. I think she was striking out because she was hurt. I doubt she meant those things she said."

"Hurt about what? She started the whole thing by interrupting me and mocking everything I've done."

"I would probably feel like you do if I were in your place. I'm saying this because of what my mom said earlier today when I stopped by the house."

"What did she say?" I wished Barbara were here right now. She always knew what to say to make me feel better.

"I told her what you'd decided to do. She asked if you had told your mom about meeting Alicia. When I told her you had, she asked how your mom was doing. I asked her why, and she said, 'It has to be hard for Nora. Kit's birth mother showing up after all these years probably feels like a threat.'"

"Why would my mom be threatened by Alicia? I don't consider Alicia to be my mother, and I never will." Even as I said the words, what Barbara meant started to sink in.

"Does your mom know that?" Adam asked quietly. "She might be afraid that Alicia will try to usurp her position as your mother."

"But why did she get so hateful? It's like she's *trying* to drive me away." I started crying again. My anger was gone, but I was frustrated and hurt.

"She probably reacted without thinking and it elevated from there. We all do that sometimes." Adam's voice was full of concern. "Are you all right, Kit?"

"I'll survive."

"For what it's worth, I think you were right to leave tonight, but I'm glad you left her a note so she won't worry. I also think you'll feel better after a good night's sleep."

His comment made me laugh—a little. "You sound like your mom now."

"I wish I were there to take care of you. Know that I love you, and I promise things will look better tomorrow."

"You're right. Maybe you could try being wrong once in a while—for a little variety."

It was his turn to laugh. "I know you're fine when you're able to muster up a little sarcasm. It's one of the things I love about you."

"Well make a list of the other things you love about me. I expect to see it when I get home. I love you, Adam Bridger."

"I love you too, Kit Bridger. Good night."

After we hung up the phone, I took the time to write the day's events in my journal. I was surprised that the anger had dissipated so quickly. Writing it all down was another outlet for some of the hurt, as well.

Before I went to sleep, I knelt down to pray. Although my mother might have mocked me for it, I prayed for her—and for me.

I prayed that we might understand each other better and be able to forgive one another.

I climbed into bed, feeling better. As I was drifting off to sleep, I remembered one more thing I wanted to pray for. I slipped out of bed one more time and added a request that Charity wouldn't be like her mother—that she might actually like me.

chapter seventeen

The emotional upheaval had taken a toll on me and I slept until ten. I felt so much better and turned on my cell phone to text Adam. There were three missed calls from my mom and she'd left a message.

"Kit, please call me. We need to talk. I'm so sorry about the way I reacted last night. Please call as soon as you get this message."

The tone of her voice told me even more than her words. She was worried. I found I was no longer angry at her, but I didn't want a repeat of the prior night.

I was starving and debated about calling her after I found something to eat. I decided I might as well get it over with and made the call.

"Kit!" She didn't even say hello. "Are you all right?"

"I'm fine, Mom."

"I was worried when I didn't hear from you. Where are you?"

"I'm at the Holiday Inn. I just barely woke up and got your message."

"Oh," was all she said. There was a few seconds of silence, neither of us speaking.

She broke the silence. "Are you getting ready to fly home then?"

"Not yet. I made a commitment, and I'm going to take care of that before I leave."

"About that," she said. "We really need to talk. I'm sorry I went off like that last night. I was surprised—but that's no excuse."

"You're right." I wasn't making it easy for her, but her words flooded back to my mind and, although the anger had subsided, the hurt was still fresh.

"Will you go to dinner with me tonight? To Milanos? We can talk there." She sounded hopeful.

"Mom, I don't want to fight with you, and I don't want you to lecture me on all of my 'mistakes.'"

"I know. I don't want to fight, either. I want to talk." She laughed and it sounded forced. "I forget you're grown up sometimes, Kit. Mothering you comes naturally to me."

The thought flashed through my mind, *Unlike Alicia.* I shoved it aside.

"What time do you want to meet there?" I asked.

"I was thinking about 6:00. Do you need me to pick you up?"

"No. I'm getting a rental car today."

"Okay. I'll make reservations for us. I'll see you then. I love you."

"I love you too, Mom." I hung up feeling relieved.

I quickly showered, braided my hair, and walked next door to get breakfast. After I'd eaten a huge plate of pecan pancakes and a side order of bacon, I felt great. Adam was right—things looked much better this morning.

I called around and found a rental car agency that would send a shuttle for me. While I waited, I tried calling a couple of my old friends but only got voice mail.

I texted Tara to get an update on the wedding plans. That girl could text faster than most people could talk—the exception being Tara, herself. Her messages were so long, it took two texts to get most of them. It occurred to me I should make sure she wasn't driving while she was texting.

Haha. Eric is driving. We're going to pick out his tux. It was her shortest text of the conversation.

For the first time in weeks, I actually enjoyed her ramble about the wedding. It took my mind off my own issues.

I picked up the rental car and pondered what to do for the

afternoon. I drove through our old neighborhood and by the house we used to live in. I drove by my high school and some of my old hangouts—a trip down memory lane.

It hadn't been quite four years since I'd lived here, but it seemed so long ago. I tried to imagine what my life would have been like if my dad hadn't taken the job at Utah State University.

I wouldn't be married to Adam, and I wouldn't have been baptized. *Would my parents have gotten divorced?* As much as I wanted them to be together, I wouldn't trade the other changes in my life to make it so—even if I could.

My phone rang. It was a number I didn't recognize. I answered it. "Hello."

"Katherine?" I recognized Alicia Haversham's voice.

"Yes." My heart started pounding and I pulled over into a parking lot.

"I've spoken with Charity, and you may meet her tomorrow at two as discussed." Her voice was about as warm as a computerized recording.

"Great." I wanted to ask, *How did she react? Is she as cold as you are? Is she excited to have a sister?* Instead, I said, "I'll need the address."

"1448 Granada Hills Lane."

"Hold on, I need to find something to write on." I fumbled in my purse for a piece of paper and a pen. "Okay, what was it again?"

"1448 Granada Hills Lane. Santa Barbara. Do you need directions?"

"No. I can download directions. I'll be there tomorrow at two." My hand shook as I wrote down the address, tracing over the numbers.

"I also made an appointment with our physician for the initial tests on Friday afternoon. I'll provide the details tomorrow." She didn't waste any time, but it was part of the agreement so it didn't really surprise me.

"Okay. I'll talk to you then." As I hung up, I perversely thought about adding "Mother" at the end—only to shock her into showing some emotion.

choosing charity

I spent the afternoon reading by the pool at the hotel. The solitude felt good, and I was more relaxed than I'd been for several days. Adam called me during his break between classes to see how I was doing. We talked for almost an hour and when I hung up, I reflected that it had been a pretty good day—I just hoped the evening with my mother wouldn't ruin it.

When I got to Milanos, my mom was already there. She stepped forward to hug me and whispered, "Kit, I'm sorry. Will you forgive me?"

"I guess I should ask you the same thing." I knew I wasn't without fault in our argument.

"Of course I forgive you. Are you hungry?" Her words made me realize I hadn't eaten since my late breakfast and the yummy smells were making my mouth water.

"Yes. Lying by the pool all afternoon is hard work," I joked, trying to lighten the mood.

"I wondered what you did today. I thought you might go to the beach again." The hostess motioned for us to follow her, and she led us back to our table.

"I called a couple of friends, but no one answered. I drove past our old house—it looks so small. Things have changed a lot in four years."

My mom agreed. "The only thing we can be sure of is that things will keep changing. So you got a rental car?"

"Yeah, I'm driving up to Santa Barbara tomorrow to meet Charity, and back there on Friday to start the testing to see if I'm a match." *There. It's out in the open. Let the fireworks begin anew.*

"I've been thinking about your decision to be a donor. I overreacted last night. I know it's your decision." My mom was much calmer than she was last night.

"It *is* my decision, but can you support me in it?" I realized how much I needed her to be with me.

"I'll do my best. I want to make sure you're considering the risks of the surgery, and I *am* bothered a little by your birth mother coming forward after all these years." Her voice quivered a little as she spoke.

"You don't need to be threatened by Alicia Haversham. I don't

101

want a relationship with her. I wanted answers from her and it was one way I could get them."

"Donating part of your liver is a high price to pay for answers." The server stopped by with water and a plate of garlic cheese sticks. It was good timing, because it gave me a minute to fight down the indignation that flared with my mother's last remark.

She turned her attention to the server. "Thank you. I think we're ready to order." After a couple of bites of a bread stick, I was able to continue the conversation rationally.

"It would be a high price just for information, but I also want to meet Charity. She might be just like her mother, but maybe not. I need to find out."

"I don't want you to be hurt. Emotionally or physically," my mother said quietly.

"I know. I don't want it either. You and dad have taught us to help others, and I believe it even more strongly now that I have the gospel in my life. Charity is only sixteen years old. She'll die without a liver transplant." As I said the words, I felt the truth of them to the center of my being.

My mom's eyes filled with tears. "She isn't your responsibility, you know. But your willingness to do this is admirable. I'm proud to be your mother."

It was my turn to blink back the tears. "Thanks, Mom." We sat quietly for a few minutes, both of us trying to control our emotions. It was hard to swallow the breadsticks with the huge lump in my throat.

"Mom, can I ask you a question?" I asked.

"Of course. What is it?"

"Did you mean what you said about prayer? Don't you believe in God?" I offered a silent prayer that she would understand I wasn't attacking her.

"I believe there's a higher power. But praying to that higher power isn't something that I believe in, personally." She spoke carefully, watching my reaction. "We've always taught you to respect the beliefs of others, and last night I didn't do that. I'm sorry I mocked you."

"So you never pray?" I asked.

"No, I don't," she said, then added, "But I'm glad it brings you comfort."

Normally, I would use that admission to press the issue that prayers are answered and God is real, but I felt like it wasn't the time. I knew she was trying to answer my questions honestly, so I asked her another one.

"Do you really believe I made a mistake in marrying Adam?"

She looked down at her water glass, tracing her finger along the rim. I was afraid of her answer.

"I think getting married at your age is a mistake." She held up her hand to stop me from replying. "However, I think Adam is a wonderful person and he treats you well. So marriage at a young age is what I'm opposed to—not marriage to Adam."

Even though she technically thought my marriage was a mistake, I was glad she didn't have anything against Adam. She lacked the eternal perspective of the gospel that Adam and I had. She discounted prayer, so she couldn't comprehend the powerful confirmation that the Spirit brings as a result.

"Are you upset?" she asked. I realized she had misconstrued my silence.

"No. I think I understand where you're coming from. Kind of."

"Can I ask you a question now, Kit?"

"Sure."

"Did you mean what you said about my appearance? Do you really think my new look is terrible?" I wasn't prepared for the change of subject, but it seemed fair, since I'd asked her about the things she'd said to me.

"Actually, you look great. You're just so different from how you used to be. You don't look like my mom anymore, and your condo is nothing like the homes we've always lived in. I feel like you rejected everything in your old life—and you hated everything about it. Sometimes I feel like you left me and Dave when you got divorced."

She smiled but still looked sad. "I did leave everything behind when I left. But I'll never stop being your mother. No matter how my looks change, that never will."

She continued. "I never thought my life would go this

way—that my marriage would end up in divorce, and I'd have to start over. It hurts, and I won't deny I'm bitter about it. I'm working on getting past it, but it still flares up sometimes."

"I'm sorry I said those things, Mom."

"And I'm sorry too."

The server interrupted us again, this time with our food, and it was every bit as good as I remembered. It was only a small thing that hadn't changed, but it helped.

chapter eighteen

Alicia answered the door so quickly, I wondered if she'd been watching out the window, which told me her aloof manner wasn't as detached as she would have me believe.

The house was massive considering only three people lived in it. It was elegantly furnished, yet seemed unlived in. It lacked any kind of warmth.

When I first saw Charity, the sight of her took my breath away. She lay back in a massive four-poster bed, a lime green coverlet draping the bed and dwarfing her. Pillows of every size, shape, and color dotted the bed and the surrounding floor. I had to step over several as I approached her.

Luminous, vibrant green eyes dominated a thin face that bore no resemblance to me—except, again, for the cheekbones. Her hair was a silky blonde copy of her mother's and was draped over her shoulder in a loose braid, intertwined with a bright pink ribbon.

I took a few steps and stopped, uncertain of how to proceed. She was my sister—my half-sister at least. What would she think of me? Of course she would welcome me as the potential life-saving donor, but would she welcome my existence in her sheltered little world?

Charity's mother—I couldn't think of her as *my* mother—hovered in the doorway. Charity's eyes were on me, and a broad smile lit up her face. Her eyes flickered past me for a moment, lighting on her mother. The beautiful mask slipped for a second, and I saw irritation briefly replace serenity.

"Mother, I'm perfectly safe. I told you I wanted to talk to Katherine alone. *Alone.*" The strong firm voice contradicted the frail girl who seemed almost ethereal. I turned and glanced at her mother, whose own look of determination faltered a bit as she turned to step out of the room.

"I want to make sure you don't need anything." Alicia hesitated, waiting. For the first time, I detected uncertainty in her voice.

"I'll text you if I need you, Mother." Charity firmly dismissed her.

She pulled the door nearly closed, leaving it cracked open, and Charity called out, "Shut it tight, Mother. And no eavesdropping."

The door clicked and Charity smiled at me. "Mothers. You know how they are. Always hovering."

I steadied my voice before I spoke. "I know how some mothers are. Not that one." My tone must have betrayed some of my animosity, and Charity picked up on it.

"Oh, Katherine, how awkward this is. I don't like feeling awkward. I should apologize, I suppose." She sounded so much like Alicia at that moment. A frown briefly flitted across her seraphic face. I shuddered to think she might be just like her mother.

She shrugged and her smile returned. "Actually, Mother should be the one to apologize. But how do you say, 'Oops, sorry I dumped you in the trash when you were a newborn. My bad'?" Charity switched from sounding much older than her sixteen years to sounding like a teenager. It was a little disconcerting. I supposed terminal illness could do that to a person. "I don't imagine Mother apologized to you, did she? She doesn't do remorse very well. Father is always the one who says he's sorry."

Charity's comment struck a nerve. Alicia had not actually apologized to me. I knew it wouldn't undo what she had done, but it sure would be easier for me if I felt she was a little bit sorry. Charity was right—Alicia *didn't* do remorse well.

"Are you always this quiet, Katherine? Sit down." She patted the bed next to her. I sat on the edge of the overstuffed pink and green chair next to the bed, keeping my distance.

Charity kept on. "I want to know everything about you. *Everything.* Like, do you go by Katherine or Kathy? What's your favorite color? Where did you grow up? Do you like being married?" Her rapid-fire questions didn't give me time to answer, but the open exuberance that resonated in her voice and her engaging smile enveloped me. I settled back into the chair, which was amazingly comfortable.

"I can't tell you anything unless you give me a chance to talk. I go by Kit." It didn't bother me a bit to let Charity call me Kit—as long as Alicia didn't.

"I love that name! You don't look like a Katherine or Kathy— just so you know. I'm sorry I'm such a chatterbox. I don't get a lot of visitors—and *never* one like you."

I smiled at the comment. I gave her a brief rundown of growing up in Ventura with my mom and dad and Dave. Her face was an open book of emotions as I spoke, and I was mesmerized by her expressiveness.

Charity clapped her hands like a child. "This is too funny! We were thirty-five miles away from each other all these years and we never knew it. Were you happy? Did you wish for a sister? I did. I never dreamed I actually had one. My mother has a lot to answer for."

Charity's reaction to me was more what I'd hoped for from Alicia. Her enthusiasm made it easy for me to talk about myself. She peppered me with questions. Whenever I revealed something about my childhood, Charity compared it to hers. It saved me the trouble of asking questions of my own.

"Mother said you live in Utah now and you're married. Tell me about your husband. Is he cute?" Adam was a subject I could go on endlessly about. I pulled out my cell phone to show Charity some pictures of him.

"He is so hot, Kit. Does he have a younger brother?" Life radiated from her gaunt face as I told her about the Bridger family. I started from the oldest, Justin, and went all the way down to the youngest of the eight children, Sarah.

Charity really perked up when I told her about Mark, Adam's

younger brother who was about to turn nineteen. She started planning how I could set them up on a date, so I told her he was getting
ready to serve a mission.

"He's a Mormon?" she cried out. "I should've known he was
too good to be true."

"You say that like it's a bad thing. I'm a Mormon." I always
felt defensive when someone Mormon-bashed, and I was suddenly
afraid Charity was one of those people.

"Being Mormon isn't the problem. I'm not an ignorant child. I
know that when Mormon guys go on missions they're gone for two
years. *Two years, Kit*—I could be dead by then." She sounded as
dramatic as Lily when she said that, but I felt a chill at the truth of
Charity's words. I had forgotten for a little while why I was there
meeting my half-sister.

My face must have mirrored the change in my emotions,
because Charity said, "Stop it right now, Kit. I have a favor to
ask: don't talk differently to me than you would anyone else. My
mother does enough tip-toeing around my illness for everyone and
it's irritating. It's true, you know. I will likely be dead by the time
he comes back from his mission."

"Not if I have anything to do with it," I stated. "You'll be waiting for him at the airport when he gets home, ready to go on a date."

"We'll see. Do you think he'd email me? Will you send me a
picture of him?"

"Missionaries are usually pretty happy to have girls write to
them while they're on their missions. They're not always the best
about writing back, though." It occurred to me that Lily would
make a perfect email pal. "You need to meet Adam's sister, Lily.
She's almost sixteen. You would love her." I scribbled down Lily's
email address and asked Charity for hers.

"Will she be shocked to hear from a skeleton in your closet,
Kit?"

"What are you talking about? *I'm* the skeleton in the closet.
And she doesn't shock easily. Besides, the whole Bridger family
knows I'm adopted. They'll welcome you as my sister. They're an
amazing family, and I can talk to them about anything."

"What about your family? Can't you talk to them about

anything?" Charity picked up on nuances, which was something I liked about myself. It felt *sisterly* to share a trait like that.

"My mom and dad just got divorced earlier this year after nearly thirty years of marriage. I still can't believe it. My mom moved back to Ventura while my dad still lives in Logan." I shrugged as if it was of little importance to me. "Life goes on."

"It does for some us," Charity said, and I cringed at her words. I'd stuck my foot in my mouth again. She smiled at me. "Sorry, Kit, I like to take things literally. It keeps things interesting. Remember what I told you? Don't worry about what you say around me."

"Usually I'm the one who messes with people. I guess I deserve it." It was odd, feeling camaraderie like this with a sister I hadn't even known existed a week ago.

"So you're not close to either of your parents? What about your brother?" Charity looked genuinely concerned, and it was the encouragement I needed to open up.

"We've never been a tight-knit family. Even though my dad lives close by, I'm having a tough time getting over what he did to my mom. He had an affair. I guess it was a mid-life crisis or something. I just don't get it, and I have a hard time being around him now."

"So why did you stay in Utah instead of coming back to Ventura with your mom?"

"*Adam.* See, I found out my parents were separated while I was in Romania. Adam and I weren't engaged yet—"

Charity cut me off. "Romania! What were you doing there?"

I described the three months I spent in Romania working with the orphans. Her questions brought back the bittersweet memories of that interlude. I told her about Marcel, the romantic medical student who had proposed to me there and almost convinced me to stay in Romania with him, helping those forgotten children.

"I'm glad you didn't stay," she said.

"Deep down I knew I shouldn't stay. Marcel was sweet and understood my love for the orphans like nobody else. But Adam is the one I want to spend eternity with. I made the right choice."

"And you wouldn't have met me if you'd stayed. I want to see pictures of Romania and Marcel."

Every story I told her brought more questions. Charity absorbed everything I said. I never talked so much about myself in so short a time.

Twice during our visit, Alicia tapped on the door and peeked in, to see if Charity needed anything. Both times Charity told her mother to leave us alone.

When Alicia knocked for the third time, before Charity could tell her to leave, she came right in and said. "I've let you have your visit, but it's time for you to get some rest." She leaned over and tucked a loose strand of pale blonde hair behind Charity's ear. When Charity started to protest, her mother was firm. "Katherine can come back tomorrow, unless you overdo it today. It's time to take your medicine and you should rest."

I glanced at the clock on the nightstand. It was five o'clock. I couldn't believe three hours had passed so quickly. I'd forgotten how sick she was, and I didn't want to make it worse. I stood up. "I need to leave now anyway. I'm coming up tomorrow for a doctor's appointment—to get the testing started." I turned to Alicia. "I'd like to stop by and visit Charity first, if that's okay with you."

Before Alicia could reply, Charity butted in. "Of course it's okay. Come as soon as you can tomorrow. We have so much to catch up on." Alicia nodded curtly to me. I sensed she would do anything for Charity—as if my very presence there didn't already attest to that fact.

"I'll walk Katherine to the door and be back to give you your medication." She said to Charity. To me she said, "I'll expect you tomorrow around eleven." I leaned around Alicia to wave good-bye to Charity.

As we walked out of the room, Charity called out. "She goes by Kit, Mother. See you tomorrow, Kit!" Alicia's only response was to give me a frigid look. She didn't say another word as she showed me to the door.

chapter nineteen

I called Adam on my drive back to my mother's condo. I left a message and he called me back quickly.

"I took my break so I only have a few minutes," he explained.

I filled up our short time on the phone rattling on about Charity.

"So I take it she accepted you a little better than Alicia did," Adam commented when I finally let him speak.

"Yeah, it was a surprise. After the way Alicia acted, I was expecting a miniature Alicia. I don't know how Charity turned out so nice, but I'm glad."

"How did Alicia act while you were there?" Adam asked.

"Charity told her to go away while we visited and then when it was time for Charity's meds, Alicia politely showed me the door. In silence, of course." Even though Alicia's behavior still puzzled me, it helped that Charity was so opposite of her.

"Now that you've got your answers and you've met Charity, do you still feel good about your decision to be a donor?"

"Definitely. I know she'll die without a liver donation, and as sad as I felt about her situation before, it is so much harder to contemplate her death now that I know her. It's unacceptable. I have to do it."

"I'm glad you feel strongly about your decision. I wouldn't want you to do it if you were unsure at all," Adam said. "So what's the next step?"

"I'm going back to see Charity tomorrow at eleven. Then I have a doctor's appointment in the afternoon to start the donor screening process. I'll know more of a timeline after that appointment. I might have to change my flight home." The thought of being away from Adam longer was depressing.

"Kit, have you considered that you might not be a match?" Adam asked.

I laughed. "I'll be a match. I know I will."

"I know you're sure, but I don't want you to be disappointed if you aren't."

"You worry too much. I guess I've taught you well. I'll call you as soon as I find out anything—*if* they can tell me something that soon. I don't know just how far they can go with the screening tomorrow."

"I have to get back to work. Call me later tonight. I love you."

I hung up just as I pulled up to my mom's condo. As I pulled into the driveway and saw a sedan that I didn't recognize, I realized that I hadn't specifically let her know I was coming to stay with her again. I just assumed she'd know. I considered leaving, but my curiosity got the better of me so I parked alongside the dark Mercedes.

I wondered if I should knock. It wasn't like it was my home, and I suddenly felt self-conscious about walking in unannounced. I knocked and then let myself in, calling out, "Hi, Mom, it's me."

I didn't see my mother, but a man I'd never seen before sat on the sofa. He stood up as I walked in. "You must be Kit." His greeting was friendly, and I got the impression that he felt more at home there than I did.

"Yes, I am." I took his extended hand and shook it. "And you are . . . ?"

"I'm Jonah Lofthouse." He offered nothing else in the way of introduction and before I could ask any questions, my mother came out of her room.

She was clearly dressed for going out. The look on her face clarified that I must not have told her I checked out of my hotel and that she hadn't heard me enter. "Kit! I wasn't expecting you. For some reason I thought you were staying in Santa Barbara tonight."

I felt a little embarrassed at the intrusion. "I, uh, thought I'd come back here for the night and drive back up tomorrow. I didn't mean to interrupt your plans."

She flushed slightly. "I wouldn't have made them if I'd realized you would be back tonight. This is Jonah Lofthouse, a business associate." Turning to him, she said, "Jonah, this is my daughter, Kit."

Jonah seemed to enjoy the discomfort my mom and I were feeling. "We introduced ourselves just before you came in, Nora." He looked directly at her. "We can reschedule our business meeting if you like." His gaze and her reaction to it told me it was much more than a business association they enjoyed.

I was acutely embarrassed at that point and feeling slightly nauseated. I shouldn't have worried, though, because they barely noticed me. Seeing them together like that was like seeing two strangers. With the high color on her cheeks and the black dress she was wearing, she barely resembled the mother I grew up with—she was beautiful.

Jonah wasn't a bad-looking guy for his age. I tried to determine just how old he was; his hair was mostly gray, but he looked fit and trim in his tailored sports coat. Maybe the same age as my mom—it was hard to tell.

I broke the silence. "You don't have to pretend you're 'business associates' for my benefit. I'm a big girl." My words startled them back to the reality that they weren't the only two people in the room.

Jonah recovered first and spoke directly to me. "Your mother brags about how smart you are. I don't think she was exaggerating." Turning back to my mom, he said, "Nora, we can go out another night if you'd like—or Kit can join us."

My mom fingered the pearl necklace that was a stunning contrast to her black dress. I didn't remember seeing those pearls before. "Would you like to come with us? We're going to dinner at Bouchon in Santa Barbara."

The awkwardness I felt overshadowed my previous embarrassment. "Uh, no. I mean, I don't want to intrude. Go ahead. I'm fine." The only thing worse than being the odd man—or woman—out on a date was if the other two people were your single mother and her boyfriend.

I think my mom sensed the weirdness, but Jonah was either clueless or just liked to get his way. "Kit, I insist. You have to eat. I'll make the call to change the reservation while you get ready."

I didn't know how to get out of it. My mother took sides with Jonah. "It'll be fun. You and Jonah can get to know each other. Hurry, go change."

"My suitcase is still in the car," I protested feebly. "I don't think I have anything nice enough to wear."

"I'm sure you've got a skirt or some slacks," my mom said. "You can borrow one of my tops if you didn't bring one." She seemed eager and pushed me toward the door. Jonah was already on his cell phone to add me to the reservation.

I muttered to myself as I went out to get my stuff. This was as bad as having dinner with my dad and Amberlie. *How can my parents be so clueless? Don't they think of anyone besides themselves?*

Although I was determined to suffer through dinner quietly as penance for my spinelessness, Jonah Lofthouse seemed just as set on drawing me out.

"Your mother told me you graduated with a bachelor's in accounting and now work for a CPA firm. Are you planning on becoming a CPA?" He glanced in the rearview mirror as he weaved seamlessly through traffic on Highway 101.

"I need to get my master's degree first, and I'm not going back to school until Adam is finished." I loved the smell of the leather interior. I could get used to a car like this.

"I keep telling her to finish her education now. It never gets easier." My mom turned halfway in her seat. I guess she thought I couldn't hear her well enough. "You should get your master's while Adam's going to school."

We'd had this conversation before. "Adam and I've agreed that I'll work full-time so he can focus more on school. Besides, I don't even know if I want to become a CPA." I was finished with this topic. "This is a beautiful car, Jonah."

"Thank you. Mercedes CLS63 AMG. Power and grace combined. It's a dream to drive." Jonah pointed out several features of the luxury sedan with such enthusiasm, if I'd been in the market for a car that probably cost half as much as a house, I would have bought it on the spot.

The restaurant was beautiful and intimate. The soft music and dim lighting added to my feeling of being an intruder on a date. My mother let Jonah order for her, and I remembered that she was always that way—even when married to my dad.

Jonah kept the conversation flowing, and to my surprise, the evening was enjoyable. Jonah praised my mom's expertise at design and raved to me about her talent, and she basked in the glow of his compliments. When my mother tried to get Jonah to talk about himself and his accomplishments, he always steered the conversation back to her—or me.

On the drive back to Ventura, I half listened to their conversation as my thoughts roamed. I thought it would be strange to be back in Santa Barbara after leaving it a couple of hours prior, but I'd hardly even thought of Alicia and Charity during dinner.

I wondered how much Jonah knew, because he didn't bring it up at all. Considering his deft ways of getting me to talk about myself at dinner, I was surprised the subject never came up. I was relieved; I didn't want to argue with my mother about it again.

I heard her laugh at something Jonah said, and it occurred to me that this "new" mom of mine laughed a lot more tonight than I had seen for a long time—maybe even years. I felt sad to know she had to be away from her family to find happiness—but there was a part of me that was glad she seemed so alive and vibrant with Jonah.

She is so different than she used to be, I thought, studying her profile from the backseat. *How can so great a change come about in so short a time?* I knew the changes were deeper than the surface ones wrought by her cosmetic surgery. Some I liked; others made me cringe.

My thoughts turned to my father. I pondered the dinner Adam and I'd had with him and Amberlie. The situation had upset me, and I now felt ashamed of how rude I'd been to Amberlie. I hadn't treated Jonah with anything other than respect, however distant and awkward I'd felt at the start of the evening.

My father, who had made choices that destroyed his marriage and drove our family apart, was now on the verge of embracing the gospel. My mother, who had always seemed to have a spiritual center, was now living for herself and enjoying worldly pleasures, even disavowing God as a loving Heavenly Father who heard and answered prayers.

Yet I was bothered more by my father's attempt at creating a new life than I was with my mother's. *Why? Why is it easier to accept Jonah with my mother, than it is to accept Amberlie with my father? Why can't I give my father the benefit of the doubt? Why can't I forgive him?*

In the back of that Mercedes, a thought came to me that shot through the center of my being. *I can accept my mom and her changes because even though I don't agree with how she's living and what she believes, I truly believe she's being honest with herself and me. I can't trust that my dad really is what he says he is. I'm afraid he is toying with something that's sacred to me. I saw what he did to our family when he got tired of it. What will he do when he gets tired of trying to live the gospel? Who will he hurt then?*

When we got back to my mom's condo, I quickly thanked Jonah and excused myself for the night.

I spent a long time writing in my journal, recapturing the time spent with Charity, and reflecting on truths I was learning about myself.

Seeing my parents as individuals makes them seem more human, and I know humans make mistakes. It seems so much easier to forgive people when they aren't so close to me. Like Claire.

I've been holding my parents to a higher standard—expecting perfection. I know better than that. Looking back, some of my hardest times—like when Janet died and when I had to leave the orphans in Romania—helped my faith grow, but I couldn't see it until later. My parents' struggles may help their faith (and mine) if we let it.

Maybe my parents moving on separately and pursuing their new lives doesn't mean they are abandoning me and won't stop loving me. Maybe it isn't all about me.

chapter twenty

Alicia answered the door again. Offering no greeting, she simply said, "You're early."

"Traffic was light." I shrugged, trying to pretend like I hadn't sweated about whether or not she'd let me in fifteen minutes early.

"Charity didn't sleep well last night," Alicia said. *Does she blame me?* Her next words confirmed it. "She isn't accustomed to long visits."

"I'm sorry," I said automatically.

She ignored my apology. "I would have canceled this visit if Charity hadn't promised she'd take it very easy for the rest of the weekend."

I read between the lines. *Don't plan on visiting her.*

Charity didn't look any worse to me today than she did yesterday. She actually looked more animated—I could tell she was excited to see me, and I was glad to see her too. It almost made up for having to deal with Alicia.

"Kit! I'm glad you're here." She turned to Alicia. "Mother, you can leave now."

Alicia started to say something but clamped her mouth shut. She shot me a frosty look as she left the room.

"Ignore Mother," Charity said. "She's always been overprotective. It's worse since I've been so sick."

"She said you didn't sleep very well. I'm sorry."

"It's not your fault. I don't sleep well most nights." She frowned. "It's so stupid because I'm always so tired. I nap a lot."

I didn't know what to say, so I changed the subject. "I brought a couple of photo albums."

"Great!" Charity patted her bed. "Come sit by me." She stuffed a fluffy green pillow behind her head and back to raise up to a sitting position.

"They're my mom's albums, so you'll have to suffer through pictures of Dave too. Sorry." I opened the first one and she pulled it closer.

"I want to see all of them." She eagerly studied the pages. She asked questions about every picture—wanting to know how old I was, where we lived, and what the occasion was.

She interspersed her questions with comparisons to her own life at the same age. By the time we finished going through the two albums, an hour had already passed.

"Do you have your photo albums?" I asked her. I wasn't sure I wanted to see them at first but curiosity won out.

"Mother said she couldn't find them," Charity said. "Which is strange because she knows where everything is. I think she just didn't want you to see them." Her frank statement caught me off guard.

"Do you really think so?" I asked. "Why would she care?"

"My mother doesn't like anyone to force her to do anything. I know you made her tell me about you."

"She told you that?" I was surprised that Alicia would admit it to Charity.

"She didn't exactly say it, but I know she never would have told me about you unless she had to. You should have seen her telling me." Charity laughed. "I've never seen her so uncomfortable. Oh, she tried to make it sound like it was her idea, but there's no way she would be open about it. She likes to control things. Since she couldn't stop us from meeting each other, she'll get even in other ways. Like not being able to find the photo albums."

"I guess I'm not surprised. I know she doesn't like me." I tried to sound nonchalant, but Charity seemed to pick up the undercurrents.

"Don't worry, Kit. It's her, not you. She doesn't like it when she's not perfect, and you're the ultimate reminder that she isn't." She patted my hand and grinned. "I like you enough for both of us."

"Thanks. It kind of hurts because I've never done anything to her—except be born." There was a lump in my throat, and I was afraid I'd start crying if I didn't talk about something else. I picked up my purse. "Guess what. I brought my camera. It's better than the one on my phone. We'll take pictures of our own."

Charity giggled. "I love it! Promise you'll email them to me."

I assured her I would, and we spent the next few minutes posing and taking pictures of each other and self-portraits of us together. I reveled in the feeling of thwarting Alicia.

"Do you ever think about dying?" Charity asked abruptly.

"Not really," I said, putting the camera away. "A couple of years ago I thought about it a lot though."

"What happened?"

"It was after I moved to Logan. Adam was on his mission and I was best friends with his sister Janet. I spent most of my spare time at their house. Adam's brother, Justin, was the one who baptized me. I was so happy . . ." My voice trailed off at the memories.

"Why did you think about dying if everything was so good?" Charity prompted.

"Janet was the kindest person I'd ever met. I could talk to her about anything and she never judged. We were coming home from her bridal shower, and she was driving. We were talking and laughing. Then we hit something big. I woke up in the hospital and she didn't. She was dead." My voice broke. Charity reached out and took my hand.

"I'm sorry," she whispered.

"It happened one month before her wedding. I felt guilty for being the one who survived, and I was mad at God. I wished I had died in her place. It took a long time to get past those feelings."

"So you weren't afraid of dying?" Charity asked.

"No. I was more afraid of living."

"I'm not afraid to die, either," she announced.

"Let's see if you still feel that way when you're ninety." I couldn't stand the thought of Charity dying and had to change the subject. "I don't think your mom is going to let me visit again before I go back."

"You're probably right, but we can text and email." We pulled out our cell phones and entered each other's information. Charity immediately texted me. *Hey big sis!*

I replied, *Hey little sis. Don't tire yourself—I'll get in trouble with your mom.* We texted each other for the next few minutes—not talking, but laughing our heads off at the stupid things we said.

There was a knock on the door, and Alicia poked her head in. "Charity, are you ready for lunch? Rita is bringing up a tray." She glanced at me. "She's bringing something for you too, Katherine. We need to leave in an hour."

"I'm not very hungry," Charity said.

"You need to try to eat something." Alicia moved aside as Rita came in with a tray.

"I know." Charity rolled her eyes. "Leave us alone while we're eating. We don't have much time."

It smelled delicious to me. My stomach growled, but I didn't want to make a move until Alicia left. She stood there until Charity complained, "Leave, Mother."

"Eat," Alicia demanded. She waited until Charity took a bite. She turned to me and said, "Katherine, make sure she eats. I'll be back in an hour."

Charity picked at her food, but I ate enough for both of us. "Don't you like it?" I asked.

"I just don't have much of an appetite." She ate a few spoonfuls of soup.

"I know you need a liver transplant, but what's wrong with you exactly?" I asked between bites. "I mean, what caused your liver to fail? Were you born that way?"

"I was born with biliary atresia. Either the bile ducts were blocked or missing. The bile can't drain from the liver so it causes liver damage. I had a Kasai procedure when I was six months old. They created a bile duct from a piece of my intestine." She paused and ate a spoonful of soup.

"So did it work?" I asked, offering her a breadstick. She pushed it away.

"Yes and no. I'm still alive, so that part's a success. But it isn't a cure and almost half of the babies that have the procedure done still need a transplant by the time they're five. I beat those odds. But most people end up needing a liver transplant by the time they're twenty. I heard the doctor tell my mother that I have the liver of a seventy-year-old alcoholic." Charity spoke matter-of-factly, and I wondered how she really felt about being so sick.

"Have you always *felt* sick? Do you spend all of your time in bed?" She looked really thin and tired, but she'd been so animated during my visits it was hard to remember she was so ill.

"It's a lot worse now. I get tired easily because I'm really anemic, so I'm in bed a lot. I get nosebleeds and I'm nauseated all the time. And you can probably tell I'm pretty yellow." She held out her arm for my inspection.

I hadn't paid attention to the color of her skin, but it definitely had a yellowish tinge now that I looked closely. "I'm sorry." I couldn't think of anything else to say.

"Don't worry, Kit. Sometimes my legs puff up like sausages—then I look really funny. But other than that I feel fine!" Her attempt at humor made me smile, but I felt terrible inside. Clearly I'd seen a more healthy side of Charity during my two visits.

"I don't want to make you feel worse," I said, remembering what Alicia told me earlier. "Should I leave?" I'd been so caught up in my own excitement at having a sister that I forgot to consider her illness.

"No, don't leave!" She was adamant. "You give me something to look forward to. And I'm not just talking about getting part of your liver. I have a sister now. That part is wonderful." She took my hand and squeezed it. "I'm glad you're here."

I blinked hard to keep from crying. Her words—*I have a sister now*—echoed my own feelings. We shared a connection, and I wanted more than anything to make her healthy again.

Rita came to get the tray, and Alicia was right behind her.

"How much did you eat?" she asked Charity.

"Most of the soup."

Alicia frowned and said to Rita. "Make her a protein smoothie. She needs more nutrition."

"Mother, I don't feel like it," Charity protested.

"Do you feel like an IV? Would that be better for you?" Alicia's words were the sharpest I'd heard her use with Charity.

"No. I'll drink it." She looked at Alicia through her long lashes. "Will you bring Kit back here after the doctor's appointment?"

"I'm afraid not. We're driving separately. I have some errands to run afterward, and I'm sure Katherine has other things to do." I was relieved when she said we'd go in separate cars because I'd been dreading the ride over with her.

Charity looked depressed. "I want to visit more."

"You need to rest and get some sleep. You were up most of the night." Alicia's tone softened at Charity's sad tone. "We'll plan another time for Katherine to visit you."

"Maybe tomorrow," I said, looking at Alicia for her assent.

"We'll see. Rita will bring your smoothie and your medication. Try to take a nap. I'll see you in a few hours." Alicia leaned down and Charity turned her cheek for a kiss.

Alicia stepped back and said, "Are you ready, Katherine?"

I nodded and Charity said, "Wait!" I turned to see what she wanted. She held her thin arms out to me. "I need a hug, Kit."

I bent down and hugged her. She felt frail and delicate in my arms.

"I love you, Kit," she whispered.

Her words overwhelmed me. I couldn't speak so I hugged her tighter. I composed myself enough to say, "Be good and I'll bring you a liver."

chapter twenty-one

I followed Alicia to the doctor's office. The drive passed too quickly, and a few short minutes later we were walking across the parking lot together, neither of us speaking.

We checked in with the receptionist who gave me a clipboard with a stack of forms to fill out. I sat down to begin the tedious process. Alicia picked up a magazine and studied it intently.

After twenty agonizing minutes, a nurse called me back. Alicia stood. *She's not coming back with me!* Aloud, I said, "No. I want to go alone." It came out a little louder than I meant to, but I panicked at the thought of her coming back with me.

She sat and picked up her magazine again, not saying a word.

After the nurse weighed me and took my vitals, I met Dr. Bartlett, the Haversham's family doctor. Charity regularly saw a hepatologist, but Dr. Bartlett would perform the initial screening physical for me to become a donor. He reminded me of my father with his slight build and serious demeanor.

He explained to me the initial exam was to evaluate my overall health, make sure my blood type was compatible, and draw blood to run preliminary tests. Assuming I passed the physical and tests at this visit, I would travel to UCLA medical center next week to meet a transplant psychologist and to begin additional testing.

I wondered if Dr. Bartlett knew my relationship to the Havershams. If he did, he didn't let on. His demeanor was professional and kind, again reminding me of my father.

His explanation was followed by the exam. It was basic and quick. After listening to my heartbeat, looking at my eyes, ears, nose and throat, he asked me several more questions. *This is easy*, I thought, my nervousness fading.

Dr. Bartlett said, "We'll need to draw some blood now and also collect a urine sample. My nurse will be in to assist you. I'll be back in to speak with you in a few minutes."

After the nurse directed me to the restroom, I was sent down the hall to get my blood drawn. I returned to the exam room and waited another fifteen minutes before the doctor came back in.

"Katherine, thanks for waiting. Your blood type is O positive. Based on that, you are an acceptable candidate to continue with the testing." He hesitated.

"But?" I asked, sensing there was some sort of problem.

"Are you aware of the restrictions on living donors? We've already discussed general health, blood type, and being of the same general size and weight."

"Right. I know all that. Are you saying I'm not healthy?" He was confusing me.

"Katherine, you cannot donate if you're pregnant."

"Oh, I'm not pregnant," I said. "My husband and I are waiting until he finishes school. I'm using birth control."

Dr. Bartlett smiled. "Katherine, no birth control method is 100 percent effective—except abstinence."

It took a few seconds for his meaning to sink in. "Are you telling me I'm pregnant?" I whispered.

"Yes, I am," he confirmed. "The urine test is positive. We'll send in the blood serum test to verify it, but I'm quite certain you're not eligible to be a living liver donor."

"Wait. How can it be?" My mind was rapidly calculating the timing.

Dr. Bartlett laughed. "I can see this is a surprise to you. Don't worry, you're not the first one to be caught unawares. When did you say the first day of your last period was?"

"I was pretty sure it was the first week in July. Like the fifth or sixth."

"Was it normal?" he asked.

I struggled to remember. With everything that had happened in the last couple of weeks, the summer seemed a distant blur. "We went camping with my husband's family, so it was early in July, but it was kind of spotty. I remember being surprised at the time, but I forgot about it."

"What about June? Can you remember the date?" Dr. Bartlett was making notes in my chart.

"It was around the 5th. It always comes around the 5th."

"But nothing in August, right?" He reached in a drawer and pulled out a little card with dates on the front and back.

"Nothing in August," I mumbled. *How had I not noticed it?*

"Katherine, based on what you've told me and my exam, I estimate you are nine or ten weeks pregnant. I would say you're due in March, probably the latter half."

"I feel ridiculous," I said, trying to make sense of it. "How could I not know?"

"It's not too uncommon for a woman to have some light bleeding in early pregnancy. I suggest you make an appointment with an obstetrician as soon as possible. An ultrasound will determine your actual due date."

He reached in the drawer and pulled out a packet of paper. "Here is some information on pregnancy. If you're using birth control pills, stop taking them. You'll need to get started on prenatal vitamins as soon as possible."

"Okay." I took the papers without really seeing them. Of all the things I'd expected when walking in to Dr. Bartlett's office, this never entered my mind.

"Katherine," Dr. Bartlett said, touching my arm to get my attention. "As far as being a liver donor for Charity Haversham goes—it's very admirable for you to consider it, but someone else will have to fill that role. It's important that you not feel guilty about that."

"Oh, right." His statement reminded me why I was there in the first place. *Oh no, how can I tell Charity the news?* Focusing back on the doctor, I asked, "Is there anything else?"

"Take this." He handed me his business card. "If your doctor wants the results of this exam or any of the tests we've run, it has our address on it." He patted my arm. "You'll be fine, Katherine. Remember to get in to see your own physician."

Alicia still sat in the waiting room, appearing to wait patiently, but the rapid tapping of her right foot clued me in on her agitation.

I had to tell her the news. I remembered Dr. Bartlett's advice to not feel guilty.

"Well?" she asked expectantly.

"My blood type matches and I'm healthy," I said, not wanting to talk about it in the waiting room.

"Good. Then we can proceed. Did Dr. Bartlett wish to speak to me?" She started toward the receptionist, likely to demand to see the doctor.

"Alicia, can we talk about this outside?" I asked quietly.

"What is it?" Her eyes narrowed suspiciously. "What's the matter?"

"Outside." I said and walked out the door. The tone of her voice warned me this would not be easy.

I stopped beside my rental car. Alicia was right behind me. "What's going on, Katherine? You're not having second thoughts are you? I kept my side of the bargain."

"No. I want to give Charity part of my liver. I just can't."

"Can't or won't?" she accused.

"I *cannot*. I'm pregnant." There, the words were out.

Alicia looked stunned and then her beautiful face contorted in rage. "Are you kidding me?" she hissed. "Is this your idea of a joke?"

"No. I'm just as surprised as you are. Adam and I weren't planning this." I didn't like her assumption that I would deceive her.

"You just found out then?" Her expression became calm—almost instantly. "Then nobody else knows. We can fix this." She nodded. "Yes, we can take care of this."

Horrified I stared at her. "What do you mean?"

"You're an ignorant girl. I *mean* we can terminate this pregnancy and move on with our plans."

"Are you talking about abortion? Are you crazy?" I couldn't believe this woman, of all people, would suggest this solution to me.

"What is your problem?" She looked at me like I was the one who had suggested murdering someone. "This is done all the time. What are you? Twenty-one years old? You're little more than a child yourself."

"There is something seriously wrong with you, Alicia. You are sadly mistaken if you think I would ever consider that alternative." I fumbled with my keys, desperate to escape this madwoman.

She grabbed my arm to stop me. "Grow up, Katherine. You can have more children. Charity is my only child. She's dying. You made a deal."

"What? You can't just replace one child with another. A child isn't *disposable*." I was shaking with anger as it dawned on me what I was saying to her. "Wait—I forgot. Children are disposable to you. At least you didn't suggest I throw this one away."

She flinched at my words, but maintained her iron grip. I hit the remote to unlock the car.

"Katherine, stop." Her fingers dug into my arm. I jerked away from her.

"Don't touch me, Alicia. Never touch me again. I'm through with you." I climbed into the driver's seat and reached to shut the door.

She blocked it.

"If that's your decision, so be it, Katherine. Just stay away from my daughter. If you contact her, I will get a restraining order against you. If Charity dies, it will be your fault!"

I slammed the door, locking it. I was half afraid she would block my way as I backed out of the parking space. She stood to the side giving me a look of pure hatred. I drove away as quickly as I dared. *How can she be such a monster?*

chapter twenty-two

I headed to Ventura, my thoughts churning and twisting. I spent most of the drive ranting out loud about what a witch Alicia was. I had never met anyone so cold-hearted and cruel.

After I'd worn out my own ears with my tirade, I thought about Charity. *Can Alicia really keep me from talking to my own sister? Can she get a restraining order against me?*

The idea of the lies Alicia would tell Charity nauseated me. I couldn't stand the thought of Charity thinking I'd abandoned her. I needed to find out if I could legally contact her.

What will happen to Charity now? What if she dies? Guilt swelled within me. Maybe she could hold on until March. *That's it. She'll be okay until then. Then I can donate. I just have to have faith that she'll be okay until I have the baby.*

Until I have the baby. That thought suddenly hit me so hard, I started shaking. I took the next exit and pulled into a gas station. I barely got the car door open when the nausea that had been threatening me took over.

Oblivious to anyone around me, I threw up right there in the parking lot. Not once or twice, but three times. Down on my knees, with heaves and sobs racking my body, I didn't have the strength to stand up or crawl away from my own mess.

Minutes passed as I knelt there, unable to pull myself together. Finally the spasms and tears subsided. I groped for my purse, pawing for a tissue. I really needed a whole pack to clean myself up. Of course I couldn't find any.

"Excuse me, are you all right?" a female voice asked. I looked up and saw a woman a little older than me standing next to my car—actually, a few feet away—she was smart enough not to get too close.

"Yes, I'm—" A hiccup cut off my words. It was so loud I started to laugh, which made me choke. She probably thought I was a lunatic.

"Can I get you anything?" she offered.

"I really need a tissue. I can't find one anywhere."

"Wait here. I'll be right back." She went into the convenience store and I kept digging for a tissue, napkin, or even a receipt. My nose was dripping, and my mouth was sour. I found a crumpled tissue in the bottom of my purse. It was just enough to smear everything across my face.

The woman came back with a box of tissues and a bottle of water. She leaned over the fender close to the front of the car and handed them to me. *Poor lady.* I didn't blame her for not coming closer.

After half a box of Kleenex and a long drink of water, I felt composed enough to look her in the face. "Thanks for helping me," I said lamely. "How much do I owe you?"

"Nothing. I just want to make sure you're okay." She looked around uncomfortably. "Do you want me to call someone for you?"

"No, I think I'm fine now. I've had a tough week. A lot of surprises. I found out I have a half-sister. She's dying, and I'm pregnant." I hiccupped again and tried hard not to cry this time.

The woman stood there turning her cell phone around and around in her hands. "I'm sorry about your sister. And congratulations about your baby—unless you're sorry." She shuffled a couple of steps sideways. "I mean—is there anything else you need. I have to go, but I don't want to leave you alone if you're not okay. Are you sure I can't call someone for you?"

"I'll be fine. I'm not far from my mom's house." I blew my nose. "Thanks for the tissues and the water. Sorry about the vomit." *That was a stupid thing to say.*

She glanced down at the ground by my car and then quickly looked away. "I hope your week gets better. Good luck."

I waited a few more minutes before I started driving again. I calmly drove the rest of the way to my mom's condo. Thankfully, she wasn't home. I needed a few minutes alone to think about things.

I lay down on the bed in the guest room and closed my eyes. I wanted to talk to Adam. I had two problems though—I didn't want to tell him this news over the phone, and I needed to sort out my own feelings on the matter.

My initial feelings of disbelief and surprise had faded, although it still seemed like a dream. I rested my hand on my tummy, trying to imagine a life growing within.

To myself I could admit I was upset about being pregnant. I felt so ashamed to have those feelings, but they were real.

This is too soon, I thought. *Adam and I haven't had enough time together as a couple—I'm not ready for a child. Our plans for me working while he finishes school are messed up. How can I tell them at work that I'm due right during the busiest season?*

My thoughts mortified me. *What kind of mother thinks this way about her unborn child? Am I just like Alicia? Am I so selfish I can't see beyond myself?*

I recalled a conversation I'd overheard between Adam and Justin. We were at the Bridgers' for Sunday dinner, and they didn't realize I was just outside their dad's office.

Justin was voicing a complaint to Adam. "I am really tired of Michelle's obsession with having a baby. She's driving me crazy with it. I wish she would let it be. Sometimes I'm not sure I'm ready to take on that responsibility." It was one of the rare times he'd spoken with anything but satisfaction regarding his perfect wife, so of course I listened.

Adam had commiserated with him. "Better you than me, man. I'm glad Kit's not pestering me to have a baby already." I felt proud of how in-sync Adam and I were. I felt bad for Justin and Michelle. *Had that been only a month ago? I was already pregnant then.*

It suddenly occurred to me that I had a bigger problem than I thought I did. Adam's comment made it pretty clear he didn't want children yet. *How will he react? Will he blame me?*

I tried to dismiss those traitorous thoughts immediately. I knew Adam well enough to know he would never blame me, and he would be happy. *At least he'll act happy. How will I know how he really feels? If he's upset, he won't tell me. Adam puts the best face on everything.*

I groaned and wished I could go back to my ignorance of this morning. I definitely couldn't tell Adam over the phone. If being pregnant upset me so much, how could it *not* upset Adam?

I was aching to talk to him. I could fly back tomorrow. My flight was booked for Sunday and I'd warned Adam that I might have to stay an extra week for testing at UCLA. There was no reason I couldn't change it to Saturday instead. There was nothing keeping me here now.

If I left tomorrow, my mom would ask why. I didn't want to tell her I was pregnant. She already thought I was too young to be married. Maybe I could tell her I missed Adam too much—it was the truth.

I dozed off with my thoughts going in circles. A light knock on the door awoke me. My mother peeked in the room.

"Oh, I didn't realize you were asleep. I was checking to see how your day went and if you were hungry."

"It's okay." My stomach growled. "I *am* hungry. What's for dinner?"

"You can choose. We can go out to eat or dig up something here. I'm flexible." She sounded way too perky. It wouldn't be easy to avoid her tonight.

"You pick something. I don't feel like going out though, so can we order in?" My face felt tight and swollen from my earlier crying jag, but I no longer felt nauseated. Just hungry—ravenously hungry. *Ugh, at least now I know why I've been eating so much lately.*

"There's a Chinese place not too far from here that delivers. The food is pretty good. Do you feel like Chinese?" She frowned at me still lying on the bed. "Are you sick, Kit?"

"No, I wasn't feeling so great earlier, but I'm better now." I rolled up to a sitting position. "I'm just a little groggy from the nap."

"Good. Come on out to the living room and I'll find the menu. We can pig out on Chinese food and watch a movie tonight. Sound fun?"

Surprisingly enough, it sounded like a great plan.

We watched a chick flick and ate so much food that we were in pain. It wasn't so painful that it stopped her from offering to dish ice cream or me from accepting it.

I forgot about my problems as we ate, watched the movie, and ate some more. When the movie ended, my mom shut off the TV and turned to me.

"So I'm dying to know. How did the testing go?" Curiosity showed on her face.

The issues I'd held at bay came surging forth again. "My blood type matched." I considered how I could word it when she asked more questions—I knew she would.

"So you qualify to be a donor?" she asked carefully, trying to keep her tone neutral. She'd made it clear she didn't want me to endanger myself by donating part of my liver. I had to give her credit for trying to be supportive of me.

"No. I was declined," I said, hoping I wouldn't have to elaborate.

Relief flooded her face before she could mask it. "Why?"

I couldn't lie to her. No matter what her reaction to my news, it couldn't be worse than Alicia's. "It seems I'm pregnant."

"What did you say?" The look on her face reminded me of what my own stunned expression probably looked like when Dr. Bartlett gave me the news.

"I'm going to have a baby." I waited for the explosion.

"Oh." That was it—her entire reaction. We both sat there, looking at each other. I wondered what she was thinking.

"I didn't know I was pregnant," I said.

"I assumed you didn't," she replied. Silence, again.

"That's it then?" I asked.

"I'm surprised. It's taking a minute to sink in." She didn't look like she was going to explode. "How do you feel about it? Does Adam know?"

Those words were enough to start the waterworks again. It felt like I was crying for the fortieth time that day. My mom pulled me over to her and hugged me as I cried it out.

"It's okay, sweetheart," she murmured as I soaked her shoulder. It was quiet except for the sounds of my crying and sniffling.

I blew my nose, and she handed me another Kleenex. I finally answered her. "I don't know how I feel, and I haven't told Adam."

"Do you want to talk about it?" she asked gently.

I cried a little more as I told her the confused thoughts I had and gave voice to the guilt I suffered for the misgivings I felt about having a baby.

"Kit, it's very normal to feel inadequate. I've never met a prospective mother who didn't have second thoughts sometimes. You're human, honey."

"What if I'm like Alicia—cold and unfeeling? What if I got some kind of 'bad mother' gene from her?" After meeting Alicia, my fears were only compounded.

"You are nothing like that woman. *Never* think that you are." My mom's voice was sharp as she spoke, and her defense of me was comforting.

"What if Adam isn't happy about the baby?" I repeated the conversation I'd overheard between Justin and Adam.

"I think he'll be happy even if the timing isn't perfect," my mom said.

"He'll *say* he is," I said. "But I'm afraid he won't tell me the truth about how he really feels. How I can know for sure if he's happy about it?" I shredded the Kleenex in my lap, feeling disloyal for admitting my husband wasn't perfect.

My mom took my chin in her hand and lifted my head up so I looked her directly in the eye. "You listen to me, Katherine Matthews Bridger. I'm about to tell you the most important thing you need to know about marriage." Her look was stern, but her touch was gentle. "Communication is vital to a marriage. You have to be able to say how you feel and what you need, and then listen to your partner in order to understand his feelings and needs. Never underestimate how important that is."

She continued. "You're shocked and surprised by this pregnancy. That's normal. But I know you well enough to say that when it processes, you'll be thrilled. Allow Adam the same privilege. Let him absorb the shock and then he'll feel the joy. The key is to speak openly and honestly about your fears, your hopes, your dreams. That was the mistake your father and I made. We didn't communicate—we didn't really listen to each other. We buried the issues deep inside, hoping they would go away. I wish I could go back and change it, but I can't." I saw tears fill her eyes.

"Kit, a marriage built on good communication will be strong. Share your feelings openly with him—don't sugarcoat them to keep the peace. Allow him to do the same. You're both human and you'll have negative feelings about things sometimes. But you can work through them. Good communication can help your marriage survive just about anything. Do you understand?"

I nodded mutely, because I couldn't speak. The lump in my throat was too big. Her support was exactly what I needed.

I called Adam just before I went to bed. I didn't want to deceive him, but I wanted to see his reaction to my news face-to-face, so I told him I was declined as a donor and I'd be home as scheduled on Sunday. When he asked me why, I told him I didn't want to go into it over the phone, but we'd talk about it in detail when I got home; that I was still upset about it all and wanted to think about it some more—all true.

My mom came to my room before I turned off the light. She hugged me again. "Now there are a couple of things we have to straighten out. I don't want to be called 'Grandma.' I'm thinking something like 'Mimi.' I've just taken ten years off my age and I'm not ready to add them again."

Her comment was as unexpected as her reaction had been. I laughed. "What's the other thing?"

"It's a good thing we have one more day. We have some shopping to do!"

chapter twenty-three

Saturday passed in a whirlwind of rampant consumerism. My mother wasn't kidding when she said "shopping." The woman was a machine.

She dragged me into half of the stores in the mall. She bought so many newborn baby clothes I had to tell her to stop. "I'm only nine or ten weeks, Mom. We have no idea if it will be a boy or a girl. Please, I'll never get them all home."

"Oh this is just the beginning," she said, laughing. "A few basic items to get you started. They're in neutral colors so it's safe. Just wait until we *know* if you're having a boy or a girl—then we'll really start shopping."

I thought nothing could top my surprise at being pregnant, but it turns out my mother's reaction managed to do just that.

After the baby-clothes frenzy, we stopped to eat lunch. Secretly relieved the ordeal was over, I thanked her for her generosity.

"We're not finished yet, Kit. We haven't bought you maternity clothes yet." She took each piece of baby clothing out of the bag and discussed it at length. I reminded myself that I lived eight hundred miles away and this was a temporary thing.

My interest was piqued once I got a look at some of the maternity clothes. They were in style and many looked like regular clothes—stretchy ones, but still trendy.

I settled on a couple of tops and bottoms from the pile my

mother had collected every time I expressed interest in any particular item.

"No, no, no," she said, pulling out half a dozen more tops and three more pairs of pants. "You need a variety."

"Mom, I can't fit all of these clothes into my luggage. I don't need to get everything right now."

"We'll get you another suitcase, Kit." She spoke like I was a child. "Don't worry, I'll pay the extra baggage fee. Let me do this."

I shook my head in defeat. It was her money.

After she paid for them, she said, "Now we need to find you some skirts or dresses for church."

We couldn't leave until we stopped at the bookstore where she let me pick out a book on pregnancy and then added two more she thought looked good. She picked up another copy of the book I'd chosen and tossed it on the pile. "One for me," she said, not the least bit embarrassed.

I texted Adam on and off throughout the day complaining about the shopping expedition. He knew I didn't like shopping, and he laughed at me.

My mother's excitement started to rub off on me, and I felt a little surge of elation when I thought about sharing all of this with Adam. When I realized I was excited, it made me even happier. She was right; Adam and I would be just fine.

He texted me to tell me Lily said "Hi." I felt a twinge of guilt, because I hadn't even thought about Lily or her struggles for a couple of days. At least she'd gotten over her anger at me. I imagined her reaction when she found out she was going to be an aunt. She'd be thrilled.

That led to the realization that this baby would be the first grandchild on both sides of the family. Barbara would be as overjoyed as my mother—well, maybe not quite as much, judging by how my mom was acting. I figured my dad and Adam's dad, Hal, would both be reserved, but happy.

My mood lightened as I anticipated the fun of telling people. Then I remembered Justin and Michelle. They'd been trying to get pregnant for months. My happiness deflated. *How would I tell them?*

My mom didn't notice my changing moods, or if she did, she didn't comment. I shoved the thought of Michelle and Justin aside, determined to enjoy this day with my mom. We had rarely felt such camaraderie, and I wanted to make the most of it.

By the time we got back to her condo, I was exhausted. She wouldn't admit to being tired, but I could tell she was. She offered to take me out to dinner on my last night there, but I convinced her to order pizza and stay in. I had to endure her going through all the clothes again, but curling up on the couch to watch made it easier.

We ended the night by opening our duplicate pregnancy books and reading passages aloud to each other about the baby's development. We started with week one and made it to week ten before I got too drowsy and had to call it a night.

As I drifted off to sleep, I realized I'd put Charity and Alicia out of my mind for a short time. I wondered what Alicia had told Charity and made a mental note to find a way to text her, call her, or at least email her. I needed to make sure that she didn't hate me like her mother did.

chapter twenty-four

The flight home was smooth—as far as airplane rides go. Mentally, it was filled with extreme turbulence.

I was giddy with excitement at the thought of seeing Adam again. With so much to tell him, I didn't want to blurt it out all at once. I knew when I started talking it would be difficult to shut myself up, so I tried to plan it out in my mind. I would be rational and logical—after all, having a baby wasn't a terrible thing; the *timing* was the surprise.

I called Adam while I waited for my bags to appear. He answered after the first ring.

"Hey, Bridger. I'm on the ground, waiting for my luggage."

"I'm in the park-and-wait lot, so I'm about a minute away."

"That's still too far!" I said. "I'll text you as soon as my bags come."

"'Kay. Love you. See you in a few."

Ten minutes later all my rational, logical thoughts disappeared as Adam wrapped me in his arms. Being with him again was like coming home even though we were still in Salt Lake. He stepped back and I reluctantly let go of him.

"I'm so glad you're home, Kit," he said, hands cupped around my face. "I missed you so much. Next time, I go with you."

"Agreed. If I ever go back," I said.

He popped the trunk and turned to pick up my bags. He saw

the big suitcase my mom bought for me and raised a brow. When he hefted it, he pretended to stagger under the weight. "Holy cow, woman! What did you and your mom buy?"

"It was my mom who bought it all. It's a long story. I'll tell you while we drive."

We pulled into traffic and Adam said, "Before I forget, my mom wanted me to tell you she's planning on us for dinner at five."

"Yum. I was hoping I didn't have to cook. But let's not stay too long tonight. I want to spend time with just the two of us."

"I agree." He reached out and squeezed my hand. "So I'm ready to hear all about it."

"Wow." I took a deep breath. "I don't know where to begin."

"Tell me everything. I was worried when you didn't want to talk on Friday night after you got back from the donor screening. I could tell you weren't doing very well."

"Yeah, Friday was a tough day," I said.

"And then you didn't even call on Saturday—just texted. That's not like you."

"I know. I'm sorry. I told you my mom was in a shopping frenzy. It wasn't very conducive to phone conversations."

"So what's up with that?" Adam asked. "It sounded like you two were having a rough time all week and then you spend an entire day shopping together. You don't even like to shop."

"I know," I repeated, shaking my head. "She was like a different person on Saturday."

"Okay, I'll stop interrupting. What happened?"

Adam, you don't know what you're asking, I thought. *You're about to have a life-changing experience.* Aloud, I said, "Dr. Bartlett is the doctor I went to see on Friday. He was only doing pre-screening. He did a basic physical and drew my blood so they could verify the type and run some other tests. And I had to pee in a cup, so they could test that too."

"You said the blood type matched."

"It did. But pregnant women can't be donors."

"What?" Adam looked at me. "Did I hear you right?"

"If you heard me say I was pregnant, then yes, you heard me

correctly." I watched him closely, trying to gauge his reaction. His eyes shifted from the road back to me.

"Wow," he said. He didn't look upset at all, but Adam rarely did.

"What are you thinking?" I desperately wanted to know.

"I'm surprised. Are you sure?"

"As sure as the doctor is. The blood test will confirm it."

"So it's still iffy?" he asked, glancing over at me.

"Not really. The urine test was positive. They'd already drawn the blood, so they sent it in. That's what Dr. Bartlett said."

Adam didn't respond, just kept driving.

"Do you need to pull over?" I asked.

"No, I'm good," he said. "Unless you need to pull over. Are you feeling sick? Are you going to throw up?" He moved to the right-hand lane.

I started laughing. "I'm not sick, you nut. Except with worry over how you feel about it."

"I'm still trying to process it. This changes things, of course. We weren't planning on this for another two or three years." He gave my hand a squeeze. "It's okay, we'll adapt."

"I know we can adapt. But how do you feel about being a dad so soon? Are you mad?" I tried to keep the quiver out of my voice.

"Of course I'm not mad! Why would you think that?"

"I heard you and Justin talking at your parents' house back in July. He was venting about Michelle obsessing over getting pregnant. You said you were glad I wasn't nagging you about having a baby. Turns out I was pregnant then. So I wonder if you're secretly upset."

Adam laughed. "I don't even remember that conversation. But haven't we always talked about having kids? If the timing has been taken out of our hands, I'm good with it."

I saw the sincerity on his face and heard it in his voice. *Of course Adam isn't upset*, I thought. *He's always had faith that things happen for a reason.*

I started crying.

"Kit, are you okay? Did I say something wrong?"

His concern made it worse, and I cried harder. I was a mess. He took the next exit. After he pulled into a parking lot, he turned off the car and unbuckled. He released my seat belt too and pulled me close to him.

"Kit, I promise I'm not mad about you being pregnant. I *want* the baby. It's exciting when you think about it."

Adam's words and embrace helped me control the waterworks this time. I was even prepared with tissues.

"I know you're good with it, Adam. You took the news far better than I did. I'm going to be a terrible mother because I wished it hadn't happened yet. I'm afraid to be a mother." I wiped my nose and looked at him. "What if I'm like Alicia and just can't love my baby?"

Understanding dawned on his face. "Kit, you are *not* Alicia. You're not a confused sixteen-year-old who has no one to turn to. There is no way you won't love our baby." He stroked my face. "*Our* baby, Kit."

The love I felt for Adam at that moment was indescribable. Tears filled my eyes again. He gently wiped them away as they trickled down my cheeks.

"Stop doubting yourself, Kit. You're incredibly beautiful, smart, and loving. Our baby will be just like you—what's not to love about that?"

I smiled at him and then buried my face in my hands, shoulders shaking.

"What's wrong?" Adam sounded anxious.

I popped my head up, so he could see I was laughing, not crying. "What if our baby's just like *you*?"

Clearly relieved I was kidding around, he said. "You should be so lucky."

"You're right—I couldn't be that lucky again." I took a deep breath, exhaling, and felt like a big weight had been lifted. "Sorry about the mood swings. It's been really bad this week."

"You've had to deal with a lot of things by yourself. I'm here now, so I'll help carry the load."

"You already have," I assured him. "That huge suitcase you lifted into the trunk? That was just the beginning. You won't believe all the stuff my mom bought. You'll have to carry that load again, and maybe even launder it."

Adam laughed. "Suddenly the shopping all makes sense. So does that mean your mom was happy about it? I'm guessing she knows."

"She's the only one who knows besides you and me. And Dr. Bartlett. And Alicia. But she *is* the only one who took me shopping. So surprising as it is—my mom is very happy. But she doesn't want to be called 'Grandma.' She wants to be called 'Mimi.'"

"I'm good with that. I'm sure my mom will be thrilled to be called 'Grandma.'"

Adam started the car and pulled on to the freeway again.

"That reminds me," I said. "I don't want to tell everyone yet."

"Why not?"

"I want to see my own doctor and get the due date confirmed. And I want more time to get used to it myself." I didn't mention Justin and Michelle. They would be at dinner tonight. I wasn't ready to deal with their disappointment when my own feelings were still so fragile.

"Okay," Adam agreed. "When is your due date anyway?"

"They're not positive, since I had spotting in July. An ultra-sound will confirm the due date. Dr. Bartlett thinks the middle or end of March."

"That seems so far away."

"I know. But I'm already nine or ten weeks along. That's about a fourth of the way there." I remembered the book I had in my backpack. I twisted and reached back so I could pull it out. "Look." I held it out so Adam could see it.

"*What to Expect When You're Expecting*," he read aloud.

"Don't read! You're driving!"

"You stuck it in front of my face. I thought you wanted me to read." He acted all innocent, but he knew what I meant.

"You drive and listen. I'll read." I flipped over to my bookmark and started sharing what I'd read. "The baby's now the size of a green olive if I'm nine weeks." I turned a few pages. "Or the size of a prune if I'm ten weeks."

"So it's either a fruit or a vegetable." Adam smirked, thinking he was funny.

"Only if he takes after you. And technically, an olive is a fruit."

We spent the rest of the drive with me quoting fun facts from the book, and Adam making clever remarks about everything I said.

I noticed his smile was practically perpetual. I realized my own jaws were aching from smiling and laughing. *What a wonderful pain to have.*

chapter twenty-five

It seemed like ages since I'd been to the Bridgers', although it had only been a little more than a week.

Lily was back to normal—at least as normal as a teenager can be. She was helping Barbara in the kitchen and squealed when she saw me. "Kit!" She ran up and hugged me. As I returned her hug, thoughts of Charity came to my mind. I hadn't thought about her since Adam picked me up at the airport.

Once I told him I was pregnant, the topic never turned back to Alicia or Charity. Now I felt the sharp contrast of Lily's exuberant hug and Charity's delicate embrace. *How can I just forget about her?*

"You sound happy," I remarked as I helped Lily set the table.

"I am. Guess what?" She didn't give me time to guess. "I'm getting a cell phone tomorrow. Mom and Dad said."

That explained her enthusiasm. "So why did they change their mind?"

"I thought I might get one for my sixteenth birthday, so I begged them to give it to me early. They finally said yes!" Her face clouded over. "It's the only thing that makes starting school tomorrow actually bearable."

I placed a glass by each plate. "You're not that excited to start, I take it."

"That's an understatement. I want to be done with high school and move on to real life." She sighed dramatically.

Again, I thought of Charity and how much she wanted to go to high school but couldn't. Maybe Charity and Lily should get together. I had an idea. *Alicia threatened me about contacting Charity, but Lily can't be held to that. Alicia doesn't even have to know who she is.*

I felt a twinge of guilt at the subterfuge. I brushed it aside. I would only use Lily as a messenger until Charity convinced Alicia to let her talk directly to me. I was afraid Charity thought I just let her down. I couldn't let her think I changed my mind about being a donor. I was certain Alicia wouldn't tell Charity the real reason.

Charity will understand if she knows I'm pregnant. Shall I have Lily call her or text her tomorrow? Probably text, since it's less conspicuous. Wait, I'll have to tell Lily I'm pregnant! She'll never keep it a secret.

I went into the living room where most of the family was gathered, waiting for the call to dinner. I leaned over the back of the couch and whispered to Adam. "Come into your dad's office. I want to talk to you."

Adam followed me in, and I shut the door to keep from being overheard. You never knew when someone was lurking in the hallway and might listen in.

"I think I want to tell your family tonight," I told him.

"Tell them what?" he asked.

Men are so thick, I thought, then saw his grin. "You know exactly what."

"Okay. But why the change of heart?"

I hadn't talked to Adam about Alicia forbidding me to contact Charity. I didn't want to tell him just then because there was a lot more to it. So I said, "I don't think I can keep it a secret."

"I didn't think you could, either, but I thought you'd last longer than three hours," he teased.

"I can, but I'm afraid you'll blow it." I tried not to feel irritated that he thought I couldn't keep a secret—even if it was true.

"Good thinking—I'd probably blurt it out at the wrong time." He drew me in close to him. "Seriously, sweetheart, I'm good if you want to tell them tonight, or if you want to wait awhile. I'll follow your lead."

"Thanks. I just wanted to know how you felt about it if I decided to say something."

Lily pounded on the door. "Come out you two! Dinner's ready!"

He gave me a quick kiss, and we went in to join the others.

"How was your California trip, Kit?" Barbara asked when the chaos of passing and dishing the food had passed.

I looked at Adam. "I don't know how much Adam has told you already. I don't want to tell you stuff you already know."

His mouth full of roast beef didn't prevent him from answering. "I didn't say much of anything. Talk away, woman."

"Everyone knows I went to Ventura to see my mom. It was good to see her. She bought a condo there and loves her job. She's changed—but they're mostly good changes. We had a lot of time to talk."

"Tell the rest," Lily urged.

What does she know? I wondered. The confusion must have shown on my face because she added, "About who you met. You know—the letter."

It dawned on me that they didn't know how the initial—or subsequent—meetings played out. Or even the reason Alicia sought me out in the first place. I guess Adam really knew how to keep his mouth shut.

"What letter?" Michelle asked. "Did you meet somebody famous?"

"More like infamous," I said. "After all these years, my birth mother decided to look me up. Turns out she lives in Santa Barbara and wanted to meet me." I tried to sound nonchalant. The thought of Alicia still made me angry.

"Are you kidding? How did she find you?" Michelle's fork stopped halfway to her mouth, mashed potatoes forgotten. It was probably the first time I'd ever actually impressed Michelle Jorgenson Bridger.

Irritation at Alicia was replaced by the satisfaction of being the center of attention. The drama queen in me naturally rose to the occasion.

"She hired an attorney who sent me a letter. She wanted to

remain anonymous until she had the DNA test results." I took a bite to let that information sink in.

"Did the test prove the relationship?" Justin asked.

Before I could answer, Lily asked, "Did you meet her?"

"Yes and yes," I said. "We set up a meeting last Monday. Her name is Alicia Haversham, and she only came forward because she wanted something. And she made sure the statute of limitations had expired before she agreed to the contact."

"What did she want?" Lily and Michelle asked simultaneously.

To tell them about Charity would lead to the inevitable questions of why I couldn't be a donor. It was a good thing I'd given Adam a heads up about making the announcement.

"Alicia has another daughter—one she kept and publicly acknowledges," I said, hearing the animosity in my own voice. "Her name is Charity and she needs a liver transplant. Alicia contacted me in hopes I would be a living donor."

The Bridger family was united in their disbelief except for Adam, who already knew the story. Michelle recovered before the others.

"I hope you told her no," she said indignantly. "What nerve!"

"I did—at first. I was so insulted I even stormed out of the meeting."

Barbara looked concerned. "What do you mean 'at first'?"

"I wanted more answers. And I wanted to meet my half-sister. I thought about it and realized I was in a position to make a deal. If Alicia gave me answers to my questions and let me meet Charity—as her sister—I would agree to donate part of my liver if I qualified."

"Did she agree?"

"Yeah, she did. She gave me answers about the circumstances of my birth. Privately, with just the two of us." I added the last bit to forestall questions I didn't want to answer. Although it wasn't part of the written agreement, I'd agreed to keep the details of my private conversation with Alicia confidential and my feelings were still very raw.

"You met Charity? How old is she? What's she like?" Lily bombarded me with questions without giving me a chance to answer.

I told them about Charity. Lily and her younger sisters listened intently as I described her appearance, her room, and a little bit about her illness.

"When do you begin the donor screening?" Barbara asked. "Is it a long process?"

"Alicia insisted I do the pre-screening while I was down there. Assuming I passed the initial physical, and my blood type matched, I'd go down to UCLA to continue the process." My heart was pounding as I anticipated the next question.

"Were you a match?" she asked. "Do you move on to the next step?"

"I was declined." I glanced over at Adam. He squeezed my hand underneath the table.

"So after all that, you weren't even a match," Michelle said, sounding a little disappointed. I think she wanted to see more drama.

She was about to.

"I was a match," I said quietly.

"Did you chicken out?" Lily asked. "I would. There's no way I'd give away part of my liver."

"No. I was ready to do it."

"Why didn't you then?" Michelle pressed for an answer.

"Because I found out I'm pregnant."

Once again, the Bridger family faces displayed identical reactions. This time it was surprise.

Justin's arm shot around Michelle's shoulders like he might have to restrain her. There was no need. She sat there—immobile.

Lily recovered about the same time as Beth, and they both squealed. They peppered me with questions and Barbara joined in with them.

She turned to Hal and asked, "What do you think about all this, Grandpa?"

Hal smiled and replied, "Probably the same as you, Grandma."

Excited reactions over the announcement of the first grand-child dominated the rest of the dinner conversation. The joy was infectious. Adam and I couldn't stop smiling.

Justin offered his congratulations; Michelle remained silent. She toyed with her food but didn't take another bite.

choosing charity

When Barbara asked who wanted chocolate cake, they took advantage of the ensuing chaos and quietly slipped out.

I doggedly dug into my cake even though my own appetite had vanished. I shoved back the twinges of guilt I felt for getting pregnant so easily while Michelle and Justin struggled.

Does anyone ever get what they hope for? Or does anybody even know for certain what they really want?

chapter twenty-six

I walked into work Monday morning marveling at how it looked the same. Only one week had passed, but I felt at least a year older. Somehow I expected my surroundings to reflect the changes inside of me.

Claire wasn't in yet, and I felt anxious about it. I went in to talk to Nadine.

"Hey, I'm back. Did you miss me?" A good night's sleep had improved my mood and I wanted to visit.

"Who are you again, dear?" Nadine asked, peering over the top of her glasses, pretending not to know me.

"Anything new happen while I was gone?"

"It's been quiet. The Partners are gone this week for a conference. How was your trip to California? How's your mother?" Nadine got up and fussed with her plants while she talked to me.

"It was good. I got to sleep in, eat a lot, and go to the beach. I'm glad to be home though." I watched her groom one of the plants, plucking off a dying leaf. If I did that to my plants at home, I'd have to pull out the whole plant.

"You look nice and rested. Almost a glow about you." Nadine's comment made me nervous. She had that knack for knowing what you thought she couldn't possibly know.

"Thanks." I changed the subject to the first thing I could think of. "So, how is Claire doing? I didn't see her when I walked in."

Nadine frowned. "I hope her tardiness isn't a habit. This will make the third time in the two weeks since she started."

"I'm sure there's a reason." I said, hoping Claire wasn't being flaky. *I'll talk to her and tell her how serious Nadine is about being on time.* "I'm going to get to work now."

I tried not to take it personally that Claire wasn't being reliable, although it had been my one hesitation in recommending her. She seemed sincere, but I hated putting my name on the line for someone else. You just couldn't predict their actions.

Nadine came out a few minutes later and announced that Claire had called in sick, and we would all need to listen for the phone since there was no receptionist. At least Nadine couldn't say she was late if she was absent.

I met Tara for lunch. The first half hour was dominated by wedding talk. Since it was less than two weeks away, I let her ramble on and even managed to show enthusiasm.

Tara refilled our soft drinks and brought them back to the table. "Thanks for listening to me, Kit. I know all I talk about is the wedding. I want to hear about California and meeting your birth mother. You texted me just enough to make me more curious."

I gave Tara an abbreviated version of my week in California—or tried to. Tara craved details and seized upon them, so it was hard to get the entire story out.

"Alicia Haversham! What a perfectly snobbish name. What did she look like?"

I described Alicia's appearance and mannerisms. Tara responded, "I hate her already! What did she want?"

"She wanted my liver," I said dramatically.

"You're kidding? For her?"

"No, for her daughter—her *real* daughter."

It was satisfying to have Tara take my side so completely. She didn't offer any words of wisdom or caution, and I didn't feel like I had to defend my position. Tara despised Alicia with me, loved Charity with me, and mourned with me when I told her I was declined as a donor. She didn't even press for reasons why.

Small wonder I couldn't keep my mouth shut. "I was turned down because I'm pregnant."

Tara's eyes widened. "Really?"

"Positively." I confessed to her that I'd stopped at the dollar store on my way to work to buy a home pregnancy test. "It seems so surreal. I wanted confirmation. So after I bought it, I went into the store bathroom and took it. It's positive—so I'm guessing Dr. Bartlett wasn't making it up."

"Were you surprised? What did Adam say?" Her questions started a whole new line of conversation. Again, Tara seemed in tune with my feelings, and I felt so thankful to have such a good friend.

I realized what time it was and quickly gathered my stuff. "I have to go. I'm going to be late."

Tara walked with me to my car. "I just had an idea!"

"What is it?" I asked.

"You just have to have a girl," she said. "Then you can name her 'Noralicia.' You know, like Bella in *Breaking Dawn*. She named her baby 'Renesmee' after her mother and Edward's adoptive mom. It will be perfect!" Tara laughed at her clever idea.

"I hope you're kidding, because Noralicia is almost as bad as Renesmee. You do know those books are fiction, don't you?" I shook my head. "I hope Eric gets to name your children."

"Just consider it!" she called. "That's all I'm saying."

Shortly before I left work, I got a text on my phone. *Guess who has a phone now!!! I have finally joined the 21st century.* I laughed knowing it was Lily. I quickly texted her back to say I'd stop by to see it on my way home.

Lily was watching for me and had the door opened before I got halfway up the walk. "Why haven't you answered my texts?"

"I answered the first one, but I don't text while I drive. That's a rule you'd better follow too."

She rolled her eyes. "Like I'll ever get a car." She tugged me inside. "You've gotta see how cool this is. Let's go downstairs, so Sarah doesn't bug us when she gets home."

I followed her to her room as she chattered on about her phone. I'd never met anyone so excited to have a cell phone.

"Answer my text. I just sent you one." My phone vibrated as she said it.

"Lily, I'm right here. You can still talk, you know." I humored her and looked at the text. It read, *Text me.*

Laughing I sent one in return, *No. Talk to me.* We texted nonsense messages back and forth to each other for a few minutes, and then I had an idea.

"Lily, I have a favor to ask."

"Sure, what is it? Text it to me."

"I'm not texting it. But it involves you texting." It sounded mysterious enough to get her attention away from her phone for a few seconds.

"Last night when I told you guys about Alicia and Charity, I didn't tell how furious Alicia was when I got declined. We got into a big fight in the parking lot of the doctor's office."

I had Lily's full attention. "A fight? Did she hit you?"

"Not that kind of a fight—it was an argument. There was a lot of yelling. She told me I couldn't contact Charity anymore. She said she'd get a restraining order if I did."

"Can she do that?" Lily asked.

"I don't know. I'd rather not deal with Alicia ever again. But I know she's probably lied to Charity. I'm sure she told her I *won't* donate, not that I *can't* donate."

"So what do you want me to do?"

"Alicia said *I* couldn't have contact with Charity. Not you." I watched her to see if my meaning sunk in. I couldn't tell, so I clarified. "I want you to text Charity."

"I'll do it, but I don't want to freak out a sick girl by sending her a text from someone she doesn't even know."

"Don't worry, I told her all about you. I already gave her your email address so she knows who you are. She needs to talk to people her own age." I added the last bit to reassure myself more than Lily.

Lily's eyes lit up and she nodded. "I'm in. But you'll have to tell me what to say."

I looked up Charity's number in my own phone and gave it to Lily. "Just say 'Hi, it's Lily, Kit's sister-in-law.'"

Surprisingly nimble for someone who never owned a cell phone, Lily had it sent almost as quickly as I finished saying it. We both sat in silence, watching Lily's phone, waiting for the chime indicating a text had been received.

We didn't have long to wait.

I'm Charity, Kit's sister.

Relieved, I said, "At least she still claims me. Tell her I didn't call her because her mom told me I couldn't." Lily obeyed, fingers flying.

No way. Is Kit there? Lily showed me the screen. I nodded.

Lily texted back, then looked up and said, "She's going to call you. Alicia didn't tell you not to accept phone calls did she?"

"Good point," I said. We switched our stares from Lily's phone to mine. When it rang, the caller ID showed it was Charity.

"Hey," I answered.

"Hi, Kit," Charity said. "Are you back in Utah?"

"Yes, I came home yesterday."

"Why didn't you come by to see me before you left—or at least call me?" I heard an accusing tone in her voice. I blamed Alicia.

"I would have. Your mother said I couldn't contact you anymore."

"She told me you probably wouldn't call me. She said you wouldn't want to face me since you'd changed your mind about being a donor."

I was livid. *I knew Alicia would lie about it.* I struggled to keep my voice level. "I didn't change my mind, Charity. I was declined as a donor."

"What? Mother said you changed your mind. Why didn't you tell her you were declined? She's upset because she thinks you backed out." Clearly Alicia had Charity fooled. She wasn't going to get away with it.

"Charity, your mom was with me at the doctor's office. She knows I was declined and she knows why. The doctor told me I'm pregnant—which was a total surprise. You can't donate part of your liver when you're pregnant. I didn't back out. I'm willing to donate after I have the baby."

There was silence on the other end of the phone. "Charity? Are you there?"

"I'm here. Why would she lie to me about it, Kit?"

"Because she was angry at me. She wanted me to terminate the pregnancy and when I told her no, she said I couldn't see you or contact you again."

"I can't believe it," Charity said.

"I swear to you I'm not making it up." It never occurred to me that Charity wouldn't believe me. I wasn't sure what to do. Her next words surprised me even more.

"I wasn't doubting you, Kit. I've seen some of the things she's done in the past to protect me." Charity laughed, but it sounded forced. "I told you she likes to punish people who don't do things her way."

"You're telling me," I said.

"Well, I'm glad you didn't just back out and disappear and there was more to it."

"I'm sorry, Charity. I want you to get better, but I can't donate right now."

"It's okay, Kit. I like you for more than your liver. At least I have a sister and I just heard I'm going to be an aunt." Her tone lightened again. "You have to keep me updated on *everything*. And you owe me pictures of Romania and Marcel. And Mark Bridger. Promise?"

"I want to, but I don't think your mom will approve. That's why I had Lily text you instead of me."

"Let me take care of my mom, Kit. I know how to handle her. But tell Lily she still has to text me and email me. I get so bored."

"Talk to your mom and let me know, okay?" I didn't want to deal with Alicia, and I knew that if anyone could get her to agree to something, it was Charity.

After we hung up, I said to Lily, "Thanks. I feel a lot better now that I've talked to her."

"No problem," Lily said. Her phone chimed again with a new text. I leaned over to see the screen.

"Is it Charity?" I asked.

Lily glanced down and turned the phone so I couldn't see the screen. "No."

"Oh, who is it?" I asked, wondering why she was shielding it.

"Just a friend," she said, quickly deleting the message.

"Lily you're acting weird. Why are you being so secretive?" It dawned on me then. "You're texting Cody, aren't you?"

"So what if I am? What's the big deal? It's just a text." Lily tried to shrug it off, but she sounded defensive.

"If you have to hide it, then it's a big deal," I said.

"You're one to talk," Lily said. "Why didn't you text Charity yourself? Is it okay if you have a secret, but not okay if I do?"

"It's not the same thing. I wasn't doing anything wrong by having you text Charity. I just needed to make sure she knew the truth."

"I'm not doing anything wrong either. I trusted your judgment, Kit. I think you can trust mine a little."

When she put it that way, I could see her point of view. I was torn because I didn't like Cody, and I knew her parents didn't either. "I don't want you to get into trouble, Lily."

She sighed. "Give me some credit for being smarter than that. We're just texting."

"Keep it that way. I've got to get going. Adam's going to beat me home and the last one home makes dinner." I leaned over and gave her a quick hug. "Thanks again, Lily."

She hugged me back. "You're welcome. You need to relax a little, you know. You're sounding like a parent already."

"Don't you forget it." I shook my finger at her and tried to look stern.

As I was climbing in the car, my phone vibrated. It was a text from Lily. *Text me.*

I replied no and hurried home so I could avoid having to cook.

chapter twenty-seven

My first doctor appointment was the day before Tara's wedding. Dr. Perry wore her brown hair in a ponytail and had a sprinkling of freckles on her face. When I commented on how young she looked, she said, "Don't worry, Kit, by the time you're due, I'll have delivered at least three babies so I'll have some experience by then."

The panic must have shown in my face because she quickly said, "I'm joking. I look much younger than I am. If I don't wear this lab coat, people think I'm one of the patients."

I liked her sense of humor.

After the initial examination, Dr. Perry sent me to have an ultrasound. I was surprised it happened so quickly, but she explained they needed to confirm the due date.

When I saw the images on the screen—although the technician had to interpret what I was seeing—it suddenly became real to me. That pulsing heartbeat confirmed it. I was going to be a mother.

Dr. Perry gave me a due date of March 14.

Armed with pamphlets, prenatal vitamins, and the knowledge that I was twelve weeks pregnant, I called Adam and told him the news.

"You already had the ultrasound?" He sounded disappointed. "I can't believe I missed it."

"I told you to come. Well, you can tell our baby you missed his first sighting because you had to go to your statistics class." I was still a little miffed that he wouldn't skip class to come with me. It served him right for missing it.

"Did you say *he*?" Adam pounced on one word, ignoring the rest of my gibe.

"I said *he* in the gender-neutral sense of the word. It's too early to tell." I took pity on him. "I'll have another ultrasound in a couple of months. That one will tell the gender if we want to know—and if the baby is cooperative."

"I'm sorry I didn't come with you. Are you still mad?"

"No. Well, maybe a little. But I scheduled my next appointment on a Thursday afternoon, so I know you won't have class. And you'd better not have work."

"I'll be there."

"I have to get back to work. It already took longer than I thought, and I don't want Claire or Nadine asking too many questions." I'd have to tell them sooner or later, but right now I opted for later.

That afternoon someone came into the office with a flower delivery. Someone getting flowers at work was rare enough that we all stopped to gawk. The guy announced, "Kit Bridger," and Claire pointed to me. I was dumbfounded.

I slipped the card out of the holder and read, "One for every week. Statistics will never take priority again. I love you. Adam." I smiled and counted the roses. Twelve red roses surrounded with baby's breath. I decided to forgive him.

"What's the occasion?" Claire asked.

"Adam's just counting his blessings," I said.

I wondered why Tara had chosen Labor Day weekend to get married instead of doing it between semesters. She wanted a September wedding, and they were going to take a long weekend for their honeymoon now and go on a cruise over Christmas break.

Whatever her reasoning, Tara got picture-perfect weather for her wedding day. She and Eric were married in the Logan Temple

Friday afternoon and the reception that evening was a work of art. All her wedding planning had paid off. Tara looked radiantly happy, and I was glad for her—and for myself as well. Not only did it herald a new beginning for Tara, it also signaled an end to the incessant wedding chatter.

We were getting ready for bed that night when my cell phone rang. It was Lily.

"Kit, where are you?" Her voice sounded strange.

"I'm home. Where are you?" I glanced at the clock. It was almost midnight.

"Is Adam there?"

"Yes. Do you want to talk to him?" I wondered why she just didn't call him directly.

"No!" It sounded liked she sniffled. *Is she crying?*

"Are you okay, Lily?" I couldn't figure out her cryptic comments.

"I need your help," she said. "But I don't want Adam to know."

I glanced at the bathroom where Adam was brushing his teeth. He probably didn't even hear the phone ring. I walked into the living room.

"I'll help if I can, Lily. But you know I don't keep things from Adam."

"Can you just come and get me?" she asked.

"Where are you?"

She gave me an address that was across town from where she lived. "I'll be out front waiting."

I bit back the questions that were churning in my head. "I'll be there in a few minutes." I had the feeling to pick her up first and ask questions later.

I walked into the bedroom and told Adam about the phone call.

"I need to go get her," I said.

"I'm coming with you." He was already grabbing his jeans.

"No. She asked me to come alone. I think I should."

"I don't feel good about this. I doubt she had permission from Mom and Dad to be out this late."

"I think you're right, Adam. But she needs a ride now. I think her immediate safety is more important. I'll talk to her and we'll figure out what to do after we hear what happened." I got dressed as I talked.

"I'm not going to lie for her."

"Don't worry. Neither will I." I kissed him good-bye and hurried out the door.

The neighborhood wasn't a very good one, and I could tell by the number of cars parked in front of the house that there was a party going on inside.

I strained to see Lily in the darkness and saw her step out of the black shadow of a tree. She slipped into the front seat. The dome light verified what I'd suspected—she'd been crying.

"What's going on?" I asked as I pulled away from the house.

"I went to a party," she said.

"It didn't really look like a Young Women activity."

"It wasn't."

I handed her a tissue. "I'm guessing your parents don't know where you are."

"They don't."

We drove in silence for a minute. I was angry at her and wanted to yell at her for being so stupid, but I kept quiet and tried to be patient.

"Cody was cheating on me," she said.

I wasn't surprised but didn't say anything.

"He kept asking me to go to the party with him. I told him no, and he called me a baby. He said maybe he should find a girlfriend who was more mature."

My anger shifted from Lily to that jerk who manipulated her. "So you decided to show him how mature you were by sneaking out?" The barb popped out before I could stop it.

Lily ignored it. "I wanted to surprise him. So I came to the party. The surprise was on me. He was making out with someone else."

"Did you talk to him?" I asked.

"Of course. I yelled at him right in front of everybody."

"Good for you. What did he do?"

Lily started crying again. "He laughed at me. He told me to stop being such a baby." She sobbed for a few minutes, and I let her cry it out.

"How did you get to the party?"

"I knew a girl from school who was going. I texted her and she gave me a ride."

"Do you want to go home or to my apartment?" I asked.

"Home, I guess. Did you tell Adam?"

"Yes. You know we won't lie for you, don't you?" I patted her arm as I said it to soften the blow. I knew she was devastated by Cody's behavior, but I needed to clarify where Adam and I stood on the matter.

"So you're going to tell Mom and Dad?" she asked.

"I think you should; then we won't have to," I said gently.

Lily started crying again. "I'm so stupid, Kit. You tried to warn me. Everyone tried to. I thought I knew him better. I can't believe I trusted him." The last words came out as kind of a wail.

I gave her some more Kleenex. I knew how crummy it was not to have enough tissues when your nose was dripping all over the place.

"You're not stupid. You made some bad decisions. A stupid person keeps making them. A smart person makes it right."

"I'll be grounded forever," she complained as I pulled into her driveway.

"Probably not past eighteen," I joked, hoping to lighten her spirits.

"True. What's two years to an idiot? Maybe by then the gossip will be about someone else." Lily blew her nose, loudly.

"That probably woke up your parents," I said. "And believe it or not, people are probably already gossiping about other things. The world doesn't really revolve around you, even though it feels that way." I leaned over and gave her a hug.

"Thanks for coming to get me," Lily said. She took a deep breath. "I'll go tell on myself so you don't have to."

"That's what true friends are for," I called after her.

chapter twenty-eight

Claire and I were in the lunchroom together alone. It seemed like a good time to talk to her about getting and staying on Nadine's good side. I emphasized that it began with being on time.

"I know it's important," she said when I brought it up. "I try to be on time. My mom gives me a ride and sometimes she just won't hurry. I'll do better."

"You could take the bus," I suggested. I wanted to offer her a ride, but Adam and I already had problems juggling one car with our work schedules and Adam's classes. I didn't feel like I could commit to giving her a ride every day.

"I thought about it," Claire said. "But I have to drop Braxton off at the babysitter's first. It's hard to get us both ready in time."

"I didn't think of that. I'm sure it's hard for you." I felt a rush of sympathy for Claire and concern for myself. *How will I be able to take care of a baby and work too?* Adam and I had discussed possibilities of me working either full-time or part-time while he watched the baby, or me quitting work altogether. We hadn't decided on anything. Adam said we had time to plan—I was a nervous wreck when I thought about it.

"What's wrong, Kit?" Claire's anxious face interrupted my thoughts. "Are you worried about me messing up this job after you recommended me?"

"No. I know you're trying. My thoughts were wandering." I wanted to change the subject. I still hadn't announced my pregnancy and although Claire was my friend, I wasn't confident she could keep a secret. "How is Braxton doing?"

"He's getting so big. He's got little fat rolls on his legs now and hasn't been sick since we got back." She pulled out her new cell phone and showed me a couple of pictures of him. He did look healthier and chubbier. So did Claire, for that matter. Being back in Logan seemed to agree with both of them.

"He's so cute," I said, even though I thought his head looked too big for his body. Again, my thoughts wandered back to myself, and whether I would have a boy or a girl. Not that either would be easy for me. I'd never even changed a diaper before. *What if I have no maternal instinct whatsoever?*

Claire knew something was bothering me. "It'll be okay, Kit. I'm saving for a car of my own." When I didn't respond, she pushed harder. "Are you sure there's nothing wrong?"

I leaned in and asked her quietly, "Claire, did you ever wonder if you'd be a good mother?"

A look of hurt bewilderment crossed her face. "Do you think I'm a bad mother?"

Understanding dawned when I saw her expression. "Oh no—I didn't mean that at all. I meant me." I looked over my shoulder to make sure Nadine wasn't lurking. "I'm pregnant," I whispered.

"That's awesome!" Claire shrieked. I grabbed her arm and shushed her.

"It's not public knowledge. I'm not ready to make an announcement yet."

"When are you due?" she mouthed in a very loud whisper.

"In March. I found out while I was in California. I keep worrying I'll be a terrible mother."

"I worry about that every day," Claire admitted. "I just try to do my best. I know I'm not perfect, but I love Braxton and he knows it."

I briefly told her about meeting Alicia and Charity. I felt the familiar rancor as I talked about Alicia. Talking about her iciness and double rejection of me brought it all bubbling to the surface.

"My biggest fear is that I'm like Alicia," I confided. "What if I reject my child like she did me?"

Claire shook her head. "Kit, there's no way you'll be like that. You're a good person. Do you want to know what I think?" I nodded and she continued.

"You said she loves Charity—so she's capable of love, right?"

"Yeah, it's like there's something wrong with *me*," I said.

"I think Alicia feels horrible about throwing you away like that. For years and years, she's just pushed back all that guilt. Her coldness is probably the way she protects herself from it."

"I think she's just a mean and nasty person."

This time Claire was the one to glance at the door to make sure nobody was around. "Kit, do you think I'm mean and nasty because I gave my first baby up for adoption?"

"No! You did what was best for Tommy—you didn't throw him in the garbage. It's not the same thing."

"I still didn't keep him. I couldn't. And sometimes I feel incredibly guilty about it. Even though I know he's with parents who love him and take good care of him, I still feel like I failed him."

"Claire, *you* did it the right way. You made sure Tommy was adopted and loved. You made the best decision you could. You shouldn't feel guilty." I hoped she didn't think I was judging her—I wasn't. It was Alicia I had issues with.

"So if I did it the right way and I feel bad about it, imagine how awful someone would feel if she didn't make sure the baby was taken care of? Don't you think that would haunt her?"

I didn't want to give Alicia any sympathy. "A normal person would be bothered. I don't think she's normal."

Claire smiled. "She probably hides it really well." She stood and threw away her sandwich bag. "I better get back to my desk. Nadine will be watching."

"Thanks for listening, Claire. Don't say anything to anyone yet, okay?"

"Don't worry, I won't." She stopped at the door of the lunchroom. "You do look a little thicker around the middle though. You won't be able to hide it for long."

I spent the rest of the day sucking in my stomach.

Once Tara's wedding was past, September seemed to fly by. Adam was back into the class, study, work routine, and I resumed my work and whine-about-missing-my-husband groove.

My mom called a couple of times every week. Our conversations didn't last long, but the connection we'd made at the end of my trip to Ventura lingered.

"How are you feeling?" It was always the first thing out of her mouth following her greeting.

"Fine."

"Are you eating enough?" was usually her second question.

"More than enough," I'd say.

Then the third item she always addressed. "Have you told your father yet?"

"No. I haven't seen him recently."

Then I'd get the mini-lecture of how I needed to tell him he was going to be a grandfather. Although she was free with chastising me, I detected a smug note in her voice. I think it's because I'd confided in her and not him—even though he only lived a couple of miles from me.

I wasn't trying to avoid my dad. He was involved in the new school semester. We'd spoken on the phone a couple of times, and I knew he was teaching two extra classes. He'd invited us to dinner, but I didn't want to go without Adam—especially knowing Amberlie would be there.

I'd barely finished talking to my mom when my dad called. Since she'd nagged me only minutes before about telling him, I wondered if she had called him as soon as she and I hung up.

"Hi, Kit. It's Dad." He always said that, as if I wouldn't recognize his voice and his name didn't pop up on my cell phone when he called me.

"Hey, Dad. What's up?"

"I stopped by the store to get some light bulbs tonight. Adam was working, so I talked with him for a minute."

"Maybe that's what I'll have to do so I can see him," I joked.

"He told me you guys have been pretty busy. He said he has next Monday night off and thought you two were probably free for dinner. Does that work for you?"

Very sneaky. That was more like a Mom move rather than a Dad move. I'd used Adam's work as an excuse once too often, I guess.

"Sure," I said. "Are you cooking?"

"No. I thought I'd treat you to dinner out. You get to pick— steak, Italian, Chinese. What sounds good?"

"Everything. I'm hungry." I wondered if he had an ulterior motive. Like getting me to spend more time with Amberlie. "If you're buying, I'll pick steak."

Dad laughed. "That's what Dave said."

"So you asked him first? What if he picked something different?"

"I knew I was safe. You two always pick steak when I'm buying." That was true. We teased him about being a cheapskate, but he was a pushover.

"Are you bringing Amberlie?" I figured I might as well ask right out.

"Yes, I'm planning on it. Are you still coming?" I guess he came right out with it too.

"Yeah, I'll be there. I went out to dinner with Mom and her boyfriend. I guess I can go out with you and Amberlie." I don't know why I said that—it kind of popped out, and I immediately regretted it.

There was silence on the other end.

"Are you there?" I asked.

"I'm here." He cleared his throat. "We'll plan on Monday then."

Accompanying my mom and Jonah on a date must have mellowed me. I didn't feel the resentment I expected when I saw my dad and Amberlie together at the restaurant. Maybe I was getting over the hard feelings.

It helped that Amberlie complimented me on my shirt. It was one that my mom bought me on our super shopping Saturday. It was maternity, but didn't look like it. At least that's what I told myself, and Adam was smart enough to agree when I asked his opinion.

Dave arrived and helped relieve the stress of making conversation. It was his first semester at college and living on his own. Adam and Dad were right at home talking about school. I felt out of the loop even though I'd only graduated a few months ago.

Amberlie joined in the conversation. It turned out her son went to Utah State as well. I knew she had kids, but I hadn't paid attention to how many or their ages.

My curiosity piqued, I asked, "How many children do you have?"

"Three. Two girls and a boy. Trey is my youngest, he's a few months older than Dave. Emily is twenty-three. She and her husband live in Smithfield. Kara just turned twenty-one, so she's your age. She's at BYU-Idaho." As Amberlie described her children to me, I saw my dad's face light up a little.

I could tell he was glad I was asking about Amberlie's children. Their proximity in age to Dave and me was interesting—but I was more impressed that she knew how old we both were. I liked her a little more.

I relaxed and found myself enjoying the evening. Over chocolate fudge torte, I decided to share my news.

"By the way, Dad, there's something you should know," I said innocently, savoring the silkiness of the fudge as it melted on my tongue.

"What's that?" he asked, knowing me well enough to sense I had an agenda.

"It's about Dave, actually." That perked up Dave's ears and my dad looked a little concerned.

"What about me?" Dave asked, forgetting about his own dessert for a moment.

"Dave's going to be an uncle."

My dad and Dave sat there dumbly, trying to figure out what I was saying. Amberlie caught it right away. "Congratulations, you two! When are you due?"

"The middle of March," I said, watching as confusion gave way to understanding and my dad grinned.

Dave still looked befuddled. "I didn't do anything."

"Of course not, you idiot. *I'm pregnant.* When I have the baby, you'll be an uncle." He was so dense sometimes. Hopefully he'd never reproduce.

"Oh," Dave said. "No wonder you're eating like a pig."

"I didn't want you to feel alone at the trough," I retorted, sticking my chocolate-coated tongue out at him.

"Enough, you two," my dad said.

We both shut up but kicked each other under the table.

"How are you feeling?" Amberlie asked me. "Have you been sick at all?"

She reminded me of my mom then, asking me how I felt. The thought seemed disloyal, so I pushed it aside.

We finished dessert as I answered questions about the pregnancy. The topic of my visit to Ventura came up, which led to the subject of Alicia and Charity.

I had forgotten that I hadn't mentioned any of it to my dad. Before the divorce, I would talk to my mom and she would automatically keep my dad apprised of things. It was a shock for me to realize that they truly lived two separate lives.

"Why didn't you tell me any of this, Kit?" My dad's tone told me he was hurt. "We had lunch right before you left for Ventura."

"I didn't know why Alicia wanted to see me, Dad. I didn't want to upset you or Mom. I told Mom because I had the meeting while I was in Ventura. I wasn't trying to keep it a secret."

"You've been home three weeks," he said. "We've talked on the phone."

"I know. I didn't think about it." I was ashamed I'd neglected to tell him. "Mom always kept you updated on stuff that was going on." It sounded lame even as it came out of my mouth, but it was true. Seeing my parents as people was hard enough. Seeing them as people with separate lives—it just hadn't occurred to me.

My dad had a pained expression on his face. "Kit, your mother and I don't talk to each other much anymore. You can't rely on that line of communication."

"I'm sorry. I should have told you." I felt awful. The dinner had been going so well. I felt like I'd ruined it.

Surprisingly, Dave bridged the awkwardness. "Well, you told

us now, so it's all good. How old did you say Charity was? What does she look like?"

His sudden shift of subject made me laugh. "She's my half-sister. And she's sick." I reached over to punch him in the shoulder.

Dave held up his hand, easily deflecting my blow. "Hey. She's not related to me. I just like to keep my options open. I'm going to see Mom over Christmas break, so you never know."

"I think your dad has an announcement," Amberlie said. She nudged him, and he shifted in his seat before he spoke.

We all looked at him, which seemed to increase his unease.

"I do." He took a drink and wiped his mouth with the napkin. "You know I've been listening to the missionary discussions. Well, I've decided to get baptized. This Saturday. You're all invited."

Amberlie smiled and hugged him. "Isn't that wonderful?"

Adam said, "That's great! Where and what time?"

Dave's reaction was typical. "I'm going to be the only heathen left in the family."

They all looked at me. *I'm glad*, I told myself. *My dad has accepted the gospel. Of course I'm glad.* Adam squeezed my hand under the table.

"Congratulations," I managed to say.

At least they didn't announce they're getting married.

chapter twenty-nine

When I attended my dad's baptismal service, I felt like I didn't know him at all. He asked Adam to baptize him, and Adam was thrilled to be a part of it.

My dad's new bishop—my bishop when I lived at home—congratulated me. He couldn't say enough about what a great guy my dad was. At least four other people approached me to rave about him.

I sat next to Dave while Adam and my dad were changing out of their wet clothing. Dave was texting even though he sat on the front row. Of course, I'd come to expect that kind of behavior from Dave.

I overheard a lady whisper to Amberlie. "What a wonderful blessing," she said. "Are you Brother Matthews' wife?"

Amberlie was turned away from me as she answered so I didn't hear her response. I seethed inside anyway.

"Doesn't it make you mad?" I asked Dave, trying to keep my voice quiet enough so it wouldn't be heard over the music.

"What?" He answered with his own dumb question. *Maybe I should text him.*

"All these people—thinking Dad's a saint. Doesn't that bug you?"

"Isn't 'saint' part of the name of your church?" Dave countered. "Why should I care what you call yourselves?"

"That's not what I mean. *He's* the one that caused the divorce. He broke up our family. Now people are greeting him like he's some amazing person. It feels so hypocritical."

"Don't you guys preach about repentance and forgiveness and all that stuff? If that's what you believe, I don't see what the problem is." Dave shrugged and went back to texting.

"Of course *you* wouldn't understand," I muttered under my breath. He wasn't listening to me anyway.

He jammed his phone into his pocket. "Why wouldn't I? Because I don't go to church on Sunday?" His voice was loud enough to draw a couple of glances.

"Whisper!" I hissed.

Dave listened for once and dropped his voice back to a hushed tone. "I think you should worry less about Dad's sincerity and more about your own."

"Are you kidding?" I couldn't believe he turned this on me. "How can you possibly know how I feel inside?"

"Exactly!" Dave smiled at his victory. Too late I realized I'd been set up. If nothing else, it immediately shut me up.

My dad and Adam came back into the room and the program continued. I tried to listen, but all I could think about were Dave's words.

I hated to admit it, but my partying, self-proclaimed "heathen" of a brother was right—I needed to stop judging and start forgiving.

I hugged my father and smiled through the introductions and congratulations after the baptismal service, but I still just wanted to go home.

Adam was in a great mood as he drove back to our apartment. "I'm so glad your dad is accepting the gospel, Kit. He has a lot of support from the ward members and that will help so much."

"I seem to be the only one who isn't thrilled," I said. I wanted to feel happy for my dad, but it was hard when I knew what he'd done.

"What's the matter, Kit?" Adam asked.

"I know I should be thankful my dad's joined the Church. I'm just afraid he isn't really converted. How can he do the things he's

171

done and suddenly be righteous? There's a part of me that wants to run and tell his bishop the truth." I was ashamed to admit that last part, but it was how I felt.

"How do you know he hasn't already talked to his bishop?"

"I don't," I admitted. "But even if he did, how do I know he's sincere? Dave—of all people—told me to practice what I preach and forgive Dad. Like *I'm* the sinner." It was humiliating to see Dave be more charitable than me.

We'd reached the parking lot, and Adam turned off the car. He turned to me and reached out to stroke my hair. "Kit, the Atonement is for everybody. Some of us may appear to need it more than others, but we all need it."

"So you're telling me the same thing Dave did. I shouldn't judge my dad—which I already know. I *want* to be happy for him and I *know* I should forgive. I just wish I knew how to do it."

"You're human. We all are. We commit sin and need Jesus Christ to make up the difference for us. No one is denied that blessing. Being human also means we don't have the same capacity as Jesus Christ to forgive, but He *will* make up that difference for us too. I know it."

As I considered what Adam was saying, something happened inside of me. It felt like a heavy burden lifted from my shoulders. Dave's earlier words had penetrated my brain, preparing me for Adam's, which penetrated my heart. Forgiveness felt possible and within my reach.

I kept waiting to hear from Charity. It had been three weeks since I spoke with her on the phone. Patience was difficult even though I knew she was the best person to handle Alicia.

I started to text her several times, but never sent them. I worried about how she was doing. Asking Lily was out of the question, since history taught me she would use it as leverage against me.

I checked my email one evening and was excited to see a message from Charity.

Hi Kit,

Sorry it's taken me so long to get back to you. I got sick and spent a week in the hospital. Nothing too serious (not like liver failure or anything—just an infection that wouldn't go away), but Mother wasn't in the mood to negotiate anything. When she's scared she's even more stubborn than usual. She thinks I can't see it, but I do.

When I got home I told her I wanted to talk to you. She tried really hard to talk me out of it. She said you abandoned me once (haha, she's one to talk) and I was just setting myself up for getting hurt again.

I told her I was old enough to make that decision myself and she lectured me. "As long as you're under 18 and living in my house . . . blah, blah, blah." You get the idea.

I said, "So never then," and she said, "What do you mean by that?" I told her that if she kept me from contacting you until I was 18, she was pretty much telling me I couldn't talk to you for the rest of my life.

Maybe I shouldn't have been so mean, but she's unreasonable as far as you are concerned. I can usually talk her into anything. She said she would think about it. That means she'll ignore it and hope I forget about it.

I waited a day, but she tried to put me off again when I asked her about it. That made me so mad, so I told her I knew the truth—that you were pregnant and couldn't donate. And that I knew she said you couldn't contact me.

I saw her expression before she could hide it. She tried to make it better by saying you didn't tell me the whole truth and you would use me to get to her.

I asked her, "Why would Kit even want to get close to you? I wouldn't if I was her." I think she would have smacked my face if I wasn't so sick.

We kept fighting and my dad came in to calm us down. He listened to both of us and came up with a "compromise."

So the deal is this—I can email you (and you can email back), but no telephone or texting until they are sure you're not using me. Those words are theirs, not mine. I tried to text you anyway. Mother even blocked your number—and Lily's.

> I'm not sure how they'll figure out your motives—
> haha. But it's not like I'm going to wake up and find
> you've stolen my organs or something. Although you
> can have the liver if you want it—I've heard it's
> rotten.
>
> Okay, enough about the epic fight. I want to hear
> about the pregnancy and you still owe me pictures—
> mainly of Adam's brother, Mark. j/k (kind of).
>
> Seriously, Kit, I want to be a part of everything.
> I can't experience it myself, but I can see so much
> more through you. We might be hundreds of miles apart,
> but we're still connected.

I could almost hear Charity's voice as I read her words. Although I was irritated by Alicia and Lawrence's lack of trust, I chose to focus on the fact they were letting us communicate at all. I would make the most of it.

I committed to keeping Charity involved in my life as much as I could. I kept my journal on my computer, so it was easy to include parts from my journal in my emails. I took pictures wherever I went. I wanted her to see the people and places I talked about.

In return she gave me details of her days. For a person whose parents provided her with so many luxuries, her life was surprisingly desolate. She talked a great deal about her doctors and their nurses—strange friends for a sixteen-year-old girl.

Charity didn't sugarcoat things. She gave me the gory details of her itching, swelling, bruising, and bleeding. Inappropriate as it seemed, I laughed at her way of looking at her illness and her way of describing the indignities she suffered because of it. She was a strange mixture of naïve child and old sage—and it put my own problems into perspective.

I reciprocated in kind. She got the details of my monthly checkups, growth spurts, and other discoveries. We were a great pair.

chapter thirty

I kept my pregnancy quiet at work until mid-October. More accurately, Claire didn't announce it until then. She followed me back to my desk one morning.

"Kit, I have an idea. I've been thinking about how you've never taken care of a baby. I'm going to teach you how. I'll bring Braxton over and you can practice on him."

To Claire's credit, she used her inside voice. To her discredit, Nadine picked up on the conversation and the implication of Claire's words.

"We'll talk about it later," I said to her as I saw Nadine approaching us. Claire followed my look and realized what she'd done.

"Sorry," Claire said. "I'd better get back to the front desk." She scurried away before Nadine parked herself in front of me.

"Good morning, Kit." She smiled knowingly. "How are you feeling?"

"I'm fine," I said, weighing my options. I'd rather spring than be sprung upon. "As a matter of fact, I have some news."

"And are you going to share that news?" Nadine asked. "Sometime before spring perhaps?"

"I'm pregnant. I'm due mid-March." I'd learned to automatically include the due date to save the inevitable follow-up question.

"Just as I suspected." She scrutinized me, making me feel like I'd been caught pilfering office supplies. I must have passed muster because her look softened, and she said, "If you have any questions, be sure and ask me. I raised six children of my own."

"Thanks. It's nice to know so many people have survived it."

She peered at me over her glasses. "Are you referring to my children or motherhood in general?"

"Motherhood in general, of course," I assured her.

"I thought so. Well, here's some advice—take better care of your baby than you do the plants I give you, and you should be fine." Nadine wandered off to her next victim.

The word spread through the office. I couldn't tell if Claire or Nadine was responsible. Making it public seemed to trigger everyone's memory of when they—or their wife or sister or landlady—were pregnant. Which they freely shared.

"I was three weeks overdue." "My sister was in labor for two and a half days." "My wife gained sixty pounds." "My landlady changed the locks." *Are these things supposed to comfort me?* I didn't even know what the last comment had to do with anything.

I smiled and nodded as they each offered their horror stories of encouragement. Why didn't anyone share this stuff *before* I got pregnant? It's not like I could change anything now.

It was exciting to have it out in the open. The question of whether or not I was coming back to work after the baby came up. Before I could answer, one of my coworkers loudly voiced her opinion.

"I would never take my baby to day care." Jaime was a little older than me and had been married a couple of months. "If you can't stay home with your baby, you shouldn't have one."

Claire looked away, and the air was filled with an uncomfortable silence. Claire wasn't the only working mother in the office with a child in day care.

Nadine's radar picked up the comment and she said, "That's a great ideal to have, Jaime. It's not always possible in the real world though."

Jaime had the grace to blush—whether it was from Nadine's words or her own realization of how she sounded, I couldn't tell. "Right. I mean you should stay home, if possible."

"Or if you don't have a job, because you stood around talking too much and got fired," Nadine added. We all took the not-so-subtle hint and got back to work.

Toward the end of October, we were at the Bridgers' house for our usual Sunday dinner. Talk often came around to the baby and this Sunday was no different. I was scheduled for another ultrasound in a couple of days, and we were going to find out if it was a boy or girl.

"You're going to have a girl," Lily announced. "I know it."

"You're just saying that because you made a pink blanket for her," Beth said.

"Wrong. I made a pink blanket *because* they're having a girl," Lily insisted.

Beth rolled her eyes. "And because you've been grounded for a month."

An unexpected boon to my being pregnant was Lily's excitement. It had given her something positive to focus on. She was more like her old bubbly self and sometimes seemed more excited than Barbara or my mother—which was hard to beat.

The downside to all the pregnancy talk was Michelle and Justin. Knowing they were going through infertility treatments—without success—made me self-conscious about my blossoming belly and all the fuss being made over me and the baby.

Lily's pink baby blanket was one of those moments where I felt that acute sense of guilt. Michelle sat quietly on the sofa as Lily presented it to Adam and me and told us she knew we were having a baby girl.

I stole a glance at Michelle as I examined Lily's handiwork. Michelle leaned over and whispered in Justin's ear. He smiled and hugged her close to him. I forced my attention back to the blanket. It was *not* my fault that I was pregnant and Michelle wasn't.

Adam told me several times I was making myself feel bad. He insisted that Justin and Michelle were happy for us. He never heard the frustration in her voice as Michelle talked about the disappointment she endured every month, and he didn't pay attention to the sorrow on her face that she tried to mask when the Bridger family went on and on about our baby.

Maybe I was overly sensitive, but he was oblivious. I realized Lily was talking to me.

"So do you like it?" She was talking about the soft blanket in my lap. It was very soft and very pink.

"I love it." I smiled at her. "But what if it's a boy?" The blanket was so pink, I didn't think I could bring myself to wrap a baby boy in it.

"It's not." She was adamant. Well, time would tell.

"If it's a boy, maybe Lily can make you a blue one," Michelle suggested. I was shocked—she never participated in these conversations.

"She'd better get started now," Beth said. "She started on this one right after you told us you were pregnant. You'll want it before the baby goes to kindergarten."

Lily pulled a face at Beth. "At least I know how to crochet. You'd have to make one out of tree bark."

"I could crochet if I felt like it. But I'd wait until I knew if it's a boy or a girl."

Michelle spoke up again, "Why don't you start on a blue one now—just in case."

"I know it's a girl," Lily insisted.

"Then give the blue one to us," Michelle said.

Conversation stopped as we all looked at Michelle. Justin sat there grinning.

Barbara spoke first. "Are you making an announcement?"

Michelle and Justin both nodded. She said, "June 22. We just found out."

Barbara and Lily shrieked and leaped on Michelle, hugging her. They demanded details and Michelle happily indulged them.

For the first time in weeks, the attention was diverted from me and my pregnancy. I felt a little twinge of jealousy watching Barbara and Lily fawn over Michelle. I pushed it back. I was truly happy for them.

I hugged the cuddly pink baby afghan close to me and snuggled into Adam's arms. Surely there was room for two grandbabies at the Bridgers'.

chapter thirty-one

"Looks like a little girl." The ultrasound technician announced, sounding as certain as Lily had, although she followed it up with the standard disclaimer that there was a slight chance she could be wrong. She gave me a towel to wipe off my tummy and stepped out of the room.

Watching the images on the screen combined with the fluttering movements I'd felt several times in the past couple of weeks hammered home the reality of it all. *I'm going to have a baby girl.*

Tears welled up in my eyes at the realization. Adam brushed one away as it trickled down my cheek. "Disappointed?" he asked softly.

"Not at all. Are you?" We'd talked about it and both agreed we were happy with either a boy or a girl, but I wanted to hear it from his mouth.

"Are you kidding? I'm thrilled!" His expression verified his words. "Lily told us it was a girl, so it's not like I'm surprised or anything."

"She'll say 'I told you so.' Maybe we should tell her it's a boy, just to mess with her."

"I like the way you think," Adam said, squeezing my hand. "Why the tears if you're not disappointed?"

"It seems real now. She's a real person. Not an 'it.' We need to think of a name."

"We already have one," he said.

"We do? What is it?" I couldn't remember deciding on anything.

"Tara suggested it. Noralicia. Remember?" I'd forgotten I'd told Adam about Tara's idea.

"Ugh. Not likely. Seriously, we have to think of a name."

"We have a few months still. You might grow to like Noralicia," he teased.

"And you might grow wings and fly." I laughed at him. "But let's tell Lily that's the name we've chosen when we tell her we're having a girl."

"She'll probably like it," Adam said.

"You're right. She's a big Twilight fan *and* she has no taste."

I called my mom to let her know the news.

"I'm so excited," she said. "Now I can go shopping."

"What? What do you call what you've been doing?"

"That was just the basics, Kit. Now I can buy little clothes for her. Do you have a name picked out?"

"Not yet. Adam says we have plenty of time. And he wants to see her first." There was no way I was telling her about "Noralicia."

"It's good to be prepared. Do you want me to send you a baby names book?"

"No thanks, Mom. We're good. I'm emailing you some ultrasound pictures though."

"I'm excited to get them." She paused and the quiet on the line made me wonder if she'd hung up.

"Mom, are you still there?"

"Yes. I was just wondering what you think of your father's news."

"His baptism? I'm good with it." I wasn't surprised by her question, but I was a little curious as to why it took her so long to bring it up. I'd talked to her several times since his baptism, and she'd never said a word.

"Oh that. I meant his other news."

"What news is that?"

"He and Amberlie are getting married. Didn't he tell you?"

"What? Are you sure? This is the first I've heard."

"Dave told me last night when I talked to him. I assumed he'd told you both. I'm sorry, I shouldn't have said anything."

"It's okay. We're going over there tonight. He probably planned on telling us then." I tried hard to keep my tone even. I hated finding out things this way. My parents were pretty good about not doing this to us, so this was doubly shocking. I didn't think she'd told me to be malicious, but I had to wonder. "How do you feel about it?" I asked.

"It's not really my place to say," she said. I could tell she was trying to keep her voice neutral. "I knew he'd been dating, so I'm not surprised. I don't imagine I'll be invited to the wedding." Her laugh didn't sound sincere. *Who can blame her?*

"I guess I'm not that surprised either," I said. "You both seemed to have moved on."

"I could either move on or wallow in self-pity. I chose to pick up the pieces and forge ahead. It seems like we've had this conversation before."

"You're the one who brought it up, Mom."

"I know that. I wanted to make sure you're doing okay with it. Dave is fine; he's caught up in his own life. I know you've struggled with the divorce, so I worried about how you were taking the news."

"Since this is the first I've heard about it, I can't really say how I'm taking it. Besides, it's not like I have a say in it. Right?" I knew that I didn't feel like discussing it with my mother. "I have to go now. I'm back at work. Talk to you later." I hung up before she replied. She'd worry about it until I talked to her again, but she'd have to work that out. I had enough on my plate.

I can't say I earned my wages that afternoon at work. I was preoccupied with knowing the baby was a girl and my dad was getting remarried. I would have a stepmother named "Amberlie."

I had the ridiculous thought I could name the baby "Noramberlicia." I was beginning to think like Tara, which led me to an entire texting conversation with her. I was glad Nadine had the afternoon off.

Adam wasn't surprised by the news of my dad getting married. "It was obvious it was coming," he said. "You seem to be doing pretty good with the news."

The indignation and anger I expected to feel just weren't there. I knew part of the reason was due to Dave and Adam. Their advice after my dad's baptism struck a nerve and I had actively tried to soften my hard-hearted attitude. I knew that my prayers were being answered by the absence of malice I felt at the news of the marriage.

Without being so caught up in my own emotions, I enjoyed watching my dad when we arrived at his house. He was clearly nervous as he fumbled around setting the table. Amberlie was there, as friendly and calm as ever.

There were only four places set at the table.

"Isn't Dave coming?" I asked.

"No. He had plans," my dad said as he dropped another fork. "He stopped by last night." Amberlie told him to sit down.

Not wanting our dinner to meet the same fate as the forks, I offered to help her. I replaced the fork and slid napkins under the silverware. I slipped one of the ultrasound pictures under my dad's utensils, leaving one edge sticking out.

When we sat down for dinner, he noticed it. "What's this?" He studied it, trying to figure it out. I kept silent, watching to see if he would come to the correct conclusion.

Amberlie knew what it was immediately. She laughed as she saw him turn it over in his hands.

"It's an ultrasound picture, Paul," she said when it became clear he was clueless.

"Of your granddaughter," I added.

His eyebrows raised and he studied again. "How can you tell?"

"Don't feel bad," Adam said, "I couldn't tell what it was without the technician pointing it out."

"Dad, did you hear me?" I asked.

"Yes. It's an ultrasound of the baby."

"Your *granddaughter*."

"My granddaughter?" he parroted. "It's a girl? How can you tell?"

Laughing at him, I explained the ultrasound. I wasn't about to admit that I needed the ultrasound tech to explain it to me also.

My dad blushed. "I'll take your word for it then. A little girl. That's just wonderful."

"Girls are so fun! There are so many cute clothes for baby girls. My daughter Emily is expecting a baby girl in December." Amberlie's enthusiasm made up for my dad's denseness.

"I didn't realize Emily was pregnant," I said. Truth be told, I hadn't really asked a lot about her children.

"Yes, I'm going to be a grandma," Amberlie sounded excited about it.

The conversation centered on babies for the next few minutes. My dad didn't contribute much. He quietly ate his dinner and wiped his sweating brow with his napkin.

I'd never seen him so nervous.

"Dad, what's up? You're acting weird."

"What do mean?" he asked.

"You seem nervous or something. You're twitching."

He glanced at Amberlie, who smiled and gave a slight nod. He mopped his forehead with his napkin one more time.

"I guess I'm a little nervous tonight." He paused and reached for Amberlie's hand. He gave it a squeeze and looked directly at me. "Kit, Amberlie and I are getting married."

He looked like he was bracing himself for an explosion. I saw Amberlie's smile falter a tiny bit and realized she was nervous, too. She just hid it better.

"Congratulations!" I said. "Do you have a date set?"

Dad's mouth gaped at my reaction. Amberlie quickly masked her own surprise.

"Thanksgiving Day," she said when my dad couldn't seem to recover his wits.

"Wow, Thanksgiving. Where are you getting married?" I asked.

My dad regained control of his faculties. "At Amberlie's house. Her bishop will perform the ceremony."

"At 10:00 a.m.," she added. "We're keeping it very small. Just our children and a few close friends. We hope you'll come."

"Of course we'll be there," I said. As much as I enjoyed their surprise at my reaction, I loved my internal reaction even more. I wasn't angry or hurt. I was happy for them, and it felt liberating.

Amberlie got up to get dessert. While she was in the kitchen, my dad said, "Kit, thank you for being so understanding. I thought you'd be upset."

"I'm sorry I've been so rude, Dad. I want you to be happy. It's taken me awhile to get over things. I do have a question, though. Where will you two live?"

"We're going to live here until we can get this house sold. We want to get a house together that is new to both of us."

Amberlie came back with blueberry pie and nodded in agreement. "We're going to rent my house out for now and decide whether or not to keep it as an investment."

The pie was good, although Lily made better. Which reminded me, we still needed to go over to the Bridgers' house to tell them the results of the ultrasound.

I reminded Adam that we needed to leave soon. He offered to help clean up before we left. He never offered that at his mom's house. Maybe Adam was getting more considerate as he matured. I'd have to test out my theory at home.

Dad and Amberlie declined our help, and we left right after dessert.

I wished I hadn't eaten so much at my dad's house, because Lily had made peach cobbler again from the peaches we'd canned earlier in the year.

I did my best to do it justice, but I was just too full. "I'm sorry, Lily. You went through all this effort to make peach cobbler especially for me and I'm too stuffed to eat it."

"I didn't make it just for you, silly. I made it for my *niece*." She patted my belly. "So did the ultrasound confirm what I've been telling you?"

I looked at Adam and said, "You tell her."

He swallowed his giant bite of cobbler and said, "Sorry, Lily, it's a boy."

"No it's not!" she argued.

Adam whipped out the ultrasound pictures faster than I could. He pointed out the baby's head, showing the profile of her face. "Isn't it obvious we're having a boy? Look at these other pictures. I think they speak for themselves."

Lily studied the pictures. Barbara leaned over her to see them too.

Lily looked crestfallen. "I was so sure you were having a girl. I jinxed it with a pink blanket."

"There's no such thing as a jinx, Lily. What's wrong with it being a boy?" Adam asked, followed by a loud belch.

"Other than the obvious," I added, motioning to my husband.

"Nothing's wrong with a boy. I just knew it was a girl." Lily looked like she was about to cry. "Now I've given you that stupid pink blanket."

"Lily, it's okay," I said. "We'll use the blanket. I promise."

"Right. I'm sure you're going to be okay with wrapping a boy in a pink blanket so everyone will think he's a girl." She sniffed and wiped her nose with the back of her hand. "I'll get started on a blue one. Will you give me the pink one back so I'll have it for Michelle—if she has a girl, that is?"

"No," I said, trying not to laugh.

"No? You won't give the blanket back? Why not?"

"It has sentimental value. It's the first blanket anyone made for my baby. I'll use it for him. Even if it means he'll need counseling later on in his life. I'll do it for you, Lily."

Either my tone or my words gave me away. Lily eyed me suspiciously. She looked over at Adam, who burst out laughing.

"You brats!" she screeched, grabbing our bowls of cobbler from our reach. Her punishment was ineffective since Adam had already finished his, and I was too full to eat anymore.

chapter thirty-two

Thanksgiving was odd, to say the least. I'd never been to a wedding in someone's home, let alone on Thanksgiving Day involving one of my parents.

Amberlie's house was small, although it fit in with the older neighborhood. I was greeted at the door by an enormously pregnant, younger-looking version of Amberlie.

"Hi, I'm Emily. You must be Kit. We're practically twins!" She was bubbly and reminded me of Tara.

She looked like she was about to give birth to twins. Her gigantic stomach made me feel almost petite. "No offense, but I hope I don't look like your twin—at least not for another three months." As soon as it came out of my mouth, I was afraid I offended her.

She just nodded and said, "I know, I'm humongous. Three more weeks. It feels more like three years. My mom told me you're having a girl too."

"I am. Are you getting excited?"

"More nervous than excited at this point. I just want to be done." She sighed then motioned me inside. "I'm supposed to greet people and introduce them to each other. Come in and meet the others."

Emily introduced us to her husband, Ian. He was talking to Trey, Amberlie's son. They said hello and went back to their conversation. Emily said, "You'll have to excuse them. They're talking computers."

A strawberry blonde girl came out of the kitchen and Emily led me toward her. "Come over and meet Kara."

Emily introduced us, and I reached out my hand to shake Kara's.

She shook my hand rather limply and said, "Emily, don't you think the turkey smell is gross?" I'd noticed the scent of roasting turkey wafting from the kitchen when I walked in. I thought it smelled good.

"It's Thanksgiving, Kara. It's supposed to smell like turkey. Find something else to worry about."

"It's not the wedding smell of choice. We should have gone out to dinner," Kara grumbled.

"Have you ever tried to go out for dinner on Thanksgiving?" Emily asked.

"Have you ever tried making reservations?" Kara replied. Their arguing reminded me of Dave and me. I liked them.

"Do you know where my dad is?" I asked them. Kara pointed to the kitchen as the doorbell rang again.

Dad and Amberlie were talking to her bishop. I hung back just inside the door, holding Adam's hand. Dad stepped over and pulled me in for a hug.

"I'm so glad you came, Kit. Have you seen Dave yet?" He sounded nervous but looked happy. Amberlie looked radiant.

"Not yet," I said. "I'm sure he'll be here any minute."

The words barely left my mouth when we heard Dave's voice. He and Trey came into the kitchen. I envied the way Dave made friends so easily.

Dave reached out to shake Dad's hand, but Dad grabbed Dave and hugged him. Dave looked over his shoulder at me and rolled his eyes. I noticed he returned the hug despite his grimace.

When he stepped back from the embrace, Dave looked at my stomach and said, "Hey, sis, maybe you should just say no to seconds."

"Hey, bro, maybe you should've just said yes to brains."

By ten thirty everyone had arrived and was seated. Amidst the aroma of roasting turkey and the muted sound of sibling insults, the bishop performed the ceremony uniting my father and Amberlie in marriage.

I felt a strange lack of emotion. I thought I would cry or something, but I was so distracted by the tantalizing smells from the kitchen all I could think about was food.

Dave slipped his cell phone out of his pocket to read a text. I elbowed him in the ribs, and he put it away. It was hard enough for me to pay attention without him distracting me too.

The ceremony was over quickly, and people were congratulating the new Mr. and Mrs. Paul Matthews. I wondered what my mom was doing right at that moment. She told me she and Jonah were going out to dinner this afternoon. She was probably sleeping in which is what I'd be doing if I was home.

Adam nudged me and suggested we offer our congratulations. After hugs and small talk, we posed and smiled for pictures. Amberlie's sister cornered me and made sure I knew who everyone was and something about each person. She lived right down the street from Amberlie. They'd kept the guest list "small," but there were still enough people that we stood shoulder to shoulder. I could never catch the bathroom empty. I could see why my dad and Amberlie had opted to live in my dad's house.

We ate a light brunch of fruit and pastries which I liked but didn't impress Adam. He wanted more substantial food. I guess I wasn't the only one salivating over that turkey cooking.

I knew Adam was as anxious as I to get over to the Bridgers' house. We were having our Thanksgiving dinner with them, and I knew Barbara wouldn't care if we grazed in the kitchen before dinner.

My dad and I had a moment alone before we left. "I have a question for you," I said.

"Fire away."

"Why in the world are you sticking around to cook a turkey dinner? I know you're going to Hawaii, so why didn't you make reservations at a nice restaurant and leave right after the wedding?" I couldn't imagine how Amberlie could stand to cook a big dinner and hang around visiting all day right after getting married.

"Amberlie wanted dinner with her children. She likes to cook, and she's the one who insisted on making the traditional Thanksgiving dinner. Her sister offered to cook this year and host us, but Amberlie wanted to have the dinner here. Dave's staying. I wish you'd reconsider."

"Sorry, Dad. This is our last Thanksgiving with Mark for two years. He goes into the MTC next Wednesday. It'll be the last time the Bridger family is all together for awhile."

"I understand. Thanks again for coming."

"You're welcome. Have fun in Hawaii." I gave him a hug.

He pulled back and looked at me. "You're growing, Sprout!"

"I know, I know. I don't need the reminder. At least I'm not as big as Emily—oops, I probably just jinxed myself."

"There's no such thing as a jinx," Adam said in my ear. He held out my coat for me. "Are you ready?"

"I'm ready." I gave my dad one more quick hug and struggled into my coat.

"Kit, will you do me a favor?" Dad asked.

"Sure, what is it?"

"Make sure you give your mom a call. She'll be really missing you and Dave today."

A little late to be worrying about Mom, I thought. Aloud, I said, "I was planning on it. I talked to her yesterday, and she has a date today." Maybe that was a rude thing to say, but he's the one who brought up the subject of Mom.

He looked relieved. "Good, I don't want her to be all alone."

Ironic that he should be concerned about my mother on his wedding day. It actually made me feel better to hear it.

Thanksgiving at the Bridgers' was full of food, laughter, and reminiscing. Mark's upcoming departure to the MTC got Justin and Adam talking about their missions.

The photo albums came out, and we marveled at how much we'd changed in just a few years.

There were pictures of the family dinner when Justin came home. Adam was on his mission then, but I'd been a fixture at the Bridger house because of Janet. There was a candid shot of Janet and me with our mouths full of brownies. Ben and Justin were talking in the background and Michelle was there, hanging on Justin's arm.

It was a sharp contrast of how quickly some things changed while others stayed the same.

I studied the picture. *How did I ever think Adam looked like Justin?* I remembered how Justin had pestered me to take the discussions and how patient Janet had been with my questions and hesitations. I recalled how much I'd disliked Michelle at the time and now we were sisters-in-law. I hoped Justin told Michelle I only flirted with him to make her jealous. My face flushed with embarrassment at the memory of Justin pointing out how my actions looked to others who knew I was waiting for Adam. I hated Justin's know-it-all attitude back then, but I was glad he was persistent in his efforts to get me baptized.

There were pictures of Janet and her fiancé, Ben, including their engagement picture and a copy of their wedding announcement. Memories of that final drive from her aunt's house flooded back. I could almost hear Janet's laughter and feel her happiness. I couldn't remember the details of the car accident, but I touched the scar on the side of my face as I reflected on that day.

There was a time when I couldn't think of her without the searing pain of loss tearing through me. The sorrow remained, but I also felt peace now. I knew Janet was the same happy, patient, and caring person—she was still Janet. The healing had come so gradually. I fingered the jagged scar and realized it had faded too. I hardly ever noticed it anymore.

It was similar to my struggle with forgiving my parents—especially my father. The changes occurred gradually, but I could definitely feel the healing.

"Are you okay?" Adam whispered. I realized I was still staring at the same photograph. Barbara was also looking at me with concern.

"I'm good," I reassured them. "I was thinking about Janet. I remember eating those brownies. Lily lured me here with them even though I didn't want to meet Justin."

"Why didn't you want to meet me?" Justin asked. "What did I ever do to you? Except convert you, baptize you, keep you from hitting on me—the list is endless."

"That was the problem. You were too perfect. I was sick of hearing about you. I wanted Adam—not some cheap imitation." I grinned at Lily. "But the brownies were worth coming over for."

"Hey, I'm anything but cheap. And I kept you in line until Adam came home. You should both thank me."

"Don't take credit for that," I said. "You told Adam to forget about me and focus on his mission. Right, Adam?"

"Keep me out of this argument. I'm getting more pie. Anyone else want more?" He conveniently escaped having to defend me.

"I'll take another piece," Justin said to Adam. "You're only telling part of the story, Kit. I only told him missionaries who left girls waiting for them either lost their girlfriends or their hair."

Michelle punched him in the arm. "I didn't hear you complaining when I waited for you."

"Waited for me?" Justin laughed. "You dated half of the singles ward—including my own brother!" He was pretty gutsy. I'd always thought Michelle was a player, but never dared say it. I guess being her husband made him feel brave.

Michelle just laughed. "I only dated half of the singles ward because the other half was female. I agree with Kit. You're full of yourself."

Justin turned his attention to his brother. "Mark, you're a smart man. You didn't get hooked on a woman before your mission. If you ever doubt your wisdom, just look at me and Adam."

Mark smirked. "What makes you think I don't have someone waiting for me?"

"You hardly even date," Beth announced. "The only thing waiting for you when you come home will be the next Star Trek movie."

Mark threw his wadded-up napkin at Beth. "You don't know everything. I've got girls lined up to write to me while I'm gone."

"Sisters and mothers don't count," Beth said, sticking her tongue out at him. She had transformed. Those kinds of comments usually came from Lily. Evidently Beth listened and learned.

Lily spoke up in Mark's defense. "Believe it or not, he does have at least one girl writing to him."

"Who?" several of us asked at the same time.

"None of your business," Mark said. "Lily, keep your mouth shut." He got up to get more pie. Barbara decided she'd better supervise since the pies were alone with her sons.

As soon as they left, I turned to Lily. "Tell me."

"You already know. You set it up. He made me promise not to tell. But I can't help it if you guess, can I?"

I tried to figure out what Lily meant. The only person I'd discussed Mark with was Charity. "Is he writing to Charity?"

Lily nodded and lowered her voice to a whisper. "I gave Mark a picture of her and told him it was her dying wish to write to him on his mission. Then I sent Charity an email telling her that Mark didn't have anyone to write to him while he was gone. They fell for it. They've been talking to each other on Facebook, and he promised to send her his address as soon as he has it."

Charity hadn't mentioned a word about it. I'd included plenty of information about the Bridgers and made sure to keep her updated about Mark after she'd expressed interest. I never dreamed that Lily would manipulate them into writing to each other.

"Aren't you a little bothered by the fact that Charity really could die? Don't you think she would be mortified to find out what you've done?" I was slightly appalled at Lily's action.

"I'm perfectly aware how sick she is. And Mark is so shy he'd never ask a girl to write to him on his own. That's why I did it. It will make them both happier. They'll never have to know that I set it up. Unless you tell them." Her mind worked in strange ways. Even scarier, I sort of understood her logic.

Adam and Mark came back in with their pie. Adam gave a piece to Justin, who dug right in without a word of thanks.

Partway through his second bite, Justin spat the pie back onto the saucer. "What did you put in it?" he accused Adam, who was laughing so hard he choked on his own pie.

"It's jalapeno-pumpkin. Just a little surprise for you for tormenting my wife." I rewarded Adam with a big kiss and glimpsed Justin running for the kitchen for a drink.

"You're my hero," I said, fluttering my eyelashes at him. "But you'd better watch your back for awhile."

"And fetch my own food," Adam said. "It was his own fault for trusting me to get his pie in the first place."

I loved Thanksgiving at the Bridger house.

chapter thirty-three

The next couple of weeks were crazy. Mark left for his mission, my dad and Amberlie came back from their honeymoon, and I gained ten pounds practically overnight.

People kept telling me how cute I was. Being unable to button up my coat over my belly didn't meet my definition of "cute."

"Adam, I'm getting so huge you won't even be able to put your arms around me," I whined as I divided up the last brownie. "I'll have to wear a tent if I don't stop growing!"

He listened as he handed me the ice cream. "Honey, I think you're cute. And we can always use the tent next summer for camping."

I flicked a brownie bit at him.

I emailed Charity and teased her about writing to Mark. She denied it.

> Really, Kit? How could I be writing to him? Do you really think Mother would mail any letters I wrote to a guy? How can I even get to the post office? Lily told me I can't send him emails, so I'm just out of luck.

She had a point—especially if Alicia connected Mark Bridger to me. Even though I didn't approve of Lily's trickery in getting them to write to each other, I agreed that it would be good for both of them. Disappointed, I kept reading.

Did you believe that line? Ha! You underestimate my skills. I may not be able to get to the post office on my own, but I do have my ways. My favorite nurse, Lorna, agreed to mail the letters for me and even buy the stamps. She thinks it's romantic that I'm writing "my young man" but didn't want me to hook up with a freak or something. I told her he was serving a Mormon mission and we'd never actually met, let alone dated. She said she knows a Mormon who seems pretty normal. I didn't tell her about you–I didn't want to burst her bubble! Just kidding. It probably helps that she doesn't like Mother very much. She thinks she's too domineering–imagine that!

My mother tries to hide it, but she's worried about time running out for me. She is more scared than I am. Believe it or not, I'm okay with whatever happens.

You asked if I knew why Mother couldn't donate part of her own liver. She can't because she had hepatitis a long time ago. She tried to bully the doctor (and probably bribe him too) but he wouldn't approve her. My father is diabetic. I don't mind you asking–we're sisters.

Don't worry about getting fatter because you're pregnant. At least you're getting something out of it. My stomach looks like I'm pregnant, but it's only fluid building up. The stupid medicine doesn't work as well as it used to. Lorna said they might have to drain some fluid out with a needle. I'm not stupid. I've seen those needles and they're huge. I might replace her with a new favorite nurse if I see her coming near me with one of those giant things.

I've got to take a nap now. I'm like a big fat baby. At least I don't have to wear diapers. (I'd better not give Lorna any more great ideas.) Write back soon.

Charity's email made me laugh, but I sensed something different in her tone. I knew she was worse than she was letting on. I wanted to see her.

I composed an email to Alicia asking if I could see Charity. Re-reading it made me cringe at how pathetic I sounded, so I deleted it instead of sending it. I wrote another one that sounded a little more mature but deleted that one too. I even dialed Alicia's number once, but ended the call before it went through.

I was a coward. I was afraid of Alicia telling me no.

My indecision came to a screeching halt a few days before Christmas when I checked my email and saw a message from Charity.

Only it wasn't actually from Charity.

> Kit,
> You don't know me, but Charity has told me about you. I can't use my own name or email, because I could get into big trouble for privacy violations. Especially if Mrs. Haversham finds out. Charity gave me her login information so I could send you a message since she can't do it herself.
> Charity is in the hospital. She's still here in Santa Barbara for now, but she's in intensive care. I shouldn't even tell you that much, but she wants to see you. I think she might be transferred to UCLA in a few days. It could happen immediately if a donor is found.
> I wouldn't tell you this except I'm afraid she might not be going home. And she wants to see you more than anything. I can't tell you how to handle Mrs. Haversham, but it seems to me if you were to show up here and it was her daughter's dying wish to see you, even that woman would be hard pressed to say no. Just my opinion.
> Do what you can to come. I don't think Charity has time on her side.

There was no signature. I was certain it was from Lorna, the nurse Charity told me about.

Adam and I were going to my mom's for Christmas. Our flight was scheduled to leave in five days. We were supposed to travel down with Dave. I couldn't shake the sickening feeling that those extra days were crucial.

I had to see Charity before it was too late.

"Adam, look at this." I shoved the laptop screen in front of his face. He quickly scanned the email.

"It's kind of dramatic. Do you think it's legit?" he asked.

"I think it is." I started crying.

"We'll be there in a few days. You can see her then."

"What if it's too late? I've had the feeling for a couple of weeks that I should contact Alicia and ask if I can see Charity. I tried to, but

I couldn't make myself ask Alicia for anything. Why didn't I listen?"

Adam set the laptop aside and gathered me in his arms, bulky belly and all. "Kit, it wouldn't have made a difference if you had called. Charity would still be in the hospital."

"I know, but at least I could have tried. Not only did I refuse to give her my liver, but I ignored the promptings. If she dies before I get there, it's all my fault!" I wailed. "And to make it worse, Alicia hasn't even told me she's going to die. She's a horrible person!"

"You don't know Charity is going to die. The email sounds serious, but blaming yourself won't help anything." He kissed the top of my head as I sobbed on his chest.

I stopped fighting the tears and let my grief flow, wrapped safely in Adam's arms.

"I've got to go down there. Now."

"I need to make some phone calls to get the shifts off work," Adam said. I loved that he was ready to leave with me immediately. I wanted him by my side, but my practical side never stayed silent for long.

"I'll change my flight. You can still fly down with Dave like we planned. My mom will pick me up at the airport and she'll let me use her car." My fingers were already flying across the keyboard to pull up our reservation.

"Kit, I don't want you to travel alone. You're seven months pregnant."

"I feel fine."

"It doesn't matter. The only reason I agreed to fly when you're this far along is because the flight is so short, and I'd be with you." He took my hands away from the keyboard. "I'm serious. I'm going with you or you're not going."

"Adam, be reasonable. The change fee is $100 per ticket. It's bad enough I have to miss work without pay. We can't afford it."

"I'll call your mother, Katherine Matthews Bridger."

"What did you say?" I couldn't believe he just threatened me with that.

"You heard me." Adam took out his cell phone and started scrolling through the contacts list.

"Don't you dare!" I lunged for the phone, dumping my laptop.

Adam easily caught the laptop while holding the phone out of my reach. "Then *you* be reasonable. If you play the 'we can't afford it' card, I have no problem telling your mother what the situation is. I know she'll be happy to pay for the change fees and help us with expenses to keep you from flying alone."

"I'm not asking my mom for the money." I folded my arms over my tummy to show him I was determined.

"Then have a little faith that things will work out. Charity is your sister. This is an emergency. I'm going with you. Now will you change the tickets or shall I?"

"Fine, you can go." I stood up and stomped off. "But your clothes are all dirty and I haven't had time to do laundry. So you can pack your own smelly stuff."

It took only a few minutes to sort the laundry and get a load started. Just enough time for me to stop grumbling about being married to such a bossy man.

chapter thirty-four

The bright sunlight contrasted sharply with my feelings of doom as we stepped off the plane into the unseasonable warmth of the day. It didn't feel like December, and it didn't feel like death.

Every time I spoke to Adam on the flight, my words sounded morbid even to myself. After the fifth time of saying, "What if she's dead?" Adam finally rebuked me with, "Stop trying to bury the living, Kit."

Of course I started to cry, and he felt terrible. I wondered if he regretted coming with me. When my inner dialog had convinced me my husband would be better off without me, he reached over and squeezed my hand three times, our code for "I love you." I started crying again.

My mom was overjoyed to see us. She squealed when she saw my stomach. I had no idea she even knew how to make a sound like that.

She hugged me, pulled back, and then patted my belly. I was used to people touching my stomach. Being pregnant seemed to melt boundaries and even strangers in the grocery store had smilingly patted my tummy.

So the gut-grasping no longer shocked me. But the squealing did. Then she said loudly, "Kit, you're so *big*!"

Even that didn't faze me too much. But I honestly was not

prepared for her to turn and announce to everyone within range of hearing, "This is my daughter! And she's pregnant!"

I felt like a freak show.

I looked to Adam for help, but he was staring at my mom. Whether it was her appearance or her loud enthusiasm, I couldn't tell. I forgot he hadn't seen her since her enhancements. Maybe her unearthly screech had paralyzed him. I elbowed him and pointed to our bags. "Let's go. Hurry."

He grabbed our luggage as my mother informed the older couple next to me that I was due in March and asked, "Don't you think she's huge?"

"Could be twins," the woman said, nodding knowingly. "Definitely a boy, the way she's carrying it all out front."

"I'm surprised she's this big, because she's so tall," my mother agreed.

I stopped abruptly causing Adam to nearly walk right over me. I whirled to face them. "I can hear you, you know."

"Of course you can, dear." Grandma Know-It-All turned back to my mother and said, "They get so emotional." Mom smiled and nodded.

"I am *not* emotional," I said a little more forcefully than I'd intended. "I'm not having twins *and* she's a girl."

Adam whispered, "It's okay, Kit. They mean well."

I was immediately sorry I'd snapped at them. I tried to apologize.

"Don't worry, dear," the old lady said. "Those emotions go up and down like an elevator. Do you remember, Thomas?" She nudged her husband.

Thomas grunted. I wasn't sure if it was in agreement or pain, but I heard him mutter, "Nothing's changed, if you ask me."

"What was that, Thomas?" she asked.

"I said be careful who you irritate, Erma. These days they all pack heat."

I wanted to go straight to the hospital. My mother insisted we stop for lunch, and Adam sided with her.

"I'm hungry so I know you must be starving," he argued when I pressed to eat later.

"Let's stop and get something quick," I conceded.

"Nice try, young lady, but you're not feeding my granddaughter fast food." She clearly had a destination in mind and was heading for it.

"Where are we going?" Since she was driving, I couldn't stop her. Maybe food would help.

"Beachside Café. I don't think you've ever been, but you'll love it. It's not far from here and right on the beach."

Adam spoke up as we pulled into the parking lot. "We came here a few times on my mission. A lot of students come here. If I remember right, they have a Cajun shrimp sandwich that's fantastic."

How strange to dine at a place familiar to my mother and husband but brand new to me.

I soaked in the sun, feeling the warmth melt some of the knots in my shoulders and back. Adam rubbed my back, and by the time our food arrived, I was feeling almost relaxed.

"So have you spoken with Alicia?" my mother asked.

"No. I want to just go visit Charity and avoid Alicia altogether."

"That may be hard to do. They may have restrictions on visitors for patients in intensive care."

"I know. I called and checked. Visiting hours are 1 p.m. to 8 p.m. and pediatric intensive care patients can have two visitors at a time. If she has a visitor already, it's probably Alicia, so I'll keep out of sight until she leaves." I'd discussed it with Adam, and we decided it was the best way to make sure I got to see Charity at least for a few minutes.

"Hopefully you won't have to deal with Alicia, but you should have a backup plan in case you have to talk to her. She can prevent you from seeing her minor child you know." I didn't need my mom reminding me of this. It was part of what had been bothering me for months.

"I'll talk to her nurse, Lorna. If she wrote to ask me to come, she'll let me in to see Charity, I'm sure of it. She'll also know when Alicia usually visits. If I don't see Charity today, I'll see her tomorrow."

Adam spoke up. "I'll be with Kit the entire time, so I've got her back. If Alicia shows up, Kit won't have to face her alone."

"Good. I'm glad you've thought it through. Since we're already in Santa Barbara, I'll stick with you too. I *am* the chauffeur."

I didn't want her to feel obligated. "You can drop us off if you have other errands you can run. We'll call you when we need a ride."

"No, dear. I'm staying. Adam may have your back, but I'll have your flank. We'll protect you." It was funny to hear my mother "rally the troops."

"Maybe you just want a glimpse of Alicia," I said.

"I wouldn't mind seeing the witch." Mom grinned, and I knew she really wanted to use a much stronger expletive. She had no good feelings for Alicia Haversham and although she used swear words sparingly, I'd heard her use a few.

"By the way, Mom, what was that whole scene at the airport? I felt like the star of a freak show the way you announced me to everyone you saw and told them I was pregnant."

"You are pregnant." She looked confused. "I didn't think it was a scene. I was very excited. Remember, last time I saw you, you weren't showing and now you've blossomed! Like Jiffy-Pop popcorn."

"That's another thing. You called me fat in front of everybody. That's embarrassing. People were staring at me."

"I never said you were fat. I said you were *big*. Pregnancy big. It's a cute big."

"Big isn't 'cute.' I already feel self-conscious, and I don't need people asking me if I'm having twins or if I'm overdue." I tried to keep my tone light, but putting on so much weight had struck a nerve deep down. My chin quivered and I tried to hide it by taking a bite of my salad. I could hardly control my chewing and a tear slipped out. How humiliating.

Adam automatically handed me a napkin and hugged me. My mom's face fell as she realized I was hurt by her comments. She reached over and took my hand and gave it a squeeze.

"Oh, baby, I'm sorry. It was said in a fun, good way. You look fabulously healthy and glowing—not fat. You're beautiful."

Adam knew kind words would make the waterworks flow

heavier, so he wisely kept quiet, lightly hugging me to him. I didn't like feeling like a huge, fat cow ready to drop a litter.

I voiced my thoughts, and Adam had something to say about it. "Cows don't drop *litters*; that would be cats or dogs. It's an 'udderly' ridiculous comparison."

His joking helped get my emotions under control. We finished lunch and then headed to the hospital.

They checked our IDs and asked who we were visiting. When I gave them Charity Haversham's name, I held my breath, expecting some kind of hassle, but we got our visitor badges without incident.

The receptionist directed us to the pediatric intensive care unit and reminded us that only two visitors at a time were allowed with a patient.

"Does she have any visitors right now?" I asked.

"None have checked in. Her mother is usually here and her father comes by in the evenings. But I haven't seen Mrs. Haversham yet today."

"Thank you." Some of my tension subsided.

We found our way to the PICU and stopped at the nurses' station. An older, grumpy-looking nurse asked if she could help us. I read her name badge, *June Alldren, R.N.*

"Is Lorna working today?" I asked.

June glanced at the board behind the desk. "Lorna's with a patient. It'll be few minutes. Are you here to see Lorna?"

"I'm actually here to see Charity Haversham, but I wanted to say hello to Lorna if she was working."

"Are you family?" June's brow was furrowed and I couldn't tell if she was suspicious or just tired. *What if Alicia has my name on a "do not admit" list? Shall I give a different name?*

Adam leaned in to talk to June. "Yes, we're family. My wife, Kit, is Charity's sister. And I'm her brother-in-law."

June's face lost its scrunched up look but her voice still sounded grouchy. "Two visitors at a time. Keep it to about fifteen minutes a visit. The patient is here to get better, not to entertain friends and family."

"Yes, ma'am," Adam said as he winked at the old crow. "Can you give us her room number, please?"

June pointed toward the closed doors. "Lorna will be out in a minute. When she comes, I'll buzz you through and she can show you the room. It's 3N09. One of you wait right here in this waiting area." June stood ready, hands on her hips to make sure someone remained behind. The doors opened and another nurse came out. Relief surged through me when I read her ID badge: *Lorna Jones, R.N.*

My mom sat on an orange vinyl chair, and Adam and I approached Lorna. She was about the same age as Nurse June, although she was dark-skinned and heavier. At least Lorna didn't look like she chewed on lemons all day long.

"Lorna," I said, stepping toward her with my hand outstretched, "I'm Kit Bridger."

Lorna smiled warmly and returned my greeting, but it was clear my name didn't ring any bells. I was surprised since I'd received the email from her only yesterday. I hoped she would know who I was, maybe even be expecting me.

"Who are you here to see, honey?" Lorna maintained her pleasant, professional demeanor as she spoke.

"Charity Haversham. I'm her sister, Kit."

Recognition dawned and Lorna said, "So you're Charity's sister. She'll be tickled to see you."

"I hope so. I came as soon as I heard. I was scheduled to come next week but I changed everything to get here sooner. I had to see her before . . . before . . ."

"I know, sugar, before Mrs. Haversham comes back. Let's get you back there."

Again her words surprised me. I was going to say "before she passed away." I was glad Lorna had filled in the words.

As we walked down the hallway to 3N09, I turned to wave at my mom. Knowing she was there encouraged me.

Lorna stopped outside the room and held her fingers to her lips. She poked her head through the doorway. "Miss Charity, I've brought you some visitors."

"Really? It can't be my mother since you never bring her back. She drops in like a tornado. Give me a hint. The visitors don't have needles, do they?" Charity's voice was high and clear like I remembered it. Maybe there was a trace of fatigue, but I detected no pain.

"Here's a hint for you," Lorna played along. "One is big, soft, and fluffy. No needles."

"The Stay Puft Marshmallow Man?" Charity giggled. "I'd like that visitor."

"Sorry, Miss Charity. It's someone who claims she's your sister." Lorna took my arm and guided me inside the door.

Charity gaped as recognition dawned on her, and then I heard an inhuman squeal for the second time in as many hours. For being so ill, Charity's shriek put my mom's rendition at the airport to shame. I expected nurses and doctors to come running to see if a patient had expired or someone had stepped on a cat.

"Kit! Kit! I knew you would come. I knew it, I knew it. Get over here! I can't get up right now."

I hurried over to hug her. I leaned down as she reached up with thin yellow arms encased with IVs and monitors. Charity's gaunt face and any bit of visible skin showed a sickly yellow tint. Her green eyes were even more vivid than I remembered, but the effect was spoiled by how yellowed the whites of her eyes were. The only thing that looked like Charity of four months ago was the colorful neon ribbons intertwined in her braid.

I bent lower and hugged her gently, not wanting to cause her pain. I tenderly kissed her bony cheek. She smelled sick. My stomach churned, and I pulled back but kept her hands in mine.

"I'm so glad you're here," she said. She took one of her thin hands from mine and reached out to rub my tummy. I didn't mind when she did it. "Kit, you've grown. We're twins." She pulled down her cover and exposed her gown-clad belly. It protruded grotesquely in contrast to the rest of her emaciated body. "Pretty gross, isn't it?"

"Yeah, it is. Did you swallow a watermelon seed?" I tried the lame joke old people cracked about me and my own big belly.

"I think it was the whole watermelon." She tried to laugh, but it didn't reach her eyes. Her eyes reminded me of a mask, kept carefully in place to guard the secrets inside. She looked past me and saw Adam.

"You must be Adam!"

Adam took her hand gently. "I'm glad to meet you Charity."

"Sit down. Pull over that chair." Charity directed and Adam obeyed.

I stood by the bed, holding her hand. "How are you doing?" The question seemed so inadequate.

"I prayed you would come before Christmas. I'm so glad you made it."

"When I got Lorna's email I changed my plans to come earlier. I had to make sure I saw you again before . . ." I let the sentence trail off.

"Before I croaked," Charity finished.

I didn't realize Lorna was still hovering in the room, logging information into Charity's chart. When I mentioned the email, Lorna stopped and looked at me. "I never sent you an email."

Confused, I thought back to the wording. True—she hadn't identified herself and couldn't because she would get in trouble for violating a patient's privacy. But I knew it was her.

"I understand. I got an email from a person who could get in trouble for revealing private patient information. There was no name. I get it." I smiled at Lorna to let her know her secret was safe with me.

She didn't smile back at me. "I did *not* send an email. I would get fired for violating patient privacy laws, and I take that seriously. I do not give out confidential patient information."

"Then who sent it?" I asked.

"That's what I'd like to know myself." Lorna's tone told me she was displeased. "When did you get this email that was supposed to be from me? What email address did it come from?"

"It came yesterday from Charity's email address. The person emailed because Charity wasn't doing very well. It said she might not make it back home and it was her dying wish to see me."

"No signature?" Lorna asked. I shook my head.

"Charity's own email address?" She clarified. I nodded.

"And it said come quick cause she was about dead?" I nodded again.

Lorna's stern look swung away from me and rested on Charity, who was lying flat on the bed with her eyes closed, lids fluttering slightly. "Uh-huh. Well, I think somebody might have exaggerated about her being 'bout dead because even today I've seen her typing on that laptop sending emails. That don't look like she's about dead to me." Lorna's sharp eyes zeroed in on me again. "Do you think she looks like she's about dead?"

It dawned on me what Lorna was implying. Charity sent the email, pretending to be Lorna, and scaring me half to death in the process.

I stared at Charity with what I hoped was a steely gaze. Her eyes were still closed, and the fluttering had slowed down. She looked very sick and wasted away, but now that I looked through eyes not fogged by the fear of my sister's imminent demise, I could see she was not on her deathbed just yet.

"Lorna, if she wasn't about dead when I got here, I think she might be by the time I leave after I finish beating her for scaring me like that."

"I'll help," Lorna said and pulled the covers down. "I know how to turn her over so we won't injure her. Except for her hind end, which we're gonna paddle till it stings."

Charity's eyes flew wide open when the covers were jerked out of her hands, and she was exposed except for her hospital gown. "Don't spank me. It'll hurt. I don't have any padding left." She scrambled spryly—unbelievably quick for a girl so "near death"— to the other edge of the bed away from Lorna. "I didn't use your name! And I didn't lie exactly. I just wanted to see Kit. I *needed* to see her." Charity looked to me for support. "Don't let Lorna beat my butt. She has hard hands."

"You're lucky I have a soft heart, Miss Charity." Lorna har-rumphed and continued her lecture. "You put my professional career at risk by doing something like that. And you could have sent your poor sister into early labor. She looks like she's about ready to pop right now."

Charity looked contrite. "I would have never jeopardized your job, Lorna. I would have 'fessed up. I had to make Kit know it was urgent. I know I said life and death, and it *will* be life and death soon. And she might not be able to get here by then. No one needs to know I sent that email."

"If your mother catches wind of that email, she'll assume it was me, and she'll use it as a way to get me fired. She already doesn't like me, and I'm too fine a nurse to be fired because of the likes of her."

"Don't feel bad, Lorna," I offered. "She doesn't like me very much either, and I never did a thing to her except make her a mother at a young age."

"That woman's your mother too? How's a woman like that get two fine daughters when I only got one boy and he's in jail. Life ain't fair, I'll tell you."

"She's my birth mother," I corrected. "My *real* mother is out in the waiting room."

"Your mom is here?" Charity conveniently changed the subject. "I want to meet her."

"As long as you give your word to stop sending emails pretending to be me." Lorna was already softening and it was easy to see that Charity was a favorite of hers.

"I'll tell her." I plopped down in the recliner by Charity's bed. "But before I do, I want to talk to you for a couple of minutes. Before your mom shows up and kicks me out."

"Oh yeah." Charity glanced at the clock. "She had a couple of appointments this afternoon, but she could be here any time. I keep asking her to let you visit, but she keeps changing the subject when I press her on it."

"So that's where you learned it," I teased her.

"What are you talking about?" With her eyes wide and her innocent tone, Charity looked about twelve instead of sixteen. "Lorna, will you keep a lookout for my mom so we have warning?"

"I'm not a kindergarten teacher," Lorna grumbled. "I'll do what I can. If I happen to see her, I'll buzz in on your speaker and tell you I'm bringing your protein shake. And you'd better drink it all."

"Thanks, Lorna, you're the best!" Charity smiled at her, and this time it reached her jaundiced eyes.

"Don't I know it," Lorna replied as she headed for the door. "Remember, you only get a fifteen-minute visit and I'm starting the clock now."

"Don't you love her?" Charity asked after Lorna left. "She makes this place bearable."

"I'm glad she watches out for you. Now explain why you sent me that email. I dropped everything—and so did Adam—so we could get down here. I've had the most awful feeling in the world the past twenty-four hours. It wasn't a very funny joke." I didn't have to fake the irritation in my voice.

"I'm sorry it worried you. I really am. But it isn't as much an exaggeration as you think. You can't honestly tell me I don't look terrible. And I *know* I'm dying. People don't want to talk about it around me, but I can see it in their eyes. They give me almost anything I want." Charity's face was defiant, but her voice quavered as she spoke.

"You don't look that great," I admitted. "But you're doing a lot better than I expected from the email."

"I'm hooked up to all this junk." She shook her arms and a sensor beeped. "I'm not stupid and I know how to use Google. I know my chances of getting a liver donated in time are crappy."

"I'm so sorry, Charity. I wish I could have donated. I'll start the donor screening process again as soon as I have the baby. I promise."

Charity shook her head. "I don't blame you, Kit. That's not what I mean. There have been other times when it looked like a donor was going to come through and it didn't. I can't just 'hang on' until you have the baby. My stupid body won't do what I tell it to do. I think I'm just meant to die."

I hated to hear her talk that way. I wanted to cheer her up and frantically tried to think of something. Fortunately, the baby chose that moment to stretch and kick. I took Charity's hand and placed it on my abdomen. "Be still and wait a minute, and you'll feel the baby kick."

The diversionary tactic worked. It only took a few seconds before she felt the tiny movements. "Wow. That's awesome! What does it feel like on the inside? Does it hurt?"

"No, it usually feels like fluttering and shifting."

We spent three or four minutes feeling the baby shift. She was being unusually active, and I made a point of telling Charity. "She never moves around this much. When I feel her kicking like this and tell Adam to check it out, she usually stops and refuses to move again. You're lucky."

"She knows it's her Aunt Charity." We were silent for another minute or so. "Do you think she really knows who I am?" she asked.

I considered the question. "I know her spirit is close by. I'm sure we knew her before we came to earth." The baby kicked hard. "I think that's a 'yes'. I'm pretty sure she knows it's you."

"I hope so. I want to see her. I want to live long enough to see my niece." Charity's brow wrinkled. "It'll be March though. I don't think I can make it until then."

So much for diverting her attention. I changed the subject. "So tell me about the food in this place. Is it any good?"

As if on cue, Lorna's voice came over the intercom. "I'll be back with your protein drink in a minute. And your mama's gonna make sure you drink it all."

"She's coming!" Charity and I said at the same time.

Adam sat there, seemingly unaware of the situation.

"Alicia's on her way back. We have to get out of here." I looked back at Charity. "Is there another exit?"

"No, you have to go through the doors, and they have to buzz you in and out." Charity's eyes were bright with excitement.

She's enjoying this, I thought.

"I'll go first and distract her," Adam said.

"I'll talk to you later," I said to Charity. I followed Adam out. He turned toward the exit, and I stepped down the hallway and stood outside another patient room with my back to the main doors.

I heard the door buzz and open. I glanced quickly over my shoulder. It was Alicia.

Alicia's heels echoed on the tile floor. Adam was walking right toward her.

"Hi," I heard him say. She ignored him. "Wait," he said. The clicking heels stopped.

What is he doing? I thought frantically.

"Excuse me," he said to Alicia, "do you know where X-ray is? I can't find it anywhere."

She sounded irritated. "I have no idea." She started walking again.

"Well, thanks anyway," Adam called cheerfully.

The doors activated at that moment and Lorna walked through. Seeing Adam she asked, "May I help you find something?"

"I'm looking for X-ray," Adam said too loudly. He wasn't a very good actor.

"X-ray?" Lorna echoed. "You're on the wrong floor. How did you get back here?"

I peered around to make sure Alicia was gone from the hallway. She'd gone into Charity's room.

I moved as fast as I could toward Adam and Lorna. She buzzed the door open and shooed us through.

"Thanks, Lorna," I said. "That was close."

Lorna gave me a stern look. "I hope you can come back tomorrow. It's my day off, so I won't have to deal with the stress."

I was pretty sure she was joking. I asked her, "Will you have Charity call me as soon as she can?"

"Do I look like a messenger?" Lorna asked in reply. I almost missed her wink. At least, I think it was a wink—maybe it was a twitch.

chapter thirty-five

Charity didn't call until the next day. We compared notes on the near miss, which was much funnier now that it was in the past.

"What did you think of Adam?" I asked.

"He's not bad looking for an old guy," she joked. "He didn't have much chance to talk with the two of us around."

"He said he could tell we were sisters." I knew that would pique her curiosity.

"Really? Does he think we look alike?"

"No. We both talk a lot. How long will you be in the hospital?"

"Until I get a liver or die." She let out an exaggerated sigh.

"Don't joke about that, okay? It's not funny."

"I'm the one dying here. If I don't joke about it, I'll cry." I knew her words were truer than she would ever let on.

"I still feel like I let you down," I said quietly.

"Don't. Look on the bright side, if you hadn't tried, we wouldn't have met."

It was hard for me to see any light in the bleakness of Charity's situation. The reality of the moment stifled our conversation.

I switched subjects. "I want to visit you again, but I'm almost as afraid of Lorna as I am of Alicia."

"Lorna's off today, but Mother will be here soon. She'll probably stay all afternoon. She said Father will bring dinner, which means I'll get to watch them eat."

"What about tomorrow?" I hoped Alicia wouldn't spend every minute of visiting hours at Charity's side.

"I'll find out what her plans are. You're lucky you timed it so well yesterday. She spends most of the days here. Even though I sleep a lot lately, she just stays here, terrorizing the nurses."

"I need about an hour's notice. I want to visit you as much as I can while I'm here."

"Okay, I'll let you know. I've got to go now. I'm so tired. I'll talk to you tomorrow."

Since I couldn't visit Charity, Adam and I decided to explore Ventura. It was interesting when our memories crossed paths at physical landmarks. The park I'd played in as a child was in the same neighborhood where he'd tracted on his mission, but it was the first time we'd been in the city together.

We walked along the beach at Marina Park. I convinced him to climb on the *San Salvador* and go down the zip line so I could take pictures.

The weather was sunny and warm. We waded in the ocean even though the water was cold. Walking on the seashore with Adam took my mind off Charity for a while.

We tried coming up with a name we could agree on for our baby girl.

"Azure," I said staring at the clear, blue sky. "Do you like that one?"

"Yeah, for a color, not a baby."

"I want a unique name, but something pretty too."

"How about Katherine, and we'll call her Katie." Adam had suggested this before. While I didn't dislike my name, I wanted my daughter to have a name of her own.

"No. I call veto power."

"You always want to talk about names, and when I come up with something you don't like—which is all of them so far—you claim veto power." He'd used this argument more than once. I'll admit the names he chose were boring, but I believed we'd be able to compromise—just not with any of the names he'd picked so far.

"Harmony or Jade," I kept trying.

"Cacophony or Seaweed," Adam countered.

"You're being silly now," I said. "Try to be serious."

He feigned surprise. "Oh, you were being serious with those suggestions?"

I rolled my eyes. "Forget it. I'll just name her when you step out to the cafeteria."

"Oh yeah? I'll re-name her when I bless her."

"You wouldn't!" I knew he was teasing me, but I pretended to be a little worried.

"Then don't name her after a color or a fruit." Adam grinned, confirming he was kidding around.

"So Kiwi and Periwinkle are both a no?"

"We can both agree on that," he said.

Spending the afternoon on the beach with Adam rejuvenated me. We got back to my mom's condo just as Jonah was bringing her home from work.

He opened the door for her and followed her into the house.

"Did you go back to the hospital?" she asked as she kicked off her shoes.

"No. Charity called and said Alicia was on her way. We talked for a few minutes, but that was it. She's going to call me as soon as she finds out Alicia's plans for tomorrow and the next day."

"So where have you two been?" Mom leaned over to pat my tummy. She said to Jonah, "Doesn't Kit look darling pregnant?"

What could the poor man say? That was as bad as asking him if her pants made her butt look big. Jonah just smiled and said, "Pregnant women have a rare beauty. It must be the glow."

Jonah was diplomatic. He would have probably replied to the fat-butt question with something like, "Your posterior has a 'rear' beauty. It really fills out your slacks."

I snorted with laughter at my inner dialog. They all looked at me, waiting. "Sometimes I just think funny thoughts." I wasn't about to tell them what I was really thinking.

"Jonah has offered to take us to dinner tonight."

"Sounds great," Adam said. "I was thinking even peanut butter and jelly sounded pretty good right now, but going out to dinner sounds much better."

I realized I hadn't introduced Adam to Jonah—not that they needed it; they seemed perfectly comfortable with each other. Still, I periodically have a flash of manners so I put them to use. "Jonah, this is my husband, Adam Bridger. Adam, this is Jonah Lofthouse, my mother's friend."

They shook hands and Jonah asked Adam the usual questions about family and school. When we climbed in Jonah's Mercedes, I nudged Adam and whispered. "This is the car I was telling you about. I want a Mercedes."

He whispered back, "We could name our daughter 'Mercedes,' then you'd have one."

I elbowed him in the ribs. "Why not call her Lamborghini?"

"That's a boy's name. Now look who's being silly." He rubbed my stomach and whispered, "You're so cute when you're pregnant."

I tried to give him the evil eye, but I couldn't keep a straight face. I settled back into the soft, supple leather and held my husband's hand, thinking, *I love my life.*

chapter thirty-six

Charity didn't call me at all the next day. I was ready to drive to Santa Barbara to take my chances, but Adam pointed out if she couldn't call, she probably couldn't visit.

When my mom got home from work I used her cell phone to call Charity's phone, figuring it wouldn't show up as me. It went straight to voice mail.

I didn't leave a message.

My brother Dave flew in to Santa Barbara on Christmas Eve, the day after I kept trying to call Charity. My mom had the day off work and planned to pick him up.

I tried calling Charity's phone a couple more times and only got voice mail. I didn't dare call straight to her room for fear Alicia would answer.

Frantic with worry, I convinced my mom to drop Adam and me off at the hospital while she went to pick up Dave from the airport.

We checked in at the front and got our visitor passes.

"I'm sure Alicia is with her but I need to make sure she's okay." I told Adam for the twentieth time. He gave my hand a squeeze and let me ramble.

The elevator opened onto the third floor and I stepped out without looking—and met Alicia Haversham face-to-face.

Frozen by shock, I stood there, unmoving. Recognition

dawned on her face and she looked like she'd seen a ghost.

She spoke first. "Katherine. What are you doing here?"

Adam gently tugged at my arm to steer me away from the elevator door, which was trying to close on him. I let him guide me aside. My mind was blank.

Adam held out his hand. "Mrs. Haversham, I'm Adam Bridger, Kit's husband. It's nice to meet you." His voice was as pleasant as if he were greeting her at a ward social.

She automatically thrust out her hand but kept her stare fixed on me.

I swallowed hard, trying to force the hammering in my chest to subside. *She does not control me*, I reminded myself. *True, but she controls Charity*, I argued back.

"I'm here to see Charity." I said, straightening my back so I could look down at her.

"How did you know?" Alicia still looked confused.

"Know what?" I asked, stalling for time while I frantically tried to think of an excuse.

"Charity's Christmas present. She asked to see you. I was on my way to call you and you—you're there, right in front of me." I'd never seen Alicia look so unsettled.

I tried to process what she'd just told me. *She was on her way to call me.* "So Charity's okay?"

"No. She's not." Alicia glanced down at my very pregnant stomach protruding. "She's dying and we haven't found a donor." Her tone seemed to accuse me. I guess she'd overcome her surprise.

My face burned at the condemnation in her eyes. "I'm sorry."

"Spare me. I agreed because it is the *only* thing Charity has asked for. Now how did you know she was here?"

"She emailed me a few days ago. I was coming to spend Christmas with *my* mother. I want to see Charity too. I'm worried about her."

"You're a little late for concern. She's been bumped up on the donor waiting list, but nothing's happening. Helplessly watching your child die is horrible." Alicia looked at Adam, but didn't seem to recognize him from the hallway conversation. "I suppose it doesn't matter if you go back with Katherine. I'm going downstairs to get some fresh air."

She stepped past us and punched the elevator button.

I tugged on Adam's hand, leading him toward the nurse's station. It suddenly seemed important for me to be the one to walk away from Alicia, rather than letting her walk away from me. A small victory, but it was mine.

Neither of us spoke until we heard the elevator ding. I refrained from glancing back, but Adam looked over his shoulder.

"She's gone," he said, stopping. "You weren't exaggerating. She acts like she despises you."

"It's not an act. She hates me." Even though my prior interactions with her had gone much the same way, the encounter felt like a punch in the gut. I realized I was shaking and I felt like crying.

"Are you okay, Kit?" Adam asked. He pulled me into his arms. "It doesn't matter what she says or what she does. You're worth ten of her. You're amazing and I love you."

"I love you too." I pulled away and sniffed back the stupid tears. "At least we don't have to sneak back to see Charity now. We have Alicia's permission."

Adam gave me another quick hug. We rounded the corner to the nurses' station.

Lorna looked up and smiled as she recognized us. "Great timing. You just missed Mrs. Haversham."

"I wish we'd missed her," I said. "Unfortunately, we had to talk to her. But at least she gave me permission to see Charity."

"Well, that's good news then. Charity isn't doing so great right now. We started her on a new procedure yesterday morning. It's a hemodiafiltration procedure that might keep her alive long enough for her to get a donor."

"So can we see her now?" I asked.

"She's been sleeping off and on all day long. Some of the meds make her even more sleepy than usual. You two can go on back, but don't wake her up if she's sleeping." Lorna hit the buzzer to let us through.

Charity's room had changed a lot in the past three days. There were more monitors and medical equipment, which meant even more tubes snaking in and around her.

The Charity of today bore little resemblance to the girl I'd seen three days ago. I remember thinking she looked frail and sick then, but she was a picture of health then compared to now. Motionless and prone, she looked like Death.

Her left arm was exposed, like a brittle, yellow stick encircled about with tape and tubing. A massive bruise covered her arm, adding to the aura of mortality heavy in the room.

I clamped my hand around Adam's like a steel claw. *No wonder she hasn't called me.* She was asleep and lay so still that if the monitor hadn't been blipping away I would have thought she was already dead.

There were no words. I stood watching her, willing her to open her eyes. I wanted to shake her awake, but I was afraid to touch her—afraid of damaging her. Besides, we promised Lorna we wouldn't wake her.

So we stood by Charity's bed, watching and waiting.

For some reason I flashed back to several years before, standing by Janet's casket, seeing her body through the filmy fabric that protected our senses from the destruction wrought by the car crash.

Repulsed at my thoughts, I tried to redirect them. *Charity isn't dead. This isn't her funeral.*

The baby woke up and vigorously kicked, pulling me out of my stupor. It felt like she was doing somersaults in there.

Charity's eyes fluttered open. In the fog of semi-consciousness, it took her a few seconds to focus on us. I could tell when it registered, because she gave us a huge smile.

"You're back." She reached up her right hand toward me, but halfway there it fell limply back to the bed. "Ugh. I'm so tired."

"Yeah. I came back even though you haven't returned my calls. What's up with that?" I joked.

"Just taking a few days off. Being lazy, you know." She tried to wave toward the chairs, but her arm flopped down again. "Sit down, you're too tall."

Adam pulled the chairs next to the bed, and we sat down. I took her frail hand in my own. I didn't know what to say to her.

"Guess what?" she said.

"What?"

"I got Mother to say you can come see me. She's going to call you." She gave a half giggle. "You're my Christmas present. Like a pet."

"I saw her outside when I got off the elevator. I showed up before she called me. You should have seen her face—utter confusion." I pretended to laugh at the memory. It was hard to put on a happy face seeing Charity like this.

She dozed off for a few minutes. When she woke up again, she talked like she hadn't been asleep. "What did Mother say when she saw you?"

"She was surprised. She was on her way to call me. If I hadn't been so shocked, I would have messed with her mind and really freaked her out."

"I wished I could've seen it. She doesn't believe in miracles, you know. She thinks I'm going to die and that's why she said you could come." Charity spoke matter-of-factly like she'd announced it was going to rain tomorrow.

"I believe in miracles," I said fiercely, even though all the evidence pointed toward Charity's imminent death. "And you believe, don't you?" I desperately wanted her to believe, as if it would assuage my own grief.

"I definitely believe in miracles," she said. "I just don't think you get to pick and choose what they are. Maybe the miracle isn't that I'm going to live . . . maybe it's that you and Mother can make peace with each other."

I snorted. "Sorry, Charity, that would take more than a miracle."

She smiled at me and said, "Try harder." She drifted off again.

My cell phone buzzed. It was a text from Dave. *Call Mom.*

Guessing she wanted an update on the situation, I asked Adam to step out to the waiting room and call her.

The door closing roused Charity again. "Where's Adam going?"

"He went to call my mom. She's picking Dave up at the airport and they're probably wondering if we're almost finished."

"I'm almost finished." She said it with a smile, trying to tease, but it gave me cold chills just the same.

"Stop talking like that," I said.

"You sound like my mother," she mumbled.

"I'm nothing like your mother," I protested as I realized she was falling asleep again.

Lorna came into the room. "How's she doing? I'm here to check her vitals."

"She keeps falling asleep right in the middle of a conversation. It's weird. But she wakes up and talks like she hasn't even been napping."

"The sleepiness is a side effect of the medication she's on. The fact she can still follow the conversation is a good sign. A lot of patients get very confused at this point." Lorna recorded Charity's stats as she talked.

"What point is she at?" I wanted to know if she was as bad as she looked.

Lorna kept typing her notes into the chart. "She's got liver failure, honey. She needs a new one, pronto. She looks so bad because her liver ain't working. We can only do so much to clean her blood, but we can't match the function of a human liver. We got to pray she gets one in time."

"I am," I whispered.

"What did you say? Speak up," Lorna demanded.

"I said, I *am* praying she gets one in time," I said it rather loudly and Charity stirred.

Lorna stopped working for a couple of seconds, watching Charity. Lorna's lined face sagged, and she sighed deeply. "I am too, child. I am too."

chapter thirty-seven

We went out to an early dinner to celebrate Christmas Eve. I wasn't surprised when Jonah joined us at the restaurant. Dave hadn't met Jonah before, but he showed no reaction when Mom introduced them to each other.

Trying to keep my mind off Charity, I watched Jonah and his interaction with my family. He led the conversation to college life and living on your own, successfully drawing Dave into the discussion. Dave loved talking about himself.

Jonah did the same thing with Adam, getting him to talk about the Bridger family and growing up in Logan. I decided all guys liked to talk about themselves.

It wasn't until I'd wolfed down half of my flourless chocolate torte that I realized Jonah had done the same thing with me. I was rambling on and on about the baby, my friends, and my job.

I was forced to face the fact that Jonah was a gifted conversationalist. My mother smiled throughout the entire dinner. I couldn't remember ever seeing her look so happy.

Jonah didn't come back to my mom's condo, and I was glad that Dave and I didn't have to share her. We settled down to watch Christmas movies, and I fell asleep before we got through the first one.

I slept in on Christmas morning and awoke to the smell of bacon and pancakes. I wandered into the kitchen to discover they were pecan pancakes—my favorite. I gave my mom a big hug of thanks and helped her set the table.

Dave and Adam were so engrossed in a video game it didn't register when I told them breakfast was ready. I walked in between them and the screen and stood there. That got their attention.

"Get out of the way!" they yelled at the same time. I wasn't surprised at Dave's reaction, but I expected better of my husband. So I kept standing there. It only took a few more seconds for the game to end when they both got shot.

"I can't believe you did that!" Dave ranted. "We just passed through a really tough level. I don't know if I saved it."

"Merry Christmas, little brother. Breakfast is ready." I smiled at him and turned to give Adam a kiss.

"Why didn't you just call us?" Adam asked.

"I did, but you'd zoned me out. Walking in between you and the screen was the only way to save your lives. You could have starved to death." I turned back to Dave. "It's my gift to you, brother."

"We were starving because you were sleeping all day," Dave grumbled. "It's about time you got up. Mom wouldn't let us open any presents until you woke up and she wouldn't let us wake you. Talk about spoiled rotten."

"Mom was just delaying the bad news that you didn't get any gifts this year—except a lump of coal."

After we'd stuffed ourselves with breakfast, we opened gifts. I laughed when I saw Dave's gift to us—a movie theater gift card.

"Why are you laughing?" he asked. "I thought it was a great idea." Then he opened our gift to him—a movie theater gift card.

"I guess great minds think alike," I said.

Dave leapt off the couch when he opened his gift from my mom. "An iPad2! Mom, you're the greatest!"

Mom gave me a Kindle, and Adam a Blu-ray player. I was thrilled.

Then she went into her room and came back with another stack of presents "for the baby." I hadn't had so much fun opening gifts in years.

"Wow," Dave said, staring at the pile of opened packages. "I guess a grandbaby outranks both kids combined." Mom didn't deny it.

When we finished clearing the wrapping paper, Adam and Dave headed for their video game, hoping to start where they'd left off. I stopped them before they could get it going.

"Adam, you should call your parents before you get carried away playing games."

"Why? I saw them less than a week ago. Besides, we're going home in a couple of days and I'll see them then." He reached for the controller.

"It's Christmas. Parents like to hear from their children on holidays. Right, Mom?"

She nodded. "They'd like it if you call." She looked at me. "And you should call your father. You too, Dave."

Dave groaned at being dragged into it. He was already setting up the game.

"You big baby," I said. "It can wait five or ten minutes longer. You've got all day."

"You won't let Adam play," he pouted. "You'll find something else for him to do. You'll drag him off to the hospital or something. You suck the fun out of everything. You'll be a great mom." He muttered the last bit, but Mom heard it anyway.

"I heard that, Dave, and I take it as a compliment." She smiled as she said it. "A mom is doing her best work when she sucks the fun out of her children's lives."

Adam called his family, Dave started messing with his iPad, and I texted Lily. I found out more in my texting than he did in the conversation. By the time he hung up from talking to his mom, I already knew what they'd all gotten for Christmas.

I rattled off all the things Lily had told me, and Adam looked at me in disbelief. "Are you serious? You made me call when you were going to text my sister anyway? What was the point?"

"To let your mom know you were thinking about her. I just got all the details I knew you'd forget to ask—or tell." It made perfect sense to me. I don't know why Adam was having a problem with it.

I called my dad and the conversation lasted about three

minutes. I handed my cell phone to Dave and he talked half as long as I did. There wasn't a lot to say, and I guessed my dad was enjoying a quiet Christmas with Amberlie. I wondered if it bothered my mom. If it did, she didn't show it.

The guys started playing their video game again. I pulled out my Kindle and searched for free e-books. My mom cleaned the breakfast mess in the kitchen and started prepping for dinner.

I halfheartedly offered to help.

"No, you sit back and enjoy your Kindle. I'm getting the ham ready to bake, and I have a few other things to prep. I hope you guys don't mind, but I invited Jonah for dinner at six."

I shrugged. "I'm good with it." Dave and Adam were so intent on the game, they didn't seem to hear her.

A thought occurred to me. "So is there going to be an announcement soon?"

Mom looked up from unwrapping the ham. "What do you mean?"

"You and Jonah. You seem to hang out with him a lot."

"You've only seen him two or three times, Kit." I could tell she was sidestepping the issue.

"I've only been here two or three times. It was pretty clear you two were together when I was here in August. Now he's spending Christmas Eve with us, and eating Christmas dinner here. I want to know if there's a wedding on the horizon."

My mom rolled her eyes. "Seriously, Kit. Just because you date someone doesn't mean you *have* to marry him."

Dave looked up from his game and smirked. "Guess that blows your pregnancy theory, Kit."

"*What?*" my mom and I asked at the same time.

"Talk to your daughter," Dave said to Mom, trying to sound innocent. "She's the one who thinks you *have* to get married."

"You are a jerk." I kicked at his controller and missed. To my mom I said, "That's not what I meant."

"I know," she answered. Her face twitched, and I could tell she was trying not to smile.

"What?" I asked. She was hiding something—I knew it.

"Nothing." She sounded about as innocent as Dave.

"You're not good at keeping secrets. Tell us."

"I don't have any secrets. I'm smiling because I'm happy."

That sounded reasonable. I turned my attention back to my Kindle.

My mom hummed "Do You Hear What I Hear?" while she finished getting the ham ready to bake. I followed along with the words in my head.

She switched from humming to singing. "Do you know what I know?"

I jumped up as fast as my bulging belly would allow. "You *do* have a secret!" I lumbered over to the kitchen. "What is it?"

"I'm making a pumpkin roll for dessert. There, you forced it out of me." She laughed at my expression. "I told you, I'm just happy."

"About what?" I pressed her.

"About life. My children are here, it's Christmas—I'm happy. Is that a crime?" She cracked eggs into the mixing bowl and added the pumpkin and sugar.

"Keeping secrets from your children is a crime," I said.

"Since when?" She added flour and spices to the pumpkin mixture.

"So you do have a secret!" I pulled out a cutting board so I could chop the walnuts.

"Why are you so obsessed with this, Kit?" she asked, pulling the chopper out of the cupboard and handing it to me.

"Because I know you're not telling me something." Neither of us spoke as I chopped the nuts.

I thought my badgering might irritate her, but she kept on smiling. She poured the batter into the jelly-roll pan and slid it into the oven to bake.

She set the timer. "It's not official, but Jonah and I have been talking about getting married."

"I knew it!" I crowed. "When?"

"I have to say I'm pleasantly surprised at your reaction, Kit. But we don't have a date yet. I told you, it's not official."

I noticed Dave and Adam had paused their game and were listening.

"But he has proposed, right?" I said.

"It's not like that. We've talked about it. This has been a tough year, and I'm not ready to rush into anything. It may be awhile." She wiped down the counter as she talked. "But you two are okay with it?"

"Cool," Dave said and went back to his game.

"Yeah, I'm fine with it. I don't want you to be alone down here. I like Jonah."

"That's a relief." Mom hugged me. "I was worried about how you kids would take it. I'm so glad you're good with it."

chapter thirty-eight

I wanted to visit Charity on Christmas Day and figured I easily had time to drive to Santa Barbara, see her for a few minutes, and make it back in time for dinner.

I told Adam my plan. I knew he would be fine going up with me. Dave pitched a fit. "Kit, why do you have to drag him off? What's he going to do up there? She's practically in a coma. If you want to sit around and watch her sleep, fine. Just don't ruin your husband's Christmas, too."

Dave's words struck a chord with me, although I didn't want him to see it. Adam had been so patient through all this—flying down early, waiting around at the hospital, listening to my tirades. He rarely got to sit around and play games just for enjoyment.

"Adam, will you come to our room where we can talk without Drama Dave?" I asked.

He followed me back, and I motioned for him to shut the door. "I don't mind driving to the hospital by myself today, if you want to stay here."

"I'll go with you. I don't want you to drive alone." I knew he'd say that.

"I'm not going to be gone that long. What Dave said is true, she'll probably be sleeping. I don't want you to feel like you have to come." I dug through my suitcase to find my other clean pair of maternity pants.

"I know I don't have to come. I want to be with you. It's Christmas." He picked up a pair of crumpled jeans from the end of the bed. "Are these the ones you're looking for?"

"No, I've worn those twice already. I know I packed my black pants." I pawed through the stacks again and found them. "Here they are." I gave him my full attention. "I know you're fine coming with me, but I want you to relax and play games with Dave. It's not like he hangs out with us a lot. It'll be good for him. I can drive to Santa Barbara alone. I have my phone. If I run into a problem, I'll call."

I could see he was wavering. Adam never shirked responsibility, but I knew he was having a lot of fun playing Xbox with Dave. I wanted him to enjoy it.

"No, I don't want you to go by yourself. I'll go with you."

"Adam Bridger, I go to work five days a week and spend at least eight hours each day away from you. I know how to drive. I'm a big girl. Let me go by myself."

He was almost convinced. I went in for the kill. "Unless you don't want to play Xbox with Dave. I know he's really annoying sometimes."

"No, I'm having fun with him. I think I should be with you though," Adam said.

"I agree—usually. But today is a little different. You can have fun *and* bond with Dave. Usually those two are mutually exclusive. You need to seize the moment."

"If you're sure . . ."

"I'm positive. Now go play with Dave before he cries. I need to get ready so I'm back in time for dinner."

I waited for the elevator, humming to myself. I hoped Charity would be awake long enough to open my gift to her. It was a framed 5 x 7 photo of the two of us—one we'd taken back in August when I'd first met her.

The frame was hot pink with neon green flowers. Orange, yellow, and green letters splashed across the bottom of the frame to spell out "SISTERS." I had one identical to it setting on my dresser at home. I knew she'd love it.

I was surprised to see Lorna at the nurse's station. "Hi, Lorna," I said. "Why are you working on Christmas?"

She peered at me over her glasses. "Someone's got to work on the holidays and it might as well be me. Have a chocolate." She pushed the open box across the counter, and I helped myself to one and bit into it.

"How is Charity today? Any improvement?" I spoke around my mouthful of chocolate.

"She's doing a little better, she's more alert. Her parents are with her right now."

"I guess I can wait until one of them takes a break." *Of course they're both with her—it's Christmas Day. What am I thinking?*

As if reading my thoughts, Lorna said, "It *is* Christmas. I don't suppose it'll hurt a thing if she has three visitors for a few minutes. You're family too. I'll buzz you back."

"Thanks, Lorna!" I went straight through the door trying not to think about intruding on Alicia, Lawrence, and Charity. After all, I was Charity's Christmas present. They probably expected me.

Charity's bed was raised up at the head, and her hair was freshly-braided and twined with red and green ribbons. Although still overshadowed by tubes and monitors, she was awake and looked far more alert than yesterday. Alicia sat on the edge of the bed, her back to the door. Lawrence appeared to be dozing in the recliner in the corner. His soft snoring confirmed it.

Charity saw me in the doorway and her face lit up. "Kit! Merry Christmas!" The fatigue in her voice belied the cheery greeting.

Alicia twisted to see me. I caught a look of pure venom before a mask of cool politeness settled on her beautiful face. "Katherine, I'm surprised you're here. I thought you would be with your family."

"I am." I struggled to maintain my own composure. *I will not let Alicia ruin my visit.* I forced a bright smile. "Charity is my sister. She's part of my family too."

Alicia stood and smoothed her flowing silk pants. "You'll need to keep the visit short. Charity is exhausted." She perched on the edge of a chair, watching like a hawk.

"I can speak for myself, Mother. I'm not dead yet." Charity

hadn't lost her droll sense of humor in joking about her own death. Alicia flinched at her words, and I inwardly cringed.

"You're not amusing, Charity," Alicia rebuked.

"Amusement is just about the only thing I still have, Mother." Charity patted the space beside her where Alicia had sat, moments before. "Sit. I hope that present's for me."

I handed her the gift and she eagerly tore into it—or attempted to. Her hands trembled as she fumbled with the wrapping. I reached over to help her tear the paper.

She stared down at the picture silently. Seconds passed. I wondered if she hated it. I wanted her to say something. She kept staring at it.

"Do you like it?" I asked. "I can get a different frame. Or a different picture."

My words broke her trance. She looked up, and for the first time I saw tears streaming down Charity's face. "It's perfect," she whispered. "I'm just memorizing it. I don't ever want to forget it." She hugged it to her tightly.

The sight of her weeping, so out of character for this girl who'd been through so much and still joked in the face of death, was too much for me. I held her close, trying not to hurt her, our tears mingling.

Why did I meet her too late? Why can't I save her? I finally found my sister and I have to let her go. She clung to me as tightly as she was able. Her frailty and my girth ended the embrace before we were ready.

I handed her a tissue and kept one for myself. "I'm glad you like it. The colors reminded me of you. I have one just like it."

"I love it." She held it out to Alicia. "Mother, look. Isn't it amazing?"

Alicia held the picture as if it might bite. "It's very colorful." She handed it back quickly and walked to the door. "I'm stepping out for some fresh air." I didn't have to be a mind reader to know what she thought of the "Sisters" frame.

"I didn't get you anything," Charity said. "I've been so busy, I just couldn't find the time."

I followed her lead. "That's all right. I already have everything."

We talked for a while longer. I was glad Alicia left as I recounted Christmas morning in detail, including the secret I forced out of my mother about Jonah. The muted snoring continued from the corner, indicating Lawrence was still asleep so I didn't worry about him.

Charity listened more than she talked, which made me feel bad because I knew it was a sign of how sick she was. I forced myself to keep talking, telling her about my family's Christmas traditions.

I realized the changes in my own family meant I'd never experience some of the old traditions again. On the other hand, by next Christmas I would have a daughter of my own and could start my own traditions.

Alicia came back in and interrupted my dialogue. "Charity needs to sleep. It's time for you to go."

I saw by Charity's heavy-lidded stare that Alicia was right and wasn't just being spiteful.

"I need to get back anyway." I leaned down to give Charity a quick hug and kiss on the cheek. "See you, Charity. Call me later if you feel like talking."

"Good-bye, Kit," Charity murmured.

I walked past Alicia, who was hovering near the doorway. She turned and followed me.

"I thought I'd walk you out," she said, falling into step beside me. Her voice did *not* sound friendly.

We walked without speaking until we got to the elevators.

"Katherine, thank you for coming to see Charity. It meant a lot to her," she said stiffly.

I knew she didn't walk me out to thank me. I mentally braced myself for the rest of it, and I didn't have long to wait.

"While I appreciate the effort you made on her behalf, I don't appreciate the liberties you've taken trying to insinuate yourself into our family. I don't know what you hope to gain by it." Her frigid tone was expected, the words not so much.

"Are you serious?" I asked. She never ceased to amaze me—and not in a good way. "Alicia, you've made it very clear that you want nothing to do with me. I am here for one reason and one reason only. For Charity. Not for you. Not for your money. *Charity.*"

"Well, you refused to help her in the way she really needed it. So I wonder what it is you want now. The obvious answer is money." Her words were insultingly ridiculous. I was glad no one else was in the hallway.

"You know what? You're wrong." I stepped right up to her and stared her down. "Haven't you figured it out by now: money doesn't bring happiness and it doesn't protect you from sickness or disease. At best, it helps you cover up your mistakes. Money might help you hide from your problems for a while. But it can't take away the pain."

"Then why *are* you here?" Alicia demanded.

"Because I care about Charity. I would think you could understand that. After all, you're her mother. Of course, motherhood doesn't mean much to you."

"How dare you?" The rage showed on her face.

"How dare *you*?" I asked. "You threw a baby in the trash. I came to meet you, to understand you. You've given me nothing but hatred." I was finally able to say all those things I wanted to for so long. "I gave you the chance to make it right. Why are you so full of hate?"

"You don't seem to grasp reality, Katherine," Alicia hissed, her manicured claws digging into my arm. "What I've done is *done*. There is no way to 'make it right.' I can't undo it. I can't go back and erase the past. I can't erase *you!*"

I jerked away from her grip, her words stabbing me to the core. I turned away from her.

I jabbed the elevator button so hard it hurt my finger. I stepped inside and hit the button for the ground level.

I stormed out to the car, furious at that woman and furious at myself for letting her get to me—again.

How many times will I allow her to discard me? How can she hate me so much that she wants to erase me? I could forgive her if she didn't hate me so intensely.

I said a prayer—one of the shortest prayers I'd ever uttered. "Please help me," I whispered. I didn't know what else to say.

Calmness flowed through me. Peace enveloped my hurting

heart and words came clearly to my mind. *She doesn't want to erase you. She wants to erase what she did to you. You are the reminder of her guilt and her pain. She honestly believes there is no way to make it right. She needs to know that forgiveness is possible. She needs charity.*

I listened.

I jotted down the feelings of my heart. The words flowed quickly as I covered every inch of the paper I scrounged from my purse. The more I wrote, the more the hurt and frustration seeped away. A feeling of forgiveness and charity for Alicia filled me. The contrast was exquisite.

When I got back to my mom's house, I took time to transcribe my hastily scribbled notes onto clean sheets of paper.

> *Alicia,*
>
> *Thank you for allowing me to visit Charity again. I'm sorry we always seem to leave each other on such a bitter note.*
>
> *We can't seem to agree on anything. But there is one thing we share—we both love Charity.*
>
> *I've been thinking about something that Charity said to me while I was visiting. We were talking about miracles. She believes in them, but doesn't think they always come in the way we think they will. Charity thinks the miracle might be you and me making peace with each other.*
>
> *Charity told me she believes in God, and it helps her not be afraid. She wishes you could feel the same comfort.*
>
> *You told me you can't undo the mistakes you've made in the past and that it is too late for you. I know it is not too late.*
>
> *I've been so hurt, angry, and caught up in myself that I forgot about something that I know is true. It's a truth that took me a long time to learn, but one that changed my whole life. I want to share it with you.*
>
> *This is it: It is possible to be forgiven. Even for terrible things.*
>
> *This is how: Jesus Christ is our Savior.*
>
> *We learn about Him and His life in the scriptures. We learn that He did what He did for us because He loves us.*
>
> *His life reflects His pure love for all people. All people. That pure love is called "charity." I don't think it was an accident*

that you named your daughter Charity. I know you love her more than anything, and everything you do is because of your love for her. You were even willing to contact me because of that love.

Jesus has commanded us to love one another as He loves us—with charity. That seems impossible to me sometimes. How can I be capable of charity? I'm only human and I make mistakes. Everyone does—some are just more visible than others.

But charity is also showing genuine concern and compassion for all people. Not by dwelling on or wallowing in the evil others have done. We forgive them, and then we move forward.

It isn't easy, but it is possible. That's how I can say I forgive you for what you did when I was born. I know, with time, I will be able to let it go completely.

But it's not enough for me to let it go. You need to let it go too. You can learn to love yourself for who you really are—a child of God. You can learn to forgive yourself. When you trust in the truth that the Savior loves you, then you open yourself to feel that love. You can feel charity for yourself—and for me.

There is a scripture universally quoted by Christians, "For God so loved the world that he gave his only begotten Son, that whosoever believeth in him should not perish, but have everlasting life"(John 3:16).

Please read the next verse—a verse that isn't mentioned as often. "For God sent not his Son into the world to condemn the world; but that the world through him might be saved."

God does not want to condemn us; He wants to save us. Each one of us.

Alicia, I want us to be friends—friends who love Charity, and friends who know we both need charity. That understanding will help heal our hearts.

My prayers are with you and Charity—I pray that you will both be healed. I know it's possible. Don't be afraid to pray and don't be afraid to forgive.

Love,
Kit

chapter thirty-nine

We flew out the day after Christmas. I felt peaceful and afraid at the same time. I wasn't sure if I'd ever see Charity again, but mailing the letter to Alicia comforted me.

We stopped by the Bridgers' house Sunday evening after we'd unpacked. When we got there, it was like Christmas morning all over again. They were all still excited about their presents and were thrilled to see us.

Chaotic joy permeated the Bridgers' house. Only four of the eight children were still living at home—Lily, Beth, Travis, and Sarah—so it wasn't nearly as crazy as it used to be around there.

After we opened gifts, Barbara told us she'd saved some dinner for us.

Adam and I ate while six-year-old Sarah showed us everything she got for Christmas and then started telling us what everyone else got as well.

In between bites and Sarah's show-and-tell, I updated them about Charity and our Christmas with my mom and Dave.

"I don't think Charity can hold on much longer." I didn't go into detail about the last showdown I'd had with Alicia, but I did tell them how fast Charity was deteriorating.

"Kit has an idea," Adam said. "She wants to hold a family fast for Charity."

"It was Adam's idea," I said. "I can't really fast right now, so when I asked Adam if he would, he agreed and suggested we involve the whole family."

"That's a wonderful idea," Barbara said, and Hal agreed. "When do you want to begin the fast?"

"Next Sunday is Fast Sunday, but I don't want to wait that long," I said. "Do you think we can start it Tuesday evening and end it Wednesday at dinner? Adam will call Justin, and I can call my dad and ask him."

"Tuesday will work." Barbara grabbed a notepad. "Do you mind if I call the aunts and uncles? I'm sure a lot of the extended family will want to participate."

Adam spoke before I did. "I think you should. The more, the better."

"I hate fasting," Sarah announced loudly. Before her mom could reprimand her, she quickly added, "But I'll do it for Charity."

I silently agreed with Sarah. I struggled with fasting, even before I was pregnant.

"Thank you, Sarah." Her generosity for someone she'd never met overwhelmed me. "I asked my mom if she would fast with us and she said yes. I was shocked. Barely four months ago, she was too bitter to pray, and now she's agreed to fast with us."

"I'm glad she's willing to do it," Barbara said. "It is amazing what the power of fasting and prayer can accomplish."

"Can we meet here Tuesday night, so we can start with a family prayer?" Adam asked.

"Of course," Hal said. "Let's start it at 7:00 p.m., if you don't mind, so people will have a chance to get home from work and eat dinner before they gather here."

"I'll make a big pot of soup and homemade bread for Wednesday's dinner and whoever wants to can meet us here on Wednesday night to break the fast." Barbara and Hal were always quick to offer their help.

By the time we left for home, I felt uplifted from the support the Bridger family showered upon me, and I even felt a glimmer of optimism that Charity might make it.

On Monday I went back to work. Although I'd been gone less than a week, everyone commented about how much bigger I was, and I tried not to let it hurt my feelings.

It certainly didn't affect my appetite. As I ate lunch with Claire, I filled her in on my visits with Charity. I showed her a couple of the pictures I'd taken on Christmas Day. Claire had seen the photos I'd had taken in August. She commented on how terrible Charity looked now.

"She looks so sick. She's gone downhill fast." Claire was nothing if not blunt.

"I know. It really hit me when I saw her last week. I don't know if she'll go home from the hospital again." I blinked back the tears that blurred my vision.

"I wish there was something we could do," Claire said.

"We're fasting for her. Do you want to join in?" I didn't know how Claire would react. We rarely talked about spiritual things.

"I can do that much," she said without hesitating. "When are you starting?" She sounded eager.

"We're going to meet at the Bridgers' house tomorrow night at seven to start with a prayer. Will you come?"

"I don't want to butt in," she said. "Except for Adam, I haven't seen any of their family since Janet died. Will it be weird?"

"Not at all. I want you to come, and I know Barbara would love to see you." Claire was convinced and agreed to come.

Adam and I arrived at his parents' house about 6:45 on Tuesday. I recognized several cars belonging to his relatives parked out front. It wasn't surprising—I'd never known any family more supportive than the Bridgers.

Caught up in greeting and updating the aunts and uncles, I didn't pay attention to the people still arriving.

Michelle came up behind me and gave me a hug. "I'm so sorry about Charity. I'm glad you invited us to fast with you.

Not that *we* can fast right now, but we can pray." Her reference to our pregnant state caused me to glance down at her stomach. It was barely thickening and she was about sixteen weeks along. I felt like a giant sloth next to her.

As if reading my thoughts, Michelle looked at my bulging belly. "Kit, you look so cute. I can't wait until I can start wearing maternity clothes." She glanced around and whispered to me. "I've put them on around the house, but Justin makes fun of me. I want to look pregnant."

"It's not as fun as you think," I muttered. Grateful for the tug I felt at my sleeve, I turned to see Claire standing there, holding Braxton on her hip. Braxton was double the size he'd been when I'd first seen him several months ago, and he looked much healthier.

"Sorry I had to bring Braxton, but my mom had other plans tonight, and I really wanted to come." She shifted him to her other hip, and he buried his face shyly against her shoulder. "I hope it's okay."

Before I could answer, Barbara was there, enveloping Claire and Braxton in a hug. "Claire, I'm so glad you finally stopped by. Kit told us you moved back. Is this your little boy?"

When she pulled away, I saw a radiant smile replace the look of uncertainty on Claire's face. Braxton peeked out at Barbara, and it was only a couple of minutes before she had coaxed him into her arms, managing to draw Claire into conversation at the same time.

Lily grabbed my arm and dragged me to the kitchen. "Kit, guess who just showed up?"

"I have no idea. I lost track ten minutes ago. These can't all be relatives."

"You're right. About six of the girls from my Laurel class showed up. Savannah and Brielle are with them." Lily waited for my reaction. I wasn't sure what she was implying then I remembered how much she hated starting school this year.

"Aren't those the same girls that gossiped about you at school?"

"Yes. But they came and *apologized*. One of them heard about the fast and got together with the others and decided to come over."

"That's good, right? Adam said the more participating, the better. Are you bothered that they're here?"

"I'm just amazed. They've stopped gossiping about me, but have pretty much ignored me. Now they're here. That's a miracle right there. And we haven't even started the fast."

I had no idea why those girls chose this night to apologize to Lily, but I felt profound gratitude as I watched her face light up like it used to, and that Lily could see a miracle in it. I remembered Charity's words. *I definitely believe in miracles. I just don't think you can pick and choose what they are.*

Miracles were possible; I prayed I would recognize them when they occurred.

chapter forty

I didn't have to wait long for the miracles to begin happening. The first came in the form of my dad and Amberlie. I hadn't seen them since I'd returned from California, and I felt a wave of happiness when they came over and embraced me—even Amberlie.

"Kit, thank you for including us in the fast," Amberlie said, gracious as always. "We want to help however we can."

"Just being here to support me is wonderful." I had to wipe away a tear from the corner of my eye. "And Charity, as well," I added.

"Of course," my dad said. "We have your Christmas present in the car. Dave got his already, but we didn't see you before you left."

"I left in a hurry. I got an email that sounded like Charity was on her deathbed. I thought it was sent from her nurse, Lorna. It turns out it was from Charity. I was kind of mad at her for tricking me, but she's gone downhill so fast that I'm glad I went earlier."

Amberlie nodded. "You made the right decision. Paul didn't tell you on the phone, but Emily had her baby on the twenty-third."

"I wondered if she'd had her yet," I said.

"She was six days overdue. She weighed eight pounds, twelve ounces. They named her Holly Nicole. They came home on Christmas Day. Emily's such a proud little mommy."

"And Grandma's pretty proud too," my dad added.

"I made matching blankets for Holly Nicole and your baby. Do you have a name picked out yet?" Amberlie asked.

"No. Adam and I can't agree on one yet."

Dad nodded like he could empathize with us. "Don't worry, just pick out one you like. He'll let you name her whatever you want, after he sees what you go through bringing a baby into this world."

"Paul!" Amberlie reprimanded him. "It's not a good idea to remind an expectant mother about how hard it is. As if you know anything about it anyway."

He laughed at her and said, "Kit's not worried, are you?"

I was, but I wasn't going to let him know so I just smiled.

"We do have something we'd like to discuss with you though." My dad looked serious, which made me a little nervous.

"What is it? Can we talk about it later?" There were already a lot of people I hadn't said hello to. I felt responsible to play hostess even though it was Barbara's home.

"It will only take a minute." He glanced over at Amberlie, and she gave an almost imperceptible nod.

"Amberlie and I have talked about it, and we'd both like to be tested to see if either of us is a match to be a liver donor for Charity."

I tried to process what I'd just heard. I'd never imagined an offer like this might result from the fast. "Really?"

"Really," they said in unison.

"You don't even know her," I protested. "And being a living donor has risks."

"We know," Dad said.

"We want to be screened as soon as possible," Amberlie added. "We both have Type O blood."

"Charity is Type B. They can draw blood locally and have it sent down to be tissue-typed and cross-matched for antigens." I couldn't help but feel excited at their willingness. "If you're sure."

"We're sure." They spoke as one, again.

Adam walked over. "Sorry to interrupt, but I have to steal Kit away for a few minutes. Grandma Bridger is very insistent." She was actually his great-grandma, and she could give bossiness lessons to a cow.

"Adam! Dad and Amberlie want to be screened as donors for Charity!"

"Really?" His reaction was the same as mine.

"Really," Amberlie repeated. "Now go talk to Grandma Bridger and your other guests. We'll stay to talk afterwards."

Elation surged through me at the thought. Not just for the hope that Charity might have a chance, but that both my dad and Amberlie were willing to make that kind of sacrifice for a stranger.

Why would they do it? I asked myself.

The answer came to my mind quietly, but clearly. *Because they love you. She isn't a stranger. She's your sister.*

I recognized the miracle.

I became aware of the press of bodies as Adam led me over to Grandma Bridger. I couldn't even count how many people there were, let alone name them all.

"Adam," I whispered, "who are all these people and where did they come from?"

"They're your friends. People who care about you; therefore, they care about Charity." He hugged me close, and we weaved our way through the jam-packed room.

We made it over to Grandma Bridger and she tried to hug me too, but her arms wouldn't reach around me. "You're a lot bigger than Michelle," she announced.

"Thanks, Grandma," I said. Even the unfavorable comparison to my beauty-queen sister-in-law didn't faze me tonight. I hugged the tiny old woman.

"Don't snap my neck," she said. "You're a strong one. You're like a sturdy farm girl—no wonder you're so big." She turned to Adam. "She'll give you a nice big brood of kids. Healthy as a horse, this one."

Adam winked at me over Grandma Bridger's head. I whinnied softly and tried to toss my mane in true horse-like fashion. "I love you," he mouthed the words over wiry gray hair.

"I know," I said.

Hal and Barbara were trying to hush everyone and get their attention. Hal banged a spoon on a cup, but it didn't seem to help.

Before I could stop him, Adam put his fingers in his mouth and let out an ear-splitting whistle.

Adam cleared his throat and spoke. "Thank you all for coming tonight to participate in this fast for Kit's sister, Charity. Kit has asked me to offer the prayer, but before I do, I'd like her to tell you a little about Charity."

I was prepared for this. We'd talked about it beforehand. I wanted them to know something about the girl they were fasting for.

I opened my mouth to speak, but when I saw the mass of kind and concerned faces, my throat closed off. My chin quivered and I fought to gain control of my emotions. Adam gave my hand a squeeze.

My struggle for composure probably took thirty seconds, but it felt like thirty minutes. I lost the battle against the tears but found my voice.

"Twenty-two years ago I was born to a young, confused teen-ager who panicked and left me in the garbage." There was a time when I was too ashamed to tell anyone what happened to me, feeling it reflected poorly on me.

"I was rescued, but all attempts to find my birth mother failed. I was adopted by my amazing parents, Paul and Nora Matthews. I always wanted a sister, but got a brother instead. I learned to live with it."

Lily snickered; she knew how Dave and I got along. I smiled at her and silently thanked her for lightening the situation a bit for me. My voice stopped quavering.

"A few months ago, my birth mother found me. She searched me out because I have a younger half-sister, Charity, who was born with a liver disorder called biliary atresia. She's had surgeries to correct it, and it bought her sixteen years. Now the cirrhosis in her liver has become so bad that a transplant is the only way she'll survive." I deliberately left out any additional details about Alicia and our relationship.

"I loved Charity as soon as I met her. I wanted to donate part of my liver to her, but during the screening process, I got a big surprise instead." I patted my tummy. "I found out that Adam and

I were going to have a baby. I'm still willing to donate, but I can't until after the baby is born.

"Charity can't wait that long. She needs a liver now. We need a miracle. So we asked you to join us in praying and fasting for this miracle. She needs your faith. *I* need your faith."

My voice broke again, and the emotions I'd tamped down bubbled over. This time sobs accompanied my tears.

Adam realized I couldn't continue, so he hugged me close, kissed the top of my head, and took over for me.

"Thank you all for choosing to be a part of this. It means so much to us." His voice shook a little. He took a deep breath and asked me, "Are you ready, Kit?"

I nodded, wiping my nose.

Adam's prayer was beautiful and heartfelt. I couldn't remember the words, but the Spirit imprinted the feelings on my heart.

Tara found me after the prayer and hugged me tightly. I hadn't even seen her come in. We couldn't talk for long because of the rush of people waiting to talk to me. Most people left after giving me a few words of encouragement and hugs—lots of hugs.

Claire held back until most people were gone. She came up to me, without Braxton. I looked around for him and saw Lily and Beth were playing with him.

"Kit, I want to ask you something," Claire said in a low tone.

Sensing she wanted some privacy, I led her into the kitchen. "What is it?"

"I know I've messed up my life in the past. I've done some pretty stupid things," she said.

"Claire, don't worry about the past. Just move forward." I searched my memory to see if I could remember saying anything that might have made her feel bad when I talked about Alicia throwing me away. I seemed to forget she'd given a baby up for adoption before she had Braxton, and I sometimes said things that hurt her feelings.

"I want to move forward," she said. "You've helped me so many times. You got me the job, you gave me clothes, and you've always been my friend—without judging me."

"That's what friends do," I said.

"I want to pay you back." She glanced around to make sure nobody else was within earshot. "I've thought of a way."

"Claire, you don't have to pay me back for anything. I did what I did because I wanted to. You would do the same for me." I didn't want Claire's money. More than anything else, I wanted her to succeed.

"I'm not talking about money," she said, shifting nervously. "I want to give part of my liver to Charity."

Once again, I was struck speechless. I never dreamed anyone would offer to be a donor for Charity. Now there were two—three, actually.

"Thank you," I said. "But donating a liver is a huge thing. I don't really think you're in a position to be a donor."

Her crestfallen look told me I'd spoken thoughtlessly—again.

"Yeah, I know. I tried to donate plasma in California, but I got turned down because I was using back then, when I was with Axel. But I'm clean now. I've been clean since I came home. I know I probably can't qualify, but I've been wondering if—if maybe part of my liver is good enough. Wouldn't even a liver like mine be better than dying?"

Claire's pleading words sank in to me. She was afraid she wasn't good enough to donate her liver but was willing to try. Her sincerity and humility nearly broke my heart.

She misinterpreted my silence. A tear rolled down her cheek. "Can't I at least get tested? I don't have any diseases that I know of."

"Claire, of course you can be tested. I'm honored that you would even consider it. I only meant that you have Braxton to think about. You're his mom and he needs you. I never thought for a minute that you're not good enough to be a donor—you just need to consider Braxton. It's risky surgery even for the donor."

Claire stood a little straighter and wiped her face. "So, you think it's possible then?"

"Of course it is. Never think that you're not good enough!" I hugged Claire close to me—as close as my rotundity would allow.

She pulled back and looked up at me. "I want to do it then. I want to be tested. Will you help me?"

"Yes. But promise me you're not doing this to 'pay me back.' You don't owe me anything."

"I promise."

"And you should talk to your mom about it too. Will you promise to talk to her?"

Claire suddenly tilted her head to the side. "Is Braxton crying? I'd better go check on him." She darted out of the kitchen before I could extract the second promise from her.

I heard Braxton squeal with laughter from the other room.

I offered a silent prayer of thanks for yet another miracle.

chapter forty-one

I called the hospital on Wednesday, hoping to catch Lorna at work. I had to leave a message, but she called me back early in the afternoon.

"How's Charity?" I asked when I heard Lorna's voice.

"Do I have to call with status reports on top of everything else I'm doing? We're shorthanded here, you know." Although Lorna sounded grumpy, I knew it was just her way. She continued in a softer tone. "That child is hanging on. She's about the same as she was on Christmas. She sleeps most of the time."

"If she feels up to talking, will you have her call me?" I asked.

"I'll let her know. Did you need anything else?" I knew Lorna was busy, but I also knew she would help expedite things or direct me to the person who could.

"There are three people here who want to be screened as liver donors for Charity. I want to know the best and fastest way to make sure the blood samples get tested right away."

"You know there's more to it than matching blood and screening for antigens, don't you?" Lorna sounded like she was about to launch into a lecture, so I interrupted her.

"I know. There's donor counseling and physicals and everything. But it's pointless if the initial screening fails. I need your help to speed up the screening. They can stop by the lab today to have blood drawn. Where should the lab send it?"

She gave an exaggerated sigh. "I don't know if there's even time. But if you get me the names of the potential donors and the lab that can send the samples, I'll get orders sent over this afternoon." She paused then added, "Even though I'm off shift in an hour."

Her answer was exactly what I hoped for. I had the information in front of me. "I have it right here. Are you ready?"

"Hold on a minute." She covered the receiver and talked to someone. I could envision her there with her hands on her heavy hips, bossing someone around. I tapped my pen impatiently.

"Okay, I'm back. Give me the names."

I rattled them off and offered to email them to her as well.

"Hold your horses, young lady. I'm still writing." On the other end I could hear her pen *scritch-scritching* on the paper.

"Thank you, Lorna. This is so exciting."

"Don't get your hopes too high. Getting a match is just the beginning. There's a lot to be done, and Charity doesn't have a lot of time to wait." Lorna sounded brusque, but I suspected she used that tone to cover up her true emotions.

"So we'd both better get busy then—right, Lorna?" I couldn't resist sassing her a bit.

"Then get your hind end off the phone, girl, and get those donors to the lab." She hung up before I could get the last word in.

I took her advice. I called Dad and told him where he and Amberlie needed to go. Then I checked with Claire and offered to take her by the lab after work.

Things were moving along.

Adam and I went back to his parents' house that evening to break the fast. This time only the immediate Bridger family was there, along with Justin and Michelle. I had invited Dad and Amberlie to come, but they were taking dinner over to Katie's house.

It was a quiet evening, a sharp contrast from the night before when people were everywhere. I enjoyed the feeling of peace. It stayed with me even when we left. I knew we were doing everything we could to help Charity.

On Thursday I followed up with the lab to make sure they'd

shipped the blood samples. The woman on the phone told me they were due to be picked up in the afternoon, so I called back around 4:00 p.m., just to check. This time she got a little snippy with me.

"We ship samples every day, and we know what we're doing. If you think you can do it faster and more accurately, please come in and fill out a job application."

Maybe calling twice in one day was a bit much.

On Friday I checked my email and my cell phone several times an hour to make sure I hadn't missed any messages. I went to Claire's desk so many times to see if she'd heard anything, that Nadine finally had to tell me to leave her alone.

I periodically tried to call Charity. Her cell phone always went straight to voice mail, and I didn't want to call her room directly.

We didn't do anything special to celebrate New Year's Eve. Adam got off work early, and we spent another quiet evening together. This time it was just the two of us.

"You know what I just thought of?" I asked as we tried to decide on a movie to watch.

"I have no clue," Adam said.

"I just realized that this is our first and last New Year's Eve as a married couple."

He raised an eyebrow at my comment. "You're planning to divorce me?"

"No, you goofball, we'll still be married. We just won't be a couple anymore." I patted my belly. "We'll be a *family*."

"You're right. Baby Katie will be here next year."

"Next year and forever. *For. Ever.*" I added the emphasis. "And her name isn't Katie—or Katherine. My dad said I could name her whatever I want to."

Adam smirked. "Well, my dad might have to beat up your dad."

"My dad and your dad will beat *you* up if you don't give me my way." I stuck my lip out in a pout.

"So what fruity name do you have picked out now?" He handed me a couple of movies. I set them aside.

"It's not really fruity—but it's *derived* from fruit. Guess."

He rolled his eyes. "Are we playing Twenty Questions?"

"Yes. Now you have nineteen left."

"Lemon? Lime? Tangerine? Grape? Apple? Pear? Kumquat? Loquat? Avocado?" He rattled them off pretty fast.

"Don't you listen? I said derived from fruit. Ten questions left."

"Don't you want to watch a movie?" He offered me a couple of Blu-rays. I waved them aside.

"No. You're down to nine questions. Remember—derived from fruit."

Adam pondered. "Jelly? Jam? Marmalade? Kool-Aid? Jello?"

I counted his guesses off on my fingers. "Lame. Four more chances."

"Pectin? Nectar?"

"You guessed it!" I yelled, clapping my hands.

"Really? I hope you don't mean Pectin?" He made a gagging sound.

"*Nectar.* Don't you like it?"

"Are you serious? *Nectar*? No way." He turned on the TV, shaking his head in disgust.

"You're right. It isn't really Nectar," I admitted.

"What is it then?"

"I don't have one. I just hoped you could brainstorm a good one. You really let me down, man." I deftly blocked the pillow he threw at me.

I was saved from further attack by the ringing of my cell phone. I picked it up and glanced at the display. The number was unfamiliar to me.

"Hello?" I answered, half expecting it to be a wrong number.

It wasn't. I quickly recognized the voice on the other end. "Katherine? It's Alicia."

chapter forty-two

That single sentence halted time for me. The instant I processed that Alicia was calling me, I simultaneously recognized the strain in her voice.

I couldn't breathe. I knew without asking that this was the phone call I'd been dreading. Adam's smile faded into a look of concern as he watched my face. His expression changed in slow motion. I felt like I was seeing him from a distance—far, far away, like the voice on the other end of the phone.

"Katherine? Are you there?" Alicia's words pierced through my fog.

"Yes. I'm here." I couldn't force the question out of my mouth, but my mind screamed it. *What is it?* There was no doubt in my mind that Alicia calling me was a bad thing.

"It's Charity. I thought you'd want to know."

She's dead then. There was no miracle, after all.

"When—when did it happen?" I asked, not wanting details, but needing to know.

"She came out of surgery last night. She was on a respirator until a couple of hours ago. She's had short periods of alertness. The doctor's are optimistic."

"What?" Somehow I was certain I'd heard wrong. I had steeled myself for news of Charity's death and the words Alicia just said made no sense with what I was expecting to hear.

Alicia clarified. "The surgery went well. Her new liver is already producing bile. She'll be in ICU for two or three days depending on how she does."

"Where are you? She had the transplant? Where did it come from?" Now that I knew Charity was still alive the questions tumbled out of my mouth.

"We are at UCLA. Charity was elevated to Level 1 and a cadaver liver became available. We got the call Thursday, and she was transferred by ambulance. She went into surgery Friday morning, and it lasted nearly ten hours. The most exhausting, nerve-wracking ten hours of my life." Alicia stopped abruptly; the sudden silence was a little awkward.

My body felt weak with relief as it all sank in. "She's doing well, though," I reiterated her words to make sure. "Can she talk or anything?"

"Not really. She can breathe on her own now but hasn't been lucid enough to talk. I—she asked me to call you right before she went into surgery. She made me promise, whichever way it went." Alicia sounded uncomfortable. "I wanted to make sure I knew— before I called."

"Thank you so much for letting me know." I was grateful Alicia had kept her promise. Even though I felt at peace after sending her the letter, I'd heard no response so had no idea if her feelings toward me had changed at all. I suspected that this call to me was very difficult for her to make.

"I promised Charity." There was another moment of silence.

"Will you ask her to call me or text me when she feels better?" I asked. I couldn't stand being in limbo, wondering how she was recovering. I didn't know if Alicia would be willing to keep me updated.

"I'll pass the message on to her when she's up to it. She can't have visitors right now though." The last bit sounded like a warning in case I had any ideas of dropping by to visit.

"I understand. I doubt I'll be traveling for awhile anyway."

"Well, I should get back to check on Charity," Alicia said.

"Tell her I said hello." I didn't know how to end the conversation. "I will."

"Alicia? Thanks again for calling me. I'll talk to you later." I hung up before she could reply.

I burst in to tears.

"Kit? Are you okay? It sounds like Charity got the transplant in time and made it through the surgery. It's an answer to prayers."

"I know," I sobbed. "I'm so relieved and so confused. I thought Alicia was calling me to tell me Charity was dead."

He pulled me close, holding me while I cried. Neither of us spoke, the only sound was my sobbing and hiccupping.

"Relax and take deep breaths," Adam said soothingly.

What would I do without Adam? I wondered. I absorbed his strength and energy. The sobs subsided and a few minutes later the hiccups did too.

"You know what's funny?" I asked Adam.

"Besides the fact that when you cry you get the hiccups and always wipe your face on my shirt?" he joked gently.

"Alicia had to make sure I knew Charity couldn't have visitors. I think she was afraid I'd suddenly appear down there. And the stupid thing is, I want to go anyway and be there for Charity."

"It wouldn't be good for either you or Charity for you to go down there," Adam said. "I'm serious. Even if she could have visitors, you're too far along in your pregnancy to be traveling that far. Christmas was a big stretch as far as I'm concerned."

"I know. I don't think Alicia will keep me updated. If she's at UCLA, I don't have Lorna around to call to see how she's doing."

"Stop worrying. I'm sure as soon as Charity feels better she'll be texting you yourself. Enjoy this moment. Enjoy the fact that she got a new liver in time and she made it through the surgery." Adam lightly massaged my shoulders.

"You're right. A major miracle just occurred. Our prayers were answered." As the realization dawned on me, a feeling of joy replaced my worry. "It's a perfect way to start a new year."

Adam kissed me. "Let's not forget to enjoy our first and only New Year's Eve as a married couple."

I returned his kiss. "I'm ready to watch a movie now—as long as it's a romantic comedy. And I get to pick it."

chapter forty-three

I quickly spread the news about Charity's successful transplant. Three days passed before I heard anything more about how she was doing. It was a short text from Charity herself.

I'm not dead yet.

I laughed out loud and replied. *Neither am I.*

It's a good day then, she sent.

I responded, *So far, so good.*

I'm out of ICU, so I got my phone back.

Great. ☺ *Text me when you can.*

That was the end of our first exchange of texts. At least I knew she was improving.

The next few days continued in much the same way as we texted back and forth. Her texts were short and sporadic, which convinced me she was sneaking texting when she wasn't supposed to be doing it.

The second week in January hit with a full blast of winter, an avalanche of assignments for Adam at school, and a huge surge in my own workload at the CPA firm.

All employees were required to work half-day on Saturdays during tax season. I didn't know how I'd make it through.

I only had eight weeks to go until my due date, but already felt eight weeks overdue. People at work took pity on me and went out of their way to let me take it easier. Even Nadine gave me special treatment. She brought a stool for me to rest my feet on while I worked.

On the third Friday in January, she called me into her office. "I spoke with the Partners." She peered at me over her glasses. "They agree you should be exempt from the Saturday work requirement."

If I could have hefted my carcass off the chair, I would have jumped for joy. "Nadine, thank you. I am so tired and this will help. Thank you."

She looked a little misty-eyed, but cleared her throat and got all business-like. "Thank the Partners. Since you're coming back only part-time after the baby, there's no point in putting you into early labor and losing what productivity we're getting from you now."

Her words didn't bother me. I was too excited at the prospects of sleeping in on Saturdays again. I intended to implement those plans the very next day.

At 8:00 a.m. my cell phone rang, interrupting my plans of sleeping until noon.

It was Charity.

She didn't even say hello first. "Do you have Skype?"

I tried to blink away the grogginess so I could think clearly. "No, but Adam can probably set it up for me. Why?"

"I'm finally home. I have my laptop. I talked my parents into setting Skype up on my machine so I can video chat with you. But I can't right now. I promised not to overdo it. So set it up and invite me. I'm emailing you my Skype name. I'll call you tomorrow."

"Okay, what time?"

"Is eight too early?" she asked.

"Yes. I *was* trying to sleep in today. We have church tomorrow from eleven till two. I'm sleeping in until ten—which is two hours later than eight in case you're wondering."

"Wow. You're grumpy. How about three, your time? Or do you need a nap too?" She laughed at her own joke. It sounded so good to hear her laugh that some of my grouchiness dissipated.

"Three is perfect. In the afternoon." I thought I'd better clarify that.

"I'll call you then. Get some rest, so you won't be so ornery."

Charity called promptly at three on Sunday. It was the first time I'd used Skype, and I loved the fact that we could see each other while we talked.

She was back in her own bed. The bright coverlet and pillows were all there. Charity looked amazingly better. Her color was normal, she'd gained some weight, and she looked alert and—alive.

"You look fabulous!" I told her.

"It's amazing the difference a working liver makes. I feel better than I've felt in years. I'm still sore from the surgery, but I actually have a little bit of energy."

"I'm so glad you're home. I'll bet you are too."

"Unbelievably glad. The past couple of months are all kind of foggy and blurry. I feel like I've been asleep forever. I'm still pretty much quarantined, so I don't get any visitors except Mother and Father. Of course, I get to visit with plenty of doctors."

"This is almost as good as visiting in person," I pointed out.

"That's why I'm so excited. Stand up, Kit. And move back from the computer so I can see you."

I complied and turned to show her my profile.

"Holy cow! You're huge! I vaguely remember you visiting at Christmas, but I don't remember you being that big."

"Of course not—I'm about four weeks further along now. I have a little over seven weeks to go. It's taking forever." I sat down again.

"No, wait!" Charity said. "Stand up again and lift up your shirt. I've never seen a pregnant belly."

"And you're not seeing mine." There was no way I was showing her my bare belly. Lily had asked me the same thing, so maybe it was a teenage girl thing. I hadn't shown it to Lily either.

"I'll show you mine," she offered. "I have a wicked-looking incision. She lifted up her pajama top and shifted the laptop so the camera was pointed at her stomach.

"Can you see it?"

Her exposed stomach revealed a giant inverted T carved into

her skin. By medical standards the incision was probably healing great, but it looked Frankenstein-ish to me and I cringed. "Yuck—that's awful!" I said, unable to avert my gaze. "Does it hurt?"

"It's getting a lot better. You should have seen it right afterwards. It was gross. I took a picture with my cell phone about a week after surgery, but I couldn't zoom out enough and Mother refused to take a picture for me. I can send you the one I took if you want." She reached for her cell phone as she said it.

"No thanks." I did *not* want an even more graphic image in my head than she'd already given me.

"Okay, but you're missing out." She lowered her cell phone. "But now you have to show me your stomach—it's only fair. And I've recently had a near-death experience." Her wheedling tone broke through my defenses.

I was self-conscious of the way I looked, but I knew it couldn't be as disgusting as what she'd just shown me.

I stood up and stepped away from the computer. "Can you still see me?"

"Step a little closer."

I lifted my shirt and displayed my distended torso.

"Whoa! That's gi-normous!" She was clearly delighted. "Turn sideways."

I obeyed. My dignity was already gone.

"It looks fake," she announced.

"It's real—believe me. I have the stretch marks to prove it." Of course, Adam chose that minute to wander back in the room.

"What are you doing?" he asked.

"I'm showing Charity my stomach." I tried to sound normal but was embarrassed at being caught with my shirt up in front of a computer screen.

Charity must have heard him because she said, "Hi Adam."

I looked back at the screen to see Charity taking a picture with her cell phone. Of her computer screen. Where I stood flashing my belly.

I jerked my shirt back down. Of course it caught on my stomach. Charity and Adam both laughed at me.

"You'd better delete that!" I warned her.

"I'm going to post it on Facebook," she said. "With the picture I took of my stomach."

"Don't you dare!"

"I'll host a contest—Sisters with Deformed Bellies. We'll see whose gets the most votes for mega-disgusting."

I laughed in spite of myself. "If you do, you'd better at least crop our heads out of the pictures so nobody can identify us."

Adam shook his head. "You two are just alike." He stepped into camera range. "Hi, Charity. I'm glad you're doing so well. You look a lot better."

"Thanks. I'm sure it's a big improvement over the last time you saw me."

"Just keep your shirt covering your belly," I said.

"And stop encouraging my wife to lift up hers," Adam added.

"I'll try, but I can't promise anything. I can blame it on the medication." Charity looked over at someone off camera. I recognized Alicia's voice, but I couldn't make out her words.

Charity turned her attention back to me. "I've got to go. Apparently, I recently had major surgery and I have to take it easy."

"We have to leave for dinner with Adam's family anyway." We agreed to Skype again the same time next Sunday.

At the Bridgers', I recounted my visit with Charity. I described her incision in graphic detail—mainly for Lily's benefit.

"I wish I could see it," Lily said.

"She took a picture and offered to send it to me. I could have her send it to you instead," I offered.

"You can probably see it on Facebook," Adam said. "She said she was going to post it next to the picture she took of Kit's stomach so people can vote on which is the most disgusting."

"She took a picture of your stomach?" Lily asked.

"Her *bare* belly," Adam volunteered. I kicked him to shut him up, but he kept on talking. "I walked in the room and she was flashing the computer."

"What?" Lily was indignant, which I also could have predicted. "You wouldn't show me your stomach when I asked. That's so unfair!"

Beth chimed in. "Yeah, I want to see your stomach too."

"Now look what you started," I accused Adam.

"Me?" His innocent tone was exaggerated. "I'm not the one exposing myself for Facebook."

Lily and Beth kept begging, and I knew caving in was the only way I'd get any peace.

"Come in the kitchen," I said. "I'm not showing you here." Sarah trailed after us.

"I feel like a freak show," I muttered, lifting up my shirt.

"Disgusting!" Beth said at the same time Lily exclaimed, "Awesome!"

Sarah stared. "It doesn't look real. Can I touch it?"

I rolled my eyes. "Go ahead. Next time I'm charging admission."

"Can I take a picture?" Lily asked.

"No!" I protested. Sarah reached out toward my stomach and the baby kicked right as she touched it. She squealed with delight.

"Did you see it? The baby kicked!" Sarah's excitement was almost worth the humiliation of being stared at.

While I was distracted, Lily snapped a picture with her cell phone. She bolted from the room. "I'm posting it on Facebook," she called behind her.

"Don't worry," Beth said. "I know her password. I'll delete it for you."

At least someone was on my side.

chapter forty-four

Valentine's Day lost a little of its appeal for me since I was thirty-six weeks pregnant, working full-time, and my calves and ankles blended into "cankles."

Adam looked relieved when I voiced my derogatory thoughts about celebrating Valentine's Day. Apparently he hadn't picked up on what I was really saying, so he failed to request it off work and was scheduled that evening.

You'd think he would know that when I said I didn't feel like celebrating Valentine's Day since I was as big as a buffalo that I really meant I wanted to be pampered by him.

I explained it to him in a tone swinging from sarcastic to self-pitying. So Adam spent our first married Valentine's Day working and feeling guilty, while I spent it at home alone with my feet up and my spirits down.

Adam really did feel bad—maybe it was the result of living with a shrieking shrew, or perhaps because he slept soundly every night and I no longer could. I woke up several times every night either to go to the bathroom or because every position I lay in was like a slow form of torture. Regardless of the reason, I was tired and grumpy even in the short amount of time we did have to spend together.

I just wanted to deliver the baby and be back to my normal self. "Helpful" people at work mentioned that I should enjoy the sleep I was getting now because it would get worse when the baby came. I wondered if I could use sleep deprivation as a defense for maiming my coworkers.

I shook myself out of my lethargy on Thursday evening and hauled myself to the grocery store while Adam was at work. We were out of everything, and I wanted to make a nice dinner for him on Friday to make up for my crabby attitude.

He had offered to take me out to dinner for a belated Valentine's date, but I snapped at him. "Valentine's Day is *over*. It's not the same."

My mood had swung back to the other end of the spectrum—something close to being human. I wandered the aisles loading my cart, hoping I could make it through the entire trip without a bathroom break, trying to figure out a nice surprise for him.

I'll make him a giant, heart-shaped chocolate chip cookie. I traipsed down the clearance aisle in search of a heart-shaped pan among the Valentine candy and other remnants. It was surprisingly crowded in the aisle, maybe because everything was 75 percent off—and there was a lot of chocolate.

The candy looked delicious. I shouldn't have come to the store hungry. I ignored my backache and searched for the perfect something—chocolate and clearance-priced.

I suddenly experienced a warm feeling spreading down my legs that had nothing to do with the anticipation of a chocolate feeding frenzy.

Embarrassed, I glanced down to see if it was obvious. I felt the warmth gush beyond my legs, splashing the floor between a Valentine's card display and a clearance bin of conversation hearts.

I stood paralyzed, clutching a bag of chocolate-covered cinnamon hearts and staring at the growing puddle. *There is no way I just wet my pants in the middle of the grocery store*, I thought frantically.

As I processed the possibilities, a child's voice came through loud and clear to everyone in the aisle, "Mommy, that lady just peed her pants!"

The mother hushed her child, and an older lady with a kind voice touched my arm. "Are you all right?"

"I'm fine," I stammered, my face burning. "I guess I had an accident."

"I think your water broke, dear," she said, patting my back. "Is your husband in the store?"

"It can't be my water," I said. "I'm not due for another three weeks and I'm not even in labor." I glanced again at Lake Michigan surrounding my feet. "But I don't think I wet my pants," I muttered.

Another woman joined the first one. "Just wait, the contractions will hit soon." She nodded knowingly. "Once your water breaks, it's hard labor from there on out."

"Hush," Kind Lady told Ms. Know-It-All. She turned back to me and said, "Don't worry. Can I call someone for you? You shouldn't drive yourself."

"Especially when the contractions hit." Ms. Know-It-All just couldn't keep quiet. "The pain is so horrible you'll crash for sure."

Kind Lady smiled at Ms. Know-It-All, but even in my fog of confused embarrassment, I could tell it was forced. Through gritted teeth, she said, "Why don't you go get someone to clean up the floor, and I'll help this young woman call her husband."

"You should call 9-1-1," Ms. Know-It-All replied. "They'll need a stretcher to wheel her out when the bad contractions hit. People say you forget, but I never forgot."

"Leave!" Kind Lady commanded in a not-so-kind tone. "You are *not* helping matters."

Without waiting to see if she was obeyed, she turned back to me. "Are you in pain? Can you walk?"

"I'm okay," I said, letting her lead me away from the flooded floor and the staring people.

I called Adam at work. "Can you come get me?" I blurted out, trying not to panic.

"Where are you?" he asked. "Are you okay?"

"My water broke at the grocery store. I'm not in labor, but I think I might have ruined some Valentines." It all came out in a rush—kind of like my water.

"What? You're not making sense."

I explained it to him again and tried to use coherent sentences this time.

"I'll be right there," he said and hung up.

I told Kind Lady that my husband was on his way and then I remembered. I had our only car. I called Adam again.

"How are you getting here? I have the car."

"Oh yeah." We were both silent, then he asked, "Can you drive?"

"I think I can drive, but I'm all wet. But a woman in the store said I would crash if I drove when the contractions started." At that point, Kind Lady snatched my cell phone out of my hand.

Kind Lady morphed into Bossy Lady before my very eyes.

"Hello. This is Ellen Gray. I'm here with your wife, and she is *not* going to drive herself. I am taking her over to the hospital right now. You find a ride, you run, or you walk—I don't care. Just get there. Do you understand me?"

I heard Adam say, "Yes, ma'am." She hung up on him. I started laughing. The situation suddenly seemed funny.

"Get in the car right now," she told me.

I followed her, soaking wet and giggling. Mrs. Gray pulled a blanket from her trunk to cover the passenger seat. Thinking about Adam being chewed out by Mrs. Gray made me laugh harder. *I left a puddle of amniotic fluid in the middle of Aisle 12. It's probably all on camera. I can never shop at that store again.*

I looked down and saw the chocolate-covered cinnamon hearts still clutched in my left hand. *I shoplifted too.* I laughed harder. *I'll make Adam go back and pay for these. They won't recognize him.*

I probably sounded borderline hysterical, but I couldn't stop laughing. Mrs. Gray kept asking me if I was okay.

Then the first hard contraction hit. Ms. Know-It-All was right. If I'd been driving, I would have crashed.

Fourteen hours, two Pitocin drips, and half a bag of chocolate-covered cinnamon hearts later—Adam would have eaten them all except I hid the rest while he was in the bathroom—our baby girl greeted the world.

She weighed in at 5 pounds 15 ounces, and her indignant screech immediately reminded me of her mother. Curly brown hair covered her head and a tiny dimple mirroring her father's flashed on her cheek as she let us all know her lungs worked as they should.

When I held her for the first time, I fell in love for the second time in my life.

She was perfect.

"Adam, I love her. I can't believe how I can love her so much already." I marveled at the way I felt holding this tiny, living miracle.

"I always knew you would," he said. "You just needed to have faith in yourself."

"That's it!" I exclaimed.

"What?"

"The perfect name for our daughter—Faith." I watched his face to see what he thought. "It's not a fruit."

"Faith Bridger. I like it." Adam took our daughter's tiny hand and her fingers curled around his index finger. He took my hand with his free one. We made a circle—Adam, Faith, and me.

Faith Bridger screwed up her face and squawked, which we interpreted as approval.

chapter forty-five

As the first grandchild on both sides of the family, Faith was showered with attention. She was so teeny, I was paranoid to take her out anywhere, but that didn't stop people from visiting us.

My mother flew in from California twice—once right after Faith was born, and again a month later, "Just for fun," as she put it. Both times she was here, I noticed my dad and Amberlie avoided stopping by. They must have planned it that way, but I was happy not to have to deal with drama, so I quietly let it pass.

Barbara Bridger stopped by practically every day the first month, usually with Lily, Beth, or Sarah in tow.

"I hope I'm not being a pest," she said one afternoon when she brought us a loaf of homemade bread and jam—and to peek in on the baby.

"As long as you bring me food, stop by anytime," I joked, half-serious. Barbara really had saved me from having to cook several times since Faith was born, and it just added to the reasons of why I loved her. "She's asleep right now, though."

"Can I just peek in on her for a minute?" Barbara asked. Lily had already headed back, so I motioned for Barbara to follow.

Even Michelle and Justin visited. They rarely came to our apartment. I proudly showed off my daughter to them.

"Just look at how tiny she is," Michelle said to Justin. "Our little baby will be here before we know it." Michelle looked up at me. "It's hard to believe you had such a small baby. You were so huge."

"I had a lot of amniotic fluid," I said stiffly. "A lot." I tried not to be offended; I knew Michelle didn't mean to be insulting—it just came naturally to her.

So I secretly hoped she would retain enough water during her pregnancy to irrigate Southern California. It was gratifying to see that Michelle's stomach was finally starting to blossom.

I shared the story with Charity via Skype—we usually talked on Sunday afternoons.

"Take a picture of Michelle—at a bad angle—and post it on Facebook. And tag her in it."

"Michelle doesn't *have* a bad angle," I complained.

"Maybe her baby will be born bald," Charity suggested. "Or maybe she'll need a C-section and she'll have a big scar. But mine will always be bigger. Have I showed it to you lately?"

I quickly covered my eyes but couldn't help laughing at her. "Stop, Charity. You show me every time we talk."

"My torso wound is the only interesting thing in my life. I feel like I know everyone there. I want to come meet them for real," Charity said. "I'm dying to hold Faith."

"We're having her blessed the first weekend in May," I said. "You should see if you can get your doctor to let you come."

"Believe me, I've asked him. He said I could travel by then if I keep doing so well."

"Really?" I was excited at the prospect of having her come.

"The doctor isn't the problem. Mother is. She's afraid of germs. She doesn't want me around anyone."

"It's still a few weeks away," I said. "Maybe you can talk her into it."

"Yeah, right. And Michelle might give you a real compliment some day."

Charity had a point—both were highly unlikely.

The first Sunday in May was beautiful and sunny. I dressed Faith in her white blessing gown, complete with matching head-band and lace-trimmed booties.

Our family and friends took up half the chapel. My mother didn't fly in this time—Jonah drove her up in his Mercedes. They shared our bench along with Dave, who had actually shaved and wore a tie for the occasion. My father and Amberlie sat a couple of rows back. I wondered what they were all thinking about—I doubted it was about Faith.

Adam did a wonderful job with the blessing. I thought my heart would burst with love as I listened to him.

We planned to gather back at the Bridger house after sacrament meeting to have lunch and visit. It took a few minutes to get out of the chapel with all of the hugs and greetings going on.

"I've got to change her before she leaks through on her dress," I whispered to Adam. He helped me clear a path and said he'd wait for me in the foyer.

I was too late in changing Faith's diaper and her dress was soiled. I finished cleaning and diapering her and was trying to scrub the spot with a diaper wipe when I heard the door open.

I glanced back out of habit and saw the person I least expected. If I'd been holding Faith, I would have dropped her.

It was Alicia Haversham.

"What are you doing here?" I asked. I threw away the wipe and picked up my daughter. "Is Charity here?"

"No. She's at home. She begged to come, but her immune system is too compromised. I can't risk her being exposed to the germs in a—a *gathering*—like this."

"Oh." I adjusted Faith's headband. "Then why are you here?'

Alicia smoothed her silk skirt, which of course had no wrinkles. She looked as beautiful and remote as ever. "I needed to come."

I watched her silently, fighting my normal instincts to talk.

"I got the letter you sent," she said. "Back in December."

"Good." I resisted the urge to ask her what she thought about it. Faith fussed and I rocked her slightly to calm her.

"I've had a lot of time to think. So much time waiting—waiting for a donor, waiting for Charity's surgery, waiting for her to recover." Alicia paused.

"It's hard to wait," I said.

"Charity told me about what you did. About the fasting and prayer you people did here. People who didn't even know Charity." Alicia's eyes glistened brightly. She swallowed and, for the first time ever, I thought she looked nervous. "And then the nurse contacted me and told me you had three people volunteer to be screened. Why would you do it? For a complete stranger."

"Because I love her. And they love me," I said simply.

"The donor liver came through right after your fast."

"I know."

"Charity calls it a miracle."

"So do I." This was the strangest conversation I'd ever had with her. *Where is this going?*

"I came to thank you."

"A letter or card would have worked. I don't understand why you came here yourself." The rocking motion had lulled Faith to sleep in my arms.

"I had to come. I started to tell you about reading your letter and thinking about the things you wrote."

"Which part?"

"The part about being forgiven. About forgiving myself." Her hands twitched to smooth the skirt again. "I never entertained the possibility of finding forgiveness for what I did to you. But your letter and all the time I've spent reflecting about it made me rethink it. I've prayed more times in the past four months than I did my entire life." She paused and looked away. I think she was struggling to maintain her composure. She met my eyes again.

"I saw the miracle of Charity getting a new liver when I thought there was no more hope. I know prayers for Charity were answered. I prayed for her as well, but I never considered praying for myself. I didn't think there was a point."

"There's always hope," I said. "For everyone."

"I'm beginning to believe there is. I've spent more than twenty years feeling my actions had condemned me and there was no way repair the damage." Her voice dropped to barely more than a whisper. "More important, I need to ask you to forgive me for what I did to you."

"I already have," I told her.

"Not just for abandoning you, Katherine. But for the way I've treated you since I met you. I blamed you and accused you wrongly. I'm sorry."

I fought back the tears. I never thought the Alicia Haversham I'd known could ever bring herself to apologize to me. "Thank you," I choked out.

"Well, that's why I came. Not to interfere with your family plans or anything. That's why I followed you in here so we could talk privately." Alicia looked around as if realizing for the first time we were having this discussion in the bathroom. "It seems we've come full circle. I left you in a bathroom, and I came to find you in a bathroom."

"Charity would probably call it a miracle." Faith stretched and started fussing again. I bounced her gently in my arms to soothe her.

"She would." For the first time, Alicia looked directly at Faith. "Being a mother comes naturally to you. I'm sure she's beautiful, but you've probably guessed I'm not the best at the baby thing."

I smiled at her comment. I'd never heard her joke before. "You seem to have done all right with Charity. Does she know you're here today?"

"No. I didn't tell anyone yet. I'll call them later. I wasn't sure how it would go, and I didn't want to get Charity worked up."

"I have a big favor to ask," I said, an idea forming in my brain.

"What is it?" Alicia looked guarded.

"Nothing too hard. I'd just like to be the one to tell Charity that you came." I reached for my cell phone in the diaper bag. "Would you mind posing for a self-portrait or two? I promised to send Charity some pictures from the baby blessing today. I think a picture of us together in this bathroom would be a great one to start out with."

Alicia didn't seem thrilled, but she didn't say no.

"It'll be our little secret," I urged. *Until Charity posts them on Facebook*, I thought.

"Well, Katherine, I guess it's the least I can do." She touched her hair, searching for wayward strands. It was already perfect.

"Call me Kit." I had the camera ready when I said it and captured a smile on Alicia's face—or at least the glimpse of one.

Alicia left as quietly as she arrived. I spent a few more moments alone with my daughter, reflecting on what had just transpired. If I didn't have the pictures to prove it, I could almost convince myself I'd imagined it.

I wanted to talk to Charity immediately but knew I had a lot of family and friends waiting for me. For now, I settled on sending Charity a text with a photo attachment. *You've shown me how well your scars are healing; now you need to see how mine are doing—I think I win. Take a look at this picture!*

acknowledgments

There are so many people to thank for helping this book become what it is:

Brianna Hansen, Carrie Lew, Susan Crawford, and Erin Longacre, who weren't afraid to tell me when Kit was whining too much. How did you all become such experts on whining?

Melissa Catmull who is a wonderful "Mimi" and cheered for Nora.

Julie Turnbow who, oddly enough, loved Alicia. Is there something we should know, Julie?

Trisha Tracy and Jane Still for being so enthusiastic to read my scribbles and listen to my rambling.

Jennifer Fielding, Melissa Caldwell, and others at Cedar Fort, Inc., who helped with the polishing and publishing.

Last, but not least, my husband, Tod, who is my Adam—only way older!

discussion questions

1. Do you know anyone who has been adopted? Have they experienced abandonment issues? Why do these issues surface even when the adoption has been successful?

2. What recurring themes surfaced throughout the book? What are some examples? Are they true to life?

3. Were the characters believable? With which character did you most identify?

4. Can you relate to Kit's turmoil about wondering if she'll be a good mother? About her lingering frustration with her own parents?

5. Did you agree with Kit's decision about becoming a living liver donor? Would you consider donating an organ or part of an organ to someone you weren't related to?

6. Do you think Lily and Charity are alike? Why or why not?

7. Did the book end the way you expected?

about the author

Terri Ferran grew up in a small town where she escaped through reading until she discovered that all roads lead to other places (except the dead-end ones).

She dreamed of being a writer but took the safe route to CPA-hood. She finally pursued her dream and realized that both sides of her brain can be used—sometimes even at the same time.

Terri is the author of the Faith, Hope, & Charity series: *Finding Faith, Having Hope*, and *Choosing Charity*, a trilogy of inspirational novels. She has also forayed into humor with *Life's Alphabet Soup: When Your Children Make You Eat Your Words*.

Terri currently lives indoors, in a house, in a cul-de-sac, in a suburb, in a county, in a state, in a country, on the Planet Earth. She loves to hear from readers at terriferran@gmail.com, and you can visit her website at www.terriferran.com.